No doubt about it, Zoe Yarberry had surprised the socks off him.

There was a big ball of fire inside that small woman. Her kiss had clean made him forget to breathe.

He thought of what she'd said about having two little girls. She viewed a relationship with him as a threat.

She could be right.

He wondered what he wanted with her, beyond the obvious.

Zoe gave him hope. Nothing big—more like a suspicious little hope that maybe he, Rory Breen, was capable of feeling something for a woman again. Suspicion that maybe he could help her and, by doing so, help himself. That he even wanted to do something for her made him realize he was still alive, still held promise as a worthwhile man.

It certainly was a long shot; he'd pretty well screwed up his life. But he had to see what would happen. . . .

Dear Reader,

Welcome to Silhouette **Special Edition** . . . welcome to romance. Each month, Silhouette **Special Edition** publishes six novels with you in mind—stories of love and life, tales that you can identify with—as well as dream about.

April has some wonderful stories for you. Nora Roberts presents her contribution to THAT SPECIAL WOMAN!—our new promotion that salutes women, and the wonderful men that win them. *Falling for Rachel,* the third installment of THOSE WILD UKRAINIANS, is the tale of lady lawyer Rachel Stanislaski's romance with Zackary Muldoon. Yes, he's a trial, but boy is he worth it!

This month also brings *Hardworking Man,* by Gina Ferris. This is the tender story of Jared Walker and Cassie Browning—and continues the series FAMILY FOUND. And not to be missed is Curtiss Ann Matlock's wonderful third book in THE BREEN MEN series. Remember Matt and Jesse? Well, we now have Rory's story in *True Blue Hearts.*

Rounding out this month are books from other favorite authors: Andrea Edwards, Ada Steward and Jennifer Mikels. It's a month full of Springtime joy!

I hope you enjoy this book, and all of the stories to come! Have a wonderful April!

Sincerely,

Tara Gavin
Senior Editor

CURTISS ANN MATLOCK

TRUE BLUE HEARTS

Silhouette®

SPECIAL EDITION®

Published by Silhouette Books New York

America's Publisher of Contemporary Romance

My thanks to Mark Whitman of Whitman Stables for his patience with all my pesky questions for this book. And I thank him, too, for his expert training of my horses—and of me.

My appreciation to my dear husband, Jim, for putting up with my horse hobby, and for his steadiness all these years.

As always, a quote to go with this book:

No one ever got sunburned by
looking on the bright side of life.
—Anna G. Henderson

SILHOUETTE BOOKS
300 East 42nd St., New York, N.Y. 10017

TRUE BLUE HEARTS

Copyright © 1993 by Curtiss Ann Matlock

ISBN: 0-373-09805-7

First Silhouette Books printing April 1993

Printed in the U.S.A.

Books by Curtiss Ann Matlock

Silhouette Special Edition

A Time and a Season #275
Lindsey's Rainbow #333
A Time To Keep #384
Last Chance Cafe #426
Wellspring #454
Intimate Circle #589
Love Finds Yancey Cordell #601
Heaven in Texas #668
*Annie in the Morning #695
*Last of the Good Guys #757
*True Blue Hearts #805

*The Breen Men

Silhouette Romance

Crosswinds #422
For Each Tomorrow #482
Good Vibrations #605

Silhouette Books

Silhouette Christmas Stories 1988
"Miracle on I-40"
To Mother with Love '92
"More Than a Mother"

CURTISS ANN MATLOCK,

a self-avowed bibliophile, says, "I was probably born with a book in my hand." When not reading or writing—which she does almost constantly—she enjoys gardening, canning, crocheting, and motorcycling with her husband and son. Married to her high school sweetheart, the author is a Navy wife and has lived in eight different states within a sixteen-year period. The nomadic Matlocks finally settled in Oklahoma, where Curtiss Ann is busy juggling two full-time careers—as homemaker and writer.

COLORADO

KANSAS

Raton

Breen Ranch

OKLAHOMA

Wings

Clayton

Sante Fe

Albuquerque

NEW MEXICO

TEXAS

Alamogordo

MEXICO

All underlined places are fictitious.

Chapter One

Rory first met Zoe Yarberry as he was leaving Kelly's Tavern. He didn't actually *meet* her; he came upon her stealing a horse trailer, with a horse in it, and she asked for his help. It wasn't quite the same as a formal introduction.

And he wasn't simply leaving Kelly's Tavern, either—he'd been *thrown out,* by his good friend Kelly, for starting a fight, which was a total injustice, because he hadn't *started* anything. That jerk Price Mitchum had started it all.

It turned out to be one of those evenings that began less than generous and got downright stingy and biting as it went along.

Rory supposed, though he didn't think others had a right to point a finger, that he had to admit to having a temper. A fuse about the size of one of his mustache hairs was how his father put it. His father, so he said, had taken one look at newborn Rory and pronounced, "This boy's wild as a winter wind blowing on a bare bottom," and had then given him the middle name of Wilder. Rory Wilder Breen was his full name. So, Rory thought, his father had labeled him and was much to blame for his nature.

Looking beyond his temper, it could just as well be said that Rory Breen was a handsome man, five feet eleven inches in his stocking feet, with twinkling eyes the color of a clear western sky and thick, wavy brown hair that women loved to run their fingers through. He was a Breen, after all, and women loved the Breen men. He hadn't made that up; it was established fact. It could as well be said that he was polite to women and his elders, a great lover of children and animals and was friendly and generous to a fault. So what if he had a short temper? He most certainly wasn't mean; and no one could say that he was.

And on this Friday night, the end of a long, hardworking week that Rory had spent cutting alfalfa and moving cattle to fresh grass, he'd intended nothing wilder than to go into Kelly's Tavern, have a few drinks, play a little pool, dance with some pretty women, just as he had each Friday night for years. He'd had no intention of getting into a fight. Just because he'd been involved in a fight each Friday night for the past month didn't mean he would be tonight. To say so was the same as saying that because it had rained each Friday night for a month, it would tonight. This was a new Friday night, and how it turned out remained to be seen. And it had been Rory's full intention to steer clear of anything that remotely resembled an altercation.

He had assured his old friend Kelly of that.

"I'm on my best behavior, Kelly. Swear on my honor." He tried to amuse Kelly by making the Boy Scout sign.

But Kelly never had had a great sense of humor. Without a whisper of a grin, he said, "I hope so, amigo." Kelly liked to pepper his speech with Spanish words such as *amigo, mañana,* and *nada.* It seemed odd, because Kelly wasn't even faintly Spanish. He was a burly, redheaded ex-Marine who dressed in tight T-shirts and pleated khaki trousers with suspenders. "Every Friday night for a month, you've managed to get drunk and get a fight started in here, and I don't want one tonight. I just got some new tables and my floor waxed, and I don't aim to get a reputation as a wild and woolly drunken place." He jabbed a finger at Rory's chest. "You're drinkin' too much, amigo. Too much."

Rory passed on the criticism of his drinking—he was sick to death of hearing about it—but he could argue the point about fighting. "I haven't started any fights. Not one. Can you name one fight that I've started?"

"Maybe not started, but you sure helped Kipp and Hooly along last week."

That wounded Rory. "I didn't *start* that. Kipp's my friend, and I had to help him. Would you just have stood there and let a fella break your friend's nose?"

"They had a one-punch disagreement until you stepped in and turned it into a free-for-all that broke half my tables and chairs. You could've pulled Kipp out of here, instead of pouncin' all over Hooly. Is he still in the hospital?"

"He didn't have to stay in the hospital. He only had a black eye and some bruised ribs," Rory said defensively. "And while we're on the subject of fightin'—aren't you callin' the kettle black?" This was a good one—old, red-headed, fiery Kelly criticizing someone else about fighting.

"I'm speakin' as the voice of experience," Kelly returned. "Drinkin' and fightin' are a high road to nowhere. And what's more, Krystal sure ain't a woman worth lettin' your life go to hell in a hand basket over. No woman is worth that, and I've learned that the hard way."

At the mention of Krystal, Rory's shoulders tightened. "Enough said, Kelly. You can keep your opinions of Crystal to yourself, and I guess my life's my own to live. Now, are you gonna get me another Jack D., or am I gonna have to drive down to Clayton?" Rory never simply asked for whiskey but for Jack Daniel's, which he called Jack D.; he wouldn't drink any other kind.

At that, Kelly got Rory's drink, saying that he didn't want Rory driving after he'd already started drinking. Rory thanked him and prudently remained quiet about not having a vehicle tonight; he'd simply thrown in the threat about going to Clayton as an extra prod. Actually, Oren usually came along to do the driving, but tonight he'd dropped Rory off and gone on down to see Ladonna Robles. He was supposed to show up later to take Rory home, but Ladonna was hotter than a firecracker, so Oren could end up side-tracked—or shot, if her father caught the two of them doing anything improper. But Rory could always find a ride home from someone.

Drink in hand, he leaned back against the bar and surveyed the dimly lit tavern from his perfect vantage point. He hadn't come to this spot at the bar by accident, either. He always stood here, at the far end, right at the seam where the bar began to curve. It belonged to him, as much as if there were a sign on the bar saying Reserved For R. Breen, and everyone knew it. On rare occasions a stranger would come in and happen to stand there. If it appeared the stranger wasn't going to move on, Rory politely made the explanation that this was his place. All through the evening people would come to speak to him, or form talking groups around him, and at times he felt a lot like some king holding court. Though he never would have said that. It was just one of those silly little things a human thought but would certainly be misunderstood if spoken of.

Though it was still early, the tavern was quite full; Rory knew most everyone, by face if not by name. For years Kelly's, as it had simply been called back then, had been an old hole-in-the-wall place where a few of the men of Wings, New Mexico, could hide away from their families and the hands from outlying ranches could wet their whistles or tie on a good one. It had been dreary, and only the depressed went there.

Then half of it had burnt to the ground, and in the process of rebuilding, Kelly had been a man reborn with the fervent desire to make his place the best of its kind in the county. He'd added on a billiard parlor—not pool but billiards, he insisted. And then, in an effort to have, as he termed it, "the most unique, bar-none, establishment in the nation," he'd implemented Sunday afternoon lemonade socials and expanded the name of the place to Kelly's Tavern and Lemonade Parlor, certainly the only tavern in America with such a name.

It was amazing that Kelly could transform the place between Saturday nights and Sunday afternoons, but he did. He covered up the neon beer signs with cute posters of cherubic children, uncovered a large skylight in the roof and put linen cloths on the tables and topped them with pitchers of lemonade made from fresh squeezed lemons. Whole families came to play pool—Rory called the game pool, no matter what Kelly said—and drink lemonade. Joe Shatto's eight-year-old son had become a champion pool player, beginning to earn his college money.

However, the six other afternoons and nights of the week—most especially Friday nights, when there was a live band—the beer signs glowed, the skylight was black, the tables were bare polyurethaned wood, and something a mite stronger than lemonade was served to customers across the long carved oak bar Kelly had bought over in Tucson and at which Doc Holliday was said to have drunk. These customers came to dance across a true sawdust floor beneath soft colored lights and a twinkling mirror ball, and to play pool on the two fancy billiard tables or darts at the fancy dart boards. They came to hoot and holler and let themselves cut loose in the dimness. No matter the fancy name, Kelly's Tavern and Lemonade Parlor, on those six days, was a smoky dark tavern where people came to drink and some of them to get drunk. And any time alcohol and the human species were mixed, fights could be expected.

That being the case, Rory thought it rather foolish of Kelly to blame *him* for fights erupting. Kelly should think about that, but Rory wasn't a man to point a finger, especially when he didn't intend to rile anyone into a fight. No, sir, he intended to spend that Friday evening being the very epitome of everyone's idea of a good guy, proving everyone wrong about the fighting.

And he'd been doing very well for nearly an hour when that jerk Price Mitchum showed up.

"That Jerk Price Mitchum" was how Rory thought of the guy—as if That Jerk was part of the guy's name, and simply put, Rory thought Mitchum was a Class A jerk. The dislike was mutual, so Rory suffered no guilt over it.

Mitchum was four or so years younger than Rory, had a build like a linebacker for the Dallas Cowboys and a face like a hacksaw, with eyes so pale they glowed in the dark. He was a braggart, a liar and a cheat, and one time Rory had come upon him disciplining a horse with a two-by-four out behind some stock trailers. Mitchum had also carried on with Krystal while she and Rory were still married.

His wife's betrayal wasn't something a man liked to admit or to talk about. Rory tried not to *think* about it; after all, he and Krystal had been divorced for more than four years. But there were times when he recalled all too clearly Mitchum and Krystal eyeing each other and the story Mitchum had circulated about the two of them after Krystal had taken off. Mitchum had been the first to date Krystal after she'd left, too, and he'd made certain Rory had known all about it, going so far as to brag about making it with her. Rory had knocked out one of his teeth for that.

This night, when Rory saw Mitchum's hulking body, he thought, uh-oh. He thought a few stronger words when Mitchum came over to where Rory and John Knotts and Bob Waggoner were talking and said, "Heard Krystal got married last week—to some dude that owns half of Vail." He winked. "The guy's gettin' a hot one, ain't he, Rory?"

Rory gazed at Mitchum's taunting grin and thought how he didn't intend to fight. He said, "Guess I don't know exactly what the guy's gotten," and then politely excused himself and walked away before Mitchum could say another word. He felt as satisfied as a fat rooster for confounding the hell out of the guy.

A little later, when Mitchum joined a table where Rory sat with several fellas, stepping on Rory's foot as he did so, Rory ignored the misstep and slipped away to the bar. When Mitchum came over, shoved himself into a space near Rory and started in bragging about this grand colt he owned, Rory kept his tongue glued in his mouth and moved away to watch two dart games in progress. When Mitchum challenged him to a game, Rory said, "I'm no good at darts. You'd beat me."

Of course that comment set Mitchum cockeyed; he didn't know what to say, because he was plainly trying to get into a set-to with Rory. But Rory was too satisfied about confounding the jerk, too satisfied with himself, to be drawn into an altercation. He didn't intend to fight, and he would drink to that.

He guessed it was his cocky self-satisfaction or several more Jack D's. that led him into a game of pool with Jada Cobb at the table right next to the one where That Jerk Price Mitchum was already playing. Of course, how could he have declined Jada's invitation? She was a charming woman—and Rory certainly wasn't going to let Mitchum's presence scare him away from the pool tables. And he had to admit to feeling the great urge to taunt Mitchum with the fact he wasn't going to fight, as well as to make the guy jealous by being the one to wrap his arm around Jada's shoulder. She let only a few select men do that, and Rory, being an old friend, was one of them—Mitchum was not.

Anyway, Rory was having a fine time playing and smiling under Mitchum's nose, as well as showing off some fancy pool shots—Rory was quite good at pool—when, just as he was about to shoot the five and three balls into separate corner pockets with one shot, Mitchum bumped his elbow with a pool cue.

"Hey, man—it was an accident," Mitchum said, backing up and acting innocent, but grinning a "come-on-and-get-me" grin at the same time. "A little tap shouldn't bother such a hotshot pool player like you."

Temptation fell all over Rory, and focusing on that grin, he felt the sweet sap of fighting spirit rise through his veins.

But the next instant Jada inserted herself between them. She was a master at getting people's attention—especially men, who couldn't help but look at her well-endowed figure and the deep cleavage where her violet-blue dress dipped in front. "Cool your jets, the both of you," she said. "Come on, Rory—" she pushed her entire shapely body at him "—you owe me a dance. You know we always dance to 'Rollin' with the Flow.'"

And so Rory's good intentions had been saved; he would be the first to admit it: his fat had been pulled from the fire.

With a grin for Mitchum, he followed Jada out onto the dance floor, where he swept her close. His head swam a bit with the motion, and he stumbled once but recovered and whirled around and around to a two-step, holding on to her tightly, inhaling her womanly scent and savoring the familiar feel of her. Jada had a figure that could stop traffic on an interstate, and she blocked Krystal's image completely from his mind.

"I'll bet you could find someone to fight with even if you were stranded in the desert," Jada said.

"It's a failing. I admit it."

"Then the least you could do is be properly penitent, not grinnin' like a wily fox. Tell me thank you for savin' your bacon."

"Savin' Mitchum's bacon, you mean."

"Your bacon—and your friendship with Kelly. Your friendship with a lot of people, because we're all gettin' a little fed up with your hot temper these last weeks."

"Thank you."

He became aware of Jada pulling away from him, and that they'd stopped dancing. "The music has stopped," she said.

He looked down at her, and she gazed up at him. "Does that mean I have to let go?" He grinned and spoke of sex with his eyes. He didn't want to let her go; she was his anchor in that moment, though he wasn't about to admit to needing one.

"Not necessarily." She chuckled and answered with a sultry look in her eyes.

"How long have we known each other—'bout ten years now?"

"I'd say it's closer to sixteen." She squinted and smiled wickedly. "I think you were about seventeen when I caught you and Oren out behind the drugstore tearin' open that package of rubbers that you two had shoplifted from our shelf."

Rory tossed back his head and laughed. "Good grief, woman! You'll never let me forget that."

"And well I shouldn't. Stealin' is serious business."

"Now, you wouldn't have *sold* me a packet." It was good, talking about old times.

"Oh, yes, I believe I would have. It would have been better than lettin' you sneak around—and fool around unprotected."

"Oren and I couldn't bring ourselves to come in and buy them right out in the open. Does it help to know you made a severe enough impression on me that I've never stolen anything again?''

"I'm glad to hear it." Her voice and eyes softened with tenderness. "Now, what sort of experience will it take for you to realize that Krystal—or any woman—isn't worth drinkin' yourself to death over?"

He was gazing into her eyes as she spoke, and seeing the glint of pity, he blinked and averted his gaze to her nose. Pride made him shoot her his best cavalier grin. "Krystal was a long time ago and forgotten, darlin'. I'm drinkin' because I like to." He lifted his hat and did a fancy bow. "Thank you for the dance."

He didn't care what she thought, what any of them thought, he told himself as he walked away from her and her irritating pity. She didn't know anything—didn't know him. No one did, so they didn't need to be telling him how to live.

With thoughts of several more glasses of Jack D., he headed for his place at the bar. And that was when the night turned stingy—that Jerk Price Mitchum was *standing in Rory's place!*

Mitchum stood there, three feet from the end of the bar, at the seam where it began to curve, propped on his right elbow and with a smirk on his hacksaw face. "Come for a drink, Breen?"

The two men on either side took note and edged away.

Rory breathed deeply and stared at Mitchum's taunting expression. Three seconds ticked by in which Rory shifted his stance and rubbed his forefinger over his mustache.

Then, with deliberate movements, he stepped up to the bar, propped his left arm on the rim and faced Mitchum, catching sight of Kelly over Mitchum's shoulder, down behind the bar several feet away and talking to someone.

Rory gazed into Mitchum's pale eyes, and Mitchum stared back. They stood so close the brims of their hats brushed and they caught each other's breath. Mitchum grinned, and Rory did, too, then saw the flicker of confusion enter Mitchum's eyes. Mitchum was waiting, and Rory figured he was, too. He'd told everyone he wasn't going to fight. They all thought he was out of control. He felt out of control. He wanted to prove he wasn't.

"This is a great spot," Mitchum said. "Think I'll keep it."

Awww... Rory's spirit moaned. He reached over and picked up Mitchum's glass, lifted it and downed the contents. It was whiskey, but not Jack D., which went to show the guy's poor taste.

He set the empty glass back on the bar, then glanced again at Kelly, who was still a few feet away. He cut his eyes to Mitchum again and thought that he could push the guy away from his place—or he could wait. After all, the guy couldn't stand there all night; he would have to take a leak sometime. Or embarrass himself, and Rory didn't care which one he did. Either way, he would eventually get his place returned.

Rory smiled and stepped away.

Mitchum said, "Well, I guess an old dog *can* be taught to jump through new hoops."

And that popped the lid off it. That was the blowing of the whistle, the opening of the chute, the firing of the gun, sending all good intentions flying south. Pivoting, Rory brought up his fist in a great swing aimed right at Mitchum's hacksaw nose.

But Mitchum was ready and blocked the punch with his right arm. The two men locked together, and Mitchum, like the sneak he was, kneed Rory in the groin. Gasping in pain, Rory pulled back to hit the guy in the belly, but the next instant, hands were jerking him roughly by the shoulders.

"That's enough!" Kelly roared. He shoved Rory backward. "I won't have it. I'm sick to death of your brawlin'!"

Rory stood with a hand propped on one knee, gasping for breath, his heart pounding and his groin throbbing. The curious faces around him merged into a blur. He wiped his sleeve across his face and felt like throwing up.

Kelly smacked his hat at him, and numbly Rory took it. He saw Mitchum, on the other side of Kelly, his chest heaving, move to the bar. He smacked his hand on the gleaming hardwood right at the curve and held on.

"I warned you about fightin' in here tonight," Kelly said, glaring at Rory. "Now get out."

That was his friend Kelly, kicking him out without knowing the full of it and not caring, as if Rory was some stranger off the street.

Rory raked back his hair and carefully settled his hat on his head, then ignored his protesting body and straightened his spine. As he walked away through the parting crowd he heard Kelly say, "Mitchum . . . you stay here. I don't want any fightin' out in my parking lot, either."

Mitchum got to stay. Rory was out. The night had just bit him in the ass.

Rory walked to the door and out it with deliberate, measured steps, which wasn't all that easy to do with his head spinning like a dropped penny and his crotch throbbing.

But he wasn't about to appear weak or done in. Nor was he about to defend himself, to his good friend Kelly or anyone else, by saying that it was Mitchum who'd started it all, that Mitchum had been after him all night long. He'd had two choices before him—to run away from Mitchum that night, and forever after, or to put a stop to it in the only way that it could be done. Maybe he could have called Mitchum outside, but he guessed he'd been too satisfied with himself to think of doing that, and besides, Mitchum probably wouldn't have gone, because the jerk had wanted everything out in public.

But Rory wouldn't have explained any of that to anyone. He certainly wasn't a snitch, nor should a person have to defend himself to his good friend. And a man didn't cry about injustice. A man took it as it came, righted it when he could, and suffered in private when he couldn't. And on certain occasions a man couldn't resist getting even.

As it turned out, Rory's chance to get even came pretty quickly, because the horse and horse trailer Zoe Yarberry was working at stealing out there in Kelly's parking lot were hooked up to Price Mitchum's pickup truck.

Chapter Two

"Hellfire and molasses!" Zoe swore in a hushed voice. She let go of the jack handle, massaged her sore palms together and bit back thoughts of stronger curses. Zoe Marie Padilla Yarberry had been brought up better than to swear. Even at this moment she could hear the whisper of her grandmother's voice: "dirty words are for people who have no better vocabulary."

Flipping her braid back over her shoulder, she straightened, breathed deeply and gazed for long seconds at the handle that lowered the jack on the tongue of the sixteen-foot stock trailer. So far, she'd gotten the jack lowered no farther than a third of the way to the ground, and the farther down the jack went, the harder the handle was to turn. Using all her strength, she could barely make it budge. The handle was bent, and the gears it turned needed greasing. Dusty never had taken care of the trailer. The only time it had gotten greased was when she did it.

Their entire married life had been like that. It could be described just like this jack: bent, misused and with Zoe applying all the grease.

She massaged her weak knee; it ached from the pressure of bracing her weight on it. Sweat dampened the edges of her hair. Her feet felt swollen, and the gravel cut into the worn soles of her boots. It always cooled off at night out on the high plains grassland, but tonight was warmer than most and with only a whisper of a southerly breeze. Inside the trailer, Blue's hooves echoed on the wood flooring as he occasionally moved, shaking off a mosquito or something. Now and then he snorted. Slices of light fell around the trailer from the two parking-lot lamps; more glow came from a full moon on the rise. Stars stretched across the black sky and twinkled brightly, almost mockingly.

The muffled sound of music came from inside Kelly's. His parking lot was full and during the fifteen minutes Zoe had been working on the trailer not a vehicle had passed along the blacktopped highway through town. Of course, Wings wasn't exactly a town. A better description would have been a bunch of buildings splattered on the earth with a black road cutting through the middle.

Across the road, Cobb's Drugstore, a two-story brick edifice of distinction, loomed eerily in the light of a single lamp, like a ghost building from another era—it was seventy-odd years old and not a thing had changed about it since it had been built. Next door to Kelly's, comparatively speaking, was Shatto's Garage. It dated from the fifties and had only recently replaced its old gas pumps with modern electronic ones. It had been such an occasion that the entire town had turned out for a party. Across from Shatto's Garage was the tiny, two-room white clapboard post office. It was from the fifties, too. Those four buildings and six houses spreading out half a mile all around made up Wings, New Mexico, a one-horse town where a person could see each end from the middle.

Zoe tucked her bottom lip between her teeth and blinked burning eyes. She wasn't one to cry easily, but she was about to now out of pure, double-D frustration. If she didn't get that jack lowered, she couldn't remove the trailer from Price Mitchum's pickup truck and take both it and Blue back home. The trailer had never been anything fancy, and Blue was at this moment simply another stud horse—but both were hers, by heaven!

Raising her eyes she looked through the metal slats of the trailer at the shadow of the horse inside, then swept her gaze to her own truck sitting fifty feet distant in the prairie grass, a battered, ten-year-old faded gold Chevy that sort of glowed with the moonlight on it. *By golly, Good Lord willing—and He was—she was gonna get this trailer and this horse!* With a silent prayer and renewed determination, she went at the handle again, gritting her teeth and giving it all she had.

She'd gotten the handle around another full circle and the jack down another inch when a voice behind her said, "Just what are you workin' at here, ma'am?"

She jumped nearly clean out of her boots and whirled to see a dark male figure standing in the deep shadow between the horse trailer and the LTD sedan parked next to it. It wasn't Price Mitchum, that much she could tell, because this guy wasn't big enough to be Price.

Just the same, a bit of fear niggled at her as she realized all too fully that she was a woman out here alone. Alone in the parking lot of a tavern. No one to hear her scream should she be attacked.

However, attacks on women in Wings, New Mexico, were unheard of, at least as far as she knew, and besides, she had concrete problems at hand.

"I'm tryin' to unhitch this trailer," she said and gestured to it. Didn't the guy have eyes? "Do you suppose you could lend a hand?"

He stepped forward out of the deep shadow, slowly, as if considering the situation—and as if he'd been drinking a lot. She had experience enough to tell her this man was at least one sheet to the wind.

A slice of light from the parking-lot lamps fell on him, showing him to be a medium to tall man, not young, not old, thick shouldered as a hardworking man gets when he reaches full manhood. Like a hundred others of the western country, he wore a Western-cut shirt and faded but creased jeans that fit like he'd been born in them. She still couldn't see his face very well, because it remained shadowed by his black cowboy hat. Yet all nervousness of him faded.

He looked at the trailer hitch, stroked his mustache with his forefinger, then looked at her and said, "That depends. *Why* do you want this trailer unhooked?"

"Because it belongs to me, and I want to take it. The truck belongs to Price Mitchum."

"Yeah, I know." He gazed at her for several seconds.

"Well, I'm not out to take his truck. It's not mine." She wanted him to know she wasn't a thief—no matter how her actions appeared.

The stranger said, "There's a horse in this trailer. Does it happen to belong to you, too?"

"Yes, sir, it does. There were two horses in that trailer, but one of them wasn't mine." She moved and pointed to where she'd tied the other horse, a flashy paint pony, to the pipe fence near the giant garbage bin. "I took him out and tied him over there."

The man looked at the paint, which could barely be seen in the shadows, then back at her. "Do you have proof of ownership on this one you're takin'?"

More concern over the ownership of the horse rather than the trailer didn't surprise her one bit. There were customs the world over that never died, and excess concern over ownership of a horse would stay with people in this part of the country until the sun fell from the sky.

She nodded. "Yes, sir, I do. I've got his registration papers over there in my truck." She indicated her Chevy. "I'll be glad to show them to you, but I'd appreciate it if you'd get to cranking pretty quick here." It wouldn't do at all to get caught at this by Price Mitchum, though she left that unsaid, because it sounded rather underhanded and spineless—not that doing this was either of those things.

The stranger pushed his hat back a tad and stepped up to the jack handle, rather like a man stepping up to swing an ax into a great log. She halfway expected him to spit on his palms, but he didn't. As he took hold, he said, "Never mind about the registration. I guess Price Mitchum could produce some kind of papers, too, if he had to."

He cranked the handle. It was tough even for him. Zoe remembered the bricks to block the trailer tires and scrambled to get them from Mitchum's truck bed and tuck them in place.

When she came back, the stranger said, "I guess you have a good reason for doin' this at night, on the sly, without goin' in there and askin' Mitchum to help you." He puffed with exertion, and she could smell the familiar rancid scent of whiskey. Whiskey poured from a bottle smelled rather nice, but coming back up in breath... There were few smells worse. She hated it with a passion.

"I guess I do, and I suppose you want to know what it is." She noticed the sexy way his jeans fit across his lean hips, which went to show, she thought, the wide range of a human's observation abilities no matter the circumstances.

He paused and twisted to look at her. "It seems only fair that I get some explanation—I *am* out here helpin' you, and I'd be counted an accomplice should you be arrested. Not to mention that Price Mitchum most probably isn't gonna be very happy about this, and he is a right big fella."

His voice had a chuckle in it, and she felt his grin. She'd always been impressed by a good sense of humor. And she herself giggled inside whenever she imagined the look on Price Mitchum's face when he sashayed out from a free and easy evening and found the trailer and horse both gone. He would know right off where they were—though he wouldn't have thought she'd do something like this, her being a woman and not a terribly big one. People misjudged her all the time because of her size. But she didn't think he would do anything about it. There wasn't a lot he could do; she was in the right.

Standing there, her left palm turned backward and tucked into a frayed back pocket, she explained. "My husband gave this trailer and horse to Price Mitchum as payment for a debt. The only problem is, they both belong to me. The trailer was mine when I married, and I'm the one who bought and paid for that horse at an auction down in Fort Worth last year. My husband took both of them when he took off six months ago. When I found out that Price had them and why, I went to him and explained they were the same as stolen property and asked for them back. He refused to give them to me. Told me it was my tough luck and that I'd have to fight him for them in court, because possession is nine-tenths of the law." She paused and decided not to mention that Mitchum had offered to let her have them—if she would sleep with him. "I don't have money for a lawyer, much less some kind of court injunction, so I'm just takin' possession. I've been waitin' my chance, and tonight, when I found out Mitchum had the trailer and horse here, I figured he'd be in Kelly's long enough for me to get them."

The stranger had the trailer jack extended to the board Zoe had placed on the ground. "Sounds reasonable to me," he said and grunted with the final exertion it took to free the trailer tongue from the ball on the back of the pickup. It popped free, and the trailer wobbled slightly. The man straightened, lifted his hat and dabbed at his face with his shirtsleeve.

"And you're helpin' me 'cause you don't like Mitchum."

He looked at her. "That, and because I was brought up to help a lady in distress." He shot her a lopsided grin, as if mocking himself. "Now, how do you propose to move this truck out of the way? Think we can push it?"

She shook her head. "No pushin' necessary. The keys are in it." And that wasn't anything unusual—the keys were probably in half the vehicles sitting in the lot right then. Things were like that in Wings. "You drive it off over there somewhere, and I'll bring over my truck."

Only after she'd started toward her own truck did Zoe realize her final words had amounted to an order. Speaking that way was about her greatest failing. People tended to take objection to being treated in that way, even if it was best all the way around. She paused to glance back to see if the stranger was going to move Mitchum's pickup.

He was already getting inside. She ran the rest of the way to hers, opened the door and took hold of the steering wheel to pull herself up onto the seat, remembering then to move and close the door quietly. She didn't want to wake her babies.

Her luck had held, with no one coming or going from Kelly's, except the helpful stranger—she should ask his name—and she prayed the Lord would continue to hold back anyone who might come along and blab her actions to Mitchum before she was done. She might go in and tell him then, just so she could see his face. He'd never had a clue she would do something like this, not one clue. He'd had her pegged as female and therefore helpless, someone who would never challenge him, someone he could just leave boot prints all over. But now there really wasn't anything he could do once she had the trailer and Blue. At least, she didn't think so. Possession being nine-tenths of the law, as he'd said, and her claims to both would hold up in court. Yep, maybe she would go in and tell him—but then, maybe it would be more prudent to keep quiet, she thought as she started the truck.

"Mama?" Glory sat up from where she lay in the seat.

"Shush, honey," Zoe cautioned and touched her daughter's silky hair. "Don't wake your sister."

Her girls had been asleep in bed when she'd had to drag them out into the night. They'd only barely awakened, though. Both of them slept like the dead, completely safe and secure, something she always considered a compliment to her as a mother. Traveling around in the truck in their pajamas in the middle of the night was nothing new to them, either. They'd been doing that since they'd been born, traveling as Zoe and Dusty had done, from one rodeo to another, one job to another. On more than one night Dusty, running from a debt or fleeing someone who wanted a piece of his hide, had had them packing up and taking off in the night.

With a warm, moist little hand on Zoe's shoulder, Glory pulled herself to her feet, stuck her thumb in her mouth and gazed out the back of the truck as Zoe maneuvered her old gold truck into the place vacated by Mitchum's fancy red job. She was an expert at backing and barely needed guidance from the stranger, who felt it his duty to wave directions at her.

"Be quiet and be sweet, darlin'," she whispered, gently squeezing Glory's hand before hopping out of the seat.

The stranger was already cranking the handle to raise the trailer jack and lower the tongue onto the ball. Out of habit, Zoe checked on Blue, who was standing there, dumb as ever. Calm horses often looked sort of dumb, but he was a stud and should by all rights have a bit more spirit. Zoe suspected Mitchum had drugged him. When the trailer tongue fell over the ball, quick as a rabbit she grabbed the bricks blocking the two trailer tires, plopped them into her truck bed and went to help the stranger hook up the trailer's safety chains and lights.

The stranger straightened and stepped backward. "Guess you're set."

"Guess I am."

Zoe wiped her palms down her thighs and ran her gaze from the dark shadow of Mitchum's pickup truck, now parked out in the grass, to the trailer and her own truck. Then she looked at the green neon sign above the tavern: Kelly's Tavern and Lemonade Parlor.

"Thinkin' of tellin' Mitchum?" the stranger said.

"Yes... thought I might."

"I wouldn't. He's pretty ornery."

She nodded. "But it seems the polite thing," she said, even as she started off toward the tavern door. She just had to see the bully's face when she told him.

Despite thoughts of her girls alone in the truck and questions as to the wisdom of her actions, she hurried inside. She could allow herself no more than two minutes.

She stood blinking, straining to locate Mitchum's big hulk and fair head among the many figures crowding the tavern.

"Hey, baby," said a skinny guy who leered extravagantly. "Can I be of help to ya?"

"Hay is for horses," she shot back. "I'm lookin' for Price Mitchum."

"Well now, I saw him a while ago. There..." He laid a hand on her shoulder as he pointed with his other. "There he is... but he can't give you nothin' I can't."

Seeing Price Mitchum standing with several other men at the far end of the bar, Zoe shook off the guy's hand and strode forward. Her eyes were fastened on Mitchum, her heartbeat pounding with rising trepidation and anger that she'd long forced back.

"Well, hello, little darlin'," Price Mitchum drawled when he caught sight of her. "Ain't this a nice surprise?" His grin and the look in his eyes held a slimy appreciation.

She stopped four feet in front of him and looked him straight in the eye, cocking her head upward to do so. "I just wanted you to know that I took possession of my trailer and horse and I'm takin' them home."

The slimy smile sank out of sight. "You what?"

"I've got my trailer and horse out there in the parking lot, and now I'm the one in possession, and I'm takin' them home. If you want to press it, *you* go take it to the law," she said, using almost the exact words he'd said to her weeks ago.

Then she turned and left, taking firm strides and ignoring Mitchum's call for her to stop. She smacked her hand on the door and burst through, heading for her pickup, her trailer, her horse and her daughters.

By heaven, she might not have much, but she would protect what was hers!

When she was halfway across the parking lot to her truck, she glanced back and saw Mitchum burst out the tavern door. A stream of people followed him, then hung back to watch the show. Fear flickered in Zoe's chest, and she checked herself from breaking into a humiliating run. She'd figured Mitchum would follow, but kept telling herself he couldn't do anything. Not much—except beat the tar out of her and take back the trailer and horse. Her pride had made her confront him, and her pride was always getting her into trouble, she thought, as he reached her in swift strides and grabbed hold of her arm. *Oh, Lord, have mercy!*

He jerked her around. "You bitch, what do you think you're doin'?" She tried to free her arm, but Mitchum's grip dug into her flesh. "You ain't takin' that stud and trailer. I got 'em fair and square for what's owed me." He shook her hard enough to loosen her teeth.

"Let her go, Mitchum."

A cold voice cut through the air. Mitchum stilled, and so did Zoe. She saw it was the stranger, standing at the rear of the trailer.

Mitchum said, "Ain't none of your business, Breen."

Zoe took the opportunity to kick Mitchum in the shin. "But it is *mine!*"

With a yell, Mitchum let go and hopped back, grabbing his leg. "You damn little bitch!" He lunged for her, but she spun and ran for her truck, thinking fear equalled good sense in this case.

In seconds Zoe had the truck started and in gear. It was mischief that made her shift into reverse when she caught sight of Mitchum ranting and raving and grabbing hold of the back corner of the trailer. Gunning the engine, she started backing up. The truck jerked a bit, then started moving, gathering speed—sending the trailer right for Mitchum, who was dancing to get out of the way.

When he let go and jumped clear, Zoe stopped and shifted into first.

"That horse and trailer ain't worth two cents anyway!" Mitchum hollered, shaking his fist at her. "Didn't begin to cover what's owed me."

"Dusty owes you that debt—not me! Go see him!"

And she started out of the gravel lot and onto the grass, fast at first, then slowing when she saw Glory's little head bobbing and remembered Mercy lying on the seat and Blue back in the trailer.

Through the open passenger window she heard someone call Mitchum's name—the stranger again.

"Look what I got, Mitchum," he called and lifted his arm, dangling something from his fingers. Then, grinning to beat the band, he drew his arm back and threw out into the dark, grassy field what Zoe knew could only be the keys to Mitchum's truck.

Chapter Three

That Jerk Price Mitchum was coming for Rory, and it was plain to see there was murder in his mind.

Egging the jerk on, Rory laughed and stood there a split second longer, then, with pure wicked delight, lit out for the girl's old Chevy that was bumping its way across the tufts of grass, heading to the road. Hot damn, but Mitchum would be fit to be tied not to be able to get hold of him! Knowing that more than made up for any regret at not standing and going at it with his fists.

With Mitchum like a mad bull hot on his tail, Rory ran alongside the traveling truck, took hold of the door handle, stumbled and pitched forward, jerked open the door and threw himself inside.

And almost plopped his rear on top of a little kid!

"Whoa!" He pushed himself up as if he'd been about to sit on a gas burner. Through the window he had one glimpse of Mitchum ranting and waving his fist before the pickup curved out onto the road and Rory was thrown against the door that he hadn't gotten closed. He hung on to the open window for dear life as his torso swung out over the road, while his feet fought to remain on the floorboard. Gritty, skin-ripping blacktop raced beneath him. His hat, already worked loose, popped up and then blew clean away into the night.

"Get that door closed before Mercy falls out!" the girl called.

"I'm tryin'!" Rory returned, gasping. *But, ooo-wee, he hadn't had so much fun in a coon's age!*

They were leaving the lights of Kelly's behind by the time Rory got the door closed and his buttocks securely shoved down on the edge of the seat. He raked a hand through his hair, then propped his arm on the opened window. The night air blew in, clearing his head and cooling the sweat on his neck. The truck headlights cut into the pitch dark, illuminating the black highway ahead like lighting up a tunnel. The kid who had been stretched out on the seat was just waking up, scooting quickly away from Rory.

There were two of them. Two kids, girls, about two, maybe three, years old, in pale nightgowns that ruffled around their ankles. Surprised, Rory looked from the shadowy little figure scooting up in the seat and rubbing her eyes to the shadowy little figure pressed against the shoulder of the woman behind the wheel. In the dimness, the two little ones were as alike as two peas in a pod. Twins. They had to be. And both regarding Rory as if seeing a spaceman. Then he looked at the woman. The dash lights lit her face with a dim, silvery glow, and wisps of hair curled around her face. Surely, Rory thought, these kids couldn't be hers. Why, she wasn't much more than a kid herself.

"Couldn't you have gone for your own vehicle?" she said irritably, flashing him a frown he felt more than saw in the dimness.

"I could have, if I'd had one." He grinned and spoke with good nature. He was a pretty happy man at the moment.

She shook her head. "Well, I'd already made him mad as a hornet, and I certainly didn't need you to involve me in your beef with him."

"You involved me when you asked for my help," Rory pointed out. "And *you* were the one to go into Kelly's and bring Mitchum out."

"I—" she put her hand to her chest *"—only asked you to help me get what was mine."* She pointed at him. *"I never asked you to toss his keys to never-never land."*

"You mean these keys?"

Grinning as proudly as a dog with two tails, he opened his fingers and jingled the key ring hanging from his middle finger. His satisfaction was more than enough repayment for the slight throb that persisted in his groin.

However, the woman did not laugh. Her eyes flicked to him again, then widened, and she slowed the pickup, glancing in the side mirror. "He's gonna come after you." She was certainly more apprehensive than impressed. That hurt—after all, he had come to her aid.

Rory stuck his head out and looked back, but the road was black, the lights of Kelly's almost a half mile back. "Not in his truck, he isn't." He considered tossing the keys out into the field, but decided that was just too low-down dirty. He would take them to Kelly's tomorrow; Kelly could just say they'd turned up.

"He does have friends—and a lot of those cars in the lot have keys in them."

"Aww... for one thing, there isn't anyone back there who'd drive him after me." At least, Rory didn't think there was, though he'd been wrong before, he thought and instinctively took another glance behind them. "And he isn't about to come fight his fight alone, or call the sheriff, either, because he knows the sheriff is my second cousin and doesn't get out of bed for foolishness."

Giving a shake of her head, she pulled the pickup to a stop. "I gotta check on Blue. I bumped him around some back there."

In a wink she was out of the truck cab, leaving her door open and Rory sitting there, the overhead light glaring in his eyes and the two kids staring at him as if he had horns or something. He was about to follow her when she reappeared, hopped back into her seat, as graceful as only a young, healthy woman can be. Her legs weren't long, but they certainly looked nice in a worn pair of Wrangler jeans. He couldn't help noticing that; he was a leg man.

"The horse okay?" he asked.

"He's on his feet, anyway," she said and shut her door, plunging them all into semidarkness again—blessedly, as far as Rory's eyes were concerned. She looked at him, gave a small sigh and extended her hand. "My name is Zoe Yarberry, and I thank you for your assistance."

"Rory Breen," he said as he shook her hand. It was small, but her shake was strong and firm. He gazed at her shadowy face and thought that her name was familiar. Even her face was becoming vaguely familiar, though he didn't recall having ever met her before.

She smiled and began to chuckle. "I think I'm gonna end up owing you for a lot more than helping with the trailer. I imagine your little stunt is gonna draw Price Mitchum's attention for weeks to come. He probably won't bother at all with me."

Rory grinned. "Glad to see you have at least some sense of humor."

She shook her head slightly, as if expressing both wonder and doubt. Rory felt quite cocky at having impressed her at last.

She said, "These are my daughters—Glory and Mercy." She didn't identify one from the other.

"Hello," Rory said and thought the names unique, on the odd side, like their mother's.

Both little girls regarded him with serious eyes. One stuck a thumb in her mouth, and the other put her face in her mother's lap, while Zoe started the truck and again checked the mirrors for someone coming after them.

As she shifted into gear, she said, "You're Oren Breen's brother, aren't you—from the ranch about eight miles down the road?"

"Yep, that's me. You know my brother Oren?" Trust that she knew of Oren, he thought; Oren made certain all women, from one to ninety-one, knew of him. Especially pretty ones like this.

"I cut his hair," she said, and then he knew where he'd heard of her.

Rory had her drop him at the entrance, insisting she not take him the mile and a half down the drive to the big house.

He had suggested going on to her place—he knew she was renting Otis Ferguson's old place only a couple of miles west of Wings.

"No need for you to go so far out of your way," he'd said about driving him home. "And I can help you get your horse unloaded, then call someone to come get me."

But she'd refused. "I can unload him. I'll take you home."

She was a cool, uppity sort, he thought as he stood on the dirt road and watched her circle around and drive off into the night, leaving him alone. After watching the red tail-lights of her trailer disappear, he turned and started down the drive. There wasn't a street lamp, porch lamp or window light in sight, but moonlight lit everything with its ethereal glow as only it can out on the great plains. The twinkling stars seemed close enough to touch. Missing his hat, he raked a hand through his hair. He was a hat man and felt almost naked without it. He sure hoped he could find it tomorrow; it was a twenty-X beaver and his favorite.

A let-down feeling swept over him.

Kicking up dust that he couldn't truly see, he thought how he would have liked to have gone with Zoe Yarberry. By going with her, he could have prolonged the fun and excitement of the night and enjoyed time with a pretty female. He could have put off the loneliness.

He knew bits and pieces about Zoe Yarberry, had seen her a couple of times at Cobb's Drugstore, though he hadn't known then who she was. Just some cute gal, he'd thought at the time.

He'd heard that old Otis Ferguson had rented his place to Dusty Yarberry, which meant Dusty must be the husband who'd taken off six months ago. Rory had come in contact with Dusty Yarberry at a number of rodeos; Yarberry showed promise at roping but was mediocre at everything else. Rory guessed Yarberry to be in his mid-twenties; he was a lanky fella with shaggy dark blond hair and a handsome face on the soft side. He'd impressed Rory as being just another rodeo bum sort, one of the thousand and one who were trying to make a name but couldn't even begin to make a living, had no gumption to do anything else and would probably end up following the circuit until he was too broken-down to ride anymore.

Zoe Yarberry was operating a beauty parlor out of the Ferguson house. Rory knew that because Oren had been going to her to have his hair cut for a couple of months now and had been telling Rory and Matt they needed to try her. Oren was careful with his hair. Matt kept his hair just like he had in his teens and went to George over in Raton, the same barber he'd used in his teens, too. He didn't trust anyone else. Rory wasn't nearly as particular as either of his brothers and got a haircut whenever he thought of it, or felt like it, which generally wasn't more than every three months or so. He would stop into the nearest barber and take it as it came. In his view, hair always grew back, so there wasn't any need to worry about it.

He wondered if Zoe Yarberry had been left all by herself with those two kids. Seemed a heavy load for such a young woman. Though she appeared up to it. He grinned, recalling how she'd stood up to Mitchum, defending what was hers. Zoe Yarberry might be young, but she certainly had a tough streak.

His thoughts drifted to That Jerk Price Mitchum, and then naturally to Krystal. He'd gone for a long time not thinking about Krystal—at least, not hurting when he thought about her, not feeling anything at all. And then last month she'd called to tell him she was getting remarried. That call had brought it all crashing back over him—the pain, the disillusionment, the humiliation, the failure.

The pain tightened his chest, and the anger that had become so familiar knotted in his gut. He wished badly for something to hit and tried to make do with a kick at the ground. It didn't ease him.

When he finally came in sight of the big house, he saw lights shining from the kitchen and Matt and Annie's room. He'd grown up in that house, which had been begun by his great-grandfather and added on to by each generation. Now he lived there with his older brother Matt, Matt's wife, Annie, and their son Little Jesse, who was the first of the next generation, and Oren. Their father, Jesse, had built himself a new house three miles to the west and brought home a new bride several months ago. And if that hadn't seemed odd enough, the new bride, Marnie, had just given birth to a new Breen—a girl at long last. Rory had a little sister. He was thirty-three, living in the family house, and his father had started a new family, while he didn't have one of his own, or any prospects, either.

Coming closer to the house, he saw Annie through the kitchen window. She had soft wavy hair. She was pretty, and he liked looking at her. He liked looking at just about all women, considered them pretty simply for being female. He guessed it could be said that he, like each of his brothers, simply *liked* women. And he supposed it had to do with losing his mother while in his teens. After growing up in an all-male household, a man appreciated a woman's touch.

His heart tightened with longing. It wasn't good for a man to envy his brother the way he did. Oh, he didn't covet Annie—not really. What he envied was what Matt had with her. Matt had a union with Annie; he had a special place with her. Rory wished for that.

He gazed at her and thought how if he went in there right now, smelling of whiskey, like he knew he did, Annie would just smile gently at him and offer him a cup of coffee. She made good coffee. And she never judged but understood him better than just about anyone.

But he didn't want to face anyone right that minute, and he sure didn't want coffee.

He walked on to the horse barn, where he pulled a quart bottle of Jack D. from its hiding place in the tack chest. It was almost full. He took it to the far end of the barn and settled himself comfortably on the sweet-smelling alfalfa hay bales stacked there. The three yearlings in the corral came to stick their necks over the rail at him, but moved away when he offered them no treat.

His depression deepened as he watched them. They wouldn't be ready to begin training until next year, and none of them showed promise of equalling his Salty Dog, who'd broken his leg two months ago and had to be put down. If Salty's leg had just been a clean break, maybe Rory could have nursed him until he healed, but the break had been the shattering kind, and Salty had been in such pain that Rory couldn't stand to see him suffer. He'd done the job himself, with his own gun, then gone off alone to bawl like a baby.

Tears came to his eyes with the vivid memory.

Lying in the darkness, he watched the yearlings in the moonlight, sipped the whiskey and let it dull the angry fire inside him.

That his wife hadn't been content with him, that somehow he'd lacked whatever it took to fulfill her, had carved a deep hole inside Rory, where demons danced to taunt him. And it took drinking to drown the demons and fill up the hole. It seemed, though, to take more drinking every day. With an edgy fear that maybe this one bottle of Jack D. wouldn't be enough, he took a heavy swig and held the bottle tightly, praying for dreamless sleep to take him.

Zoe turned into the dirt drive. The lone pole lamp lit the sandy, grass-tufted yard between the house and the barn, glinted on the house's tin roof and showed clearly the peeling white paint of all the buildings—house, barn, empty cockeyed chicken coop and dilapidated tool shed.

With expert maneuvering, she backed the trailer into the wide, open door of the barn, got out and pulled the chain that turned on the single light bulb hanging in the center from a frayed cord. A dingy yellow glow dispelled the blackness.

The barn was fifty years old, with plenty of cracks, but it had been built of good seasoned hardwood and remained sturdy yet. On one side were three spacious stalls with openings to outside corrals. Each held only a bucket for water and a wooden hay feeder, but they were clean, solid and safe stalls nonetheless. On the other side was open space for storage. An old broken wagon sat there, along with a small stack of alfalfa hay bales.

The girls had followed, not about to miss a thing. "Come here, darlin's." Zoe lifted first Mercy and then Glory into the bed of the old wagon. "Now, you two stay up here, no matter what. I don't want either of you to get kicked. It could kill you. You hear me?" She didn't mind scaring them—it could save their lives. She gave each of them her firm mother's eye, and they nodded obediently. Glory stuck her thumb in her mouth.

Zoe opened the gate of the trailer and went inside to get Blue. In the deep shadows, she couldn't clearly see him, but her senses put her on alert. He quivered when she touched him. She carefully led him toward the gate and out into the dull light of the barn. Her eye lit upon the welts across his hips at about the same moment he began snorting, prancing and pulling away from her.

She jerked hard on the lead rope, once, twice. "Whoa...whoa!" She felt about the size of a flea, and the image of a man she'd seen have half his head kicked off filled her mind.

Eyes rolling wide and wild, Blue reared. Zoe threw all of her slight one hundred and five pounds into his massive twelve hundred, sticking her puny right shoulder against his muscular left one and dancing around as fast as he did to keep herself glued to him, all the while saying "Whoa" in her best imitation of a calm man.

The safest place was against the horse, and she needed to pull him in a circle to get control. She did it all automatically, hearing her father's instructions from memory. It was a lot like trying to rope the wind, but fear that he might hurt the girls or get away and hurt himself kept her at it and overrode all consideration of getting stomped.

They circled together until Blue quieted. He trembled against her, and Zoe trembled against him. At the same instant that she saw she'd made a great mistake in not having the stall gate open, Mercy and Glory darted over to open it. Glory's pudgy little fingers fumbled with the latch. Together the girls flung open the gate, then scurried back to the shelter of the wagon, peeking through the spokes of the wooden wheel.

Zoe led Blue into the stall, carefully removed the halter and quickly backed herself out, securing the stall gate with shaking hands. Blue sniffed around, nervous and gruff.

She looked at the girls. They grinned, Glory proudly, Mercy hesitantly. __

"We help-ded," Glory said with an expression that clearly said she knew Zoe couldn't scold them. Mercy looked hopeful.

"Yes, you both helped, and I thank you," Zoe said. She took a deep breath and shook off the tension, moving to get the horse a big block of hay. Nothing shut a horse up like good alfalfa hay.

"He's hurt...." Glory gazed at Blue with wide, serious eyes.

Zoe nodded. "Yes, darlin'... but he'll be okay. Help me get the water hose."

As she filled his water bucket, she studied the welts across his hips. They looked to have been made by about a one-by-two board and were recent.

They fed and watered Blue and told him they loved him. Then Zoe said, "Come on, little darlin's, time to get back to bed," and reached to turn out the light.

She grabbed up the girls, one in each arm, propping them on her hips.

"You two are gonna break my back," she said, and they both giggled and wrapped their legs tight around her. Following the yellow glow of the porch light, she lugged them across the grass-clumped yard to the house, managing not to trip over the gray striped cat who rubbed at her ankles. With no other house in sight, no other lights at all, the sky stretched midnight blue, sprinkled with glittering stars and the large, forty karat moon.

Zoe went up the cracked concrete back steps and into the kitchen through the door that wasn't locked. There was no need, because not only were thieves few, but there wasn't anything inside worth stealing. The sparse furnishings belonged to the Fergusons, all but a few dishes, the linens and Zoe's old television with aluminum foil stuck on the antennas, and if anyone wanted that, they were welcome.

Her steps echoed on scuffed and peeling linoleum, and the floorboards beneath squeaked. The house was what they called a shotgun design—thin and long, each room leading to the next, and it was said a shotgun could be fired from the front room and exit the back, hitting everyone in between. It was as old as the barn, circa World War II, but, unlike the barn, had been built with green lumber, so it wasn't nearly as sturdy. In strong winds, which were common as jackrabbits out on the high grassland, Zoe could feel the walls shaking. About the only modification since it had been built was some electrical wiring, and not nearly enough of that.

She plunked each girl to the counter, one on either side of the deep, chipped enamel sink, and pulled the chain to turn on the light above.

"Hands," she instructed.

Each girl held her hands over the sink. She washed them, then took a wet cloth to their faces.

Gratitude rose, as it always did when she looked at her girls, for their perfection. With silky straight hair the color of dried wheat and golden button eyes, they were beautiful. Everyone said so, and Zoe most often replied, "I know. Thank you." Wasn't any use being modest about the obvious.

And these little girls were the most angelic souls on earth. From birth, they both had slept the night through and had done much more laughing than crying. Only on rare occasions did they get into mischief. Glory did have a propensity for stubbornness, which Zoe thought of as a strong will, and Mercy did have a streak, a very small streak, of selfishness, which Zoe considered necessary for survival. She thought them as close to perfect as human beings could be and still live on this earth. That they were her children she considered her due for having both of them at once.

She kissed each beautiful forehead, then urged both girls toward the bathroom. She changed their nightgowns for fresh ones, worn but clean. By the light shining from the bathroom, because there wasn't one in the girls' room, she tucked them into bed on the mattress stretched on the floor. She didn't mind not having a bedstead for them, because this way they couldn't hurt themselves if they fell out of bed.

The Padilla family's fortunes had bounced from very low to comfortably high and back again to lower than low more than once. Zoe had grown up knowing how to make do, to make pennies stretch like rubber, and she also possessed a strong artistic streak. For the girls' room, she'd painted the old dresser a glossy rose pink to match the woodwork and covered the walls with images of rainbows and butterflies and trees and friendly animals. She'd sewn—by hand, because she didn't have a machine—lacy curtains for the windows. It was a cheerful room for two children.

As she kissed them, Mercy said, "Song, Mama." With one look, Mercy could coax the stripes off a zebra.

So Zoe sang, "Hush, little baby, don't say a word, Mama's gonna buy you a mockin' bird. And if that mockin' bird don't sing, Mama's gonna buy you a diamond ring...." As she'd learned the words, it was *Papa's gonna buy,* but the girls didn't have a papa anymore, and it was Mama doing all the buying. At least Dusty's leaving hadn't seemed to affect them. They'd quit asking after him months ago, remaining happy as always. He'd been an elusive figure in their lives at best, anyway. They'd been only an inconvenience to him.

Both girls were asleep before Zoe finished the song. She adjusted the thin summer quilt over them, moved the gray cat to the foot of the bed, started to pull Glory's thumb from her mouth, then left it. On the way out, she stepped on a plastic cow and had to choke back a yowl. She picked it up, along with a stuffed monkey and a jack-in-the-box, and put them on the toy bench, where they could talk to each other in the night.

In her own room, she turned on the lamp that sat on the three-legged table beside the bed. It cast a dull yellow glow over the brown iron bedstead, the scratched oak dresser, the long crack across the ceiling. But Zoe had worked on this room, too. She'd covered the bed with an almost new dusty blue chenille spread, and had dyed nearly the same color a fluffy string rug and lace for curtains. On top of the dresser was a lovely clear glass vase with a dried-flower arrangement, along with her collection of crystal cosmetic bottles—all five of them, a small collection, but she liked it. The room was cozy. She considered that having pretty things to look at was a most important thing in life, though she could admit what one person found pretty, like morning sunshine spilling across the weathered gray walls of the barn, others would find no big deal.

Her gaze fell to the bed, and she thought of Dusty. She wondered if he was sleeping alone, and the fantasy of bursting into a motel room where he was with some woman filled her mind. She saw them jerking the sheets up to their chins and staring at her with popping eyes. What would she do? She pictured herself standing in the door with a gun— no, change that to a hose, a fire hose, aiming the water at them and washing them right off the bed.

Lord save her from bitterness. Bitterness was like a boomerang that came right back and smacked a person in the head. It hurt her much more than it could ever hurt Dusty.

Slowly she sat, took off her boots and the rest of her clothes, then rubbed her weak knee. It throbbed a little but hadn't swollen, as it sometimes did. When she'd been nine, in a freak accident, her brother had run over her knee with his motorcycle; since that time her knee had been unstable. Occasionally it popped out of joint, and she'd learned to maneuver it to pop it back into place. The weakness was simply something she lived with.

She stood beside the open window, allowing the night air to caress her bare skin while she unplaited her hair, ran her fingers through it and shook it down across her shoulder blades. She looked down at her body. Her skin, even though she was a quarter Mexican, was the color of ivory. It was her best feature, inherited from her mother, as was her shiny honey-brown hair. It appeared naturally wavy, but it wasn't—she had a perm. As a beautician, she knew how to do it just so, to make it look natural.

She took a cotton nightgown off the hook on the back of the bathroom door and slipped it on. She'd showered earlier and wouldn't now, but she did wash her face again, with glycerin soap and a nubby cloth, and liberally applied a fresh mixture of almond and peanut oil, with extra castor oil around her eyes, because she was out of rich eye cream and had no money to buy more. The air out here was dry as day-old toast, and skin became just like that if not taken care of. Her grandmother, a Western lady of the old order, had ingrained early into Zoe and her sister the responsibility of taking care of themselves. Lucinda Padilla had been fond of saying, "Beauty does come from within, but a woman has to help it get out."

Zoe stared for a long moment into the mirror and wondered who she was trying to stay beautiful for. There had certainly never been anything beautiful enough about her to have kept her husband interested. Dusty had married her because he'd gotten her pregnant, plain and simple—and honorable on his part. He'd loved her in his way, as much as he was able to love anyone. And she'd been so crazy about him, she'd deluded herself about everything.

She supposed she was now taking care of herself for herself. Herself and her girls. She was all they had now.

Originally from Virginia, her mother had never adjusted to the West and had left to return East when Zoe had been eight; she'd died in a car crash back in Virginia. Her father had died two years ago, her grandmother the year before that. Her elder sister, Astera, lived out in California and was involved with her own family, two girls and a boy. Brother Ulysses had survived the Gulf War and was intent on becoming an officer, working his way up from the ranks in the Marine Corps. Odd how she'd been so close to her grandmother and father but never her sister and brother. They each had their own busy lives and problems. Only if she were dying would Zoe impose on either of them. She had her mother's pride—and her father's heart, her grandmother had always said, meaning the latter as a compliment.

Zoe had adored her father and supposed she wasn't adverse to having a heart like his. She just liked to think herself more dependable than he had been. Though he'd made something of a name for himself as a horse trainer, Joseph Padilla had been a cowboy through and through. His world had been horses and cows and cows and horses, with a little left over for his children, drinking and women, in that order. Responsibility, time and money hadn't counted at all.

The phone beside the bed rang, jarring her from her thoughts.

"Yes?" she answered timidly, placing a hand to her chest as if for some sort of protection against hearing Price Mitchum on the other end of the line. Hope of hearing Dusty's drawl flickered, too.

"It's Jada, honey."

Not Price Mitchum. And not Dusty, either.

Zoe plopped onto the bed. "Oh, Jada . . . hi."

"Is everything all right with you and the girls?"

"Yes, we're just fine, thanks. The girls are back to sleep, and Blue is safe in his stall. I sure do thank you for callin' me about Price havin' the trailer and Blue at Kelly's tonight. I might never have had another chance to get them—I mean, I bet he almost never used that trailer. He has one a lot nicer. The angels were just lookin' out for me tonight."

Jada said, "Someone was lookin' out for you. The whole reason Price had your trailer and horse was that he'd taken them to a sale. I heard him talkin' about it. He'd been to an auction down in Dalhart but couldn't get either bid up to what he wanted, so he'd pulled them and was takin' them to another sale down in Amarillo tomorrow. You are one lucky girl to have gotten them tonight."

Zoe's heartbeat picked up tempo as she thought how close she'd come to losing Blue forever. "I sure thank you for helpin' me out, Jada."

"No problem. Although, missy, I was afraid I was gonna have your blood on my hands. Why in the world did you come in and tell him? I do believe he's the type that wouldn't have let you bein' a woman stop him from grindin' you into dust."

"It wasn't one of the smartest things I ever did," Zoe admitted with a heavy breath. She lay back on her pillows and bent one knee, propping the other leg on it, bobbing her foot in the air. She needed a pedicure; she liked to keep her toenails painted in blushing rose.

"Amen to that, honey. You put a firecracker under him," Jada said with her deep, throaty chuckle. "And then when he saw Rory throw his keys out into the field, I thought he was gonna choke on his own spit! What was Rory doin' with Price's keys?"

"He helped me get my trailer. Price had left his keys in his pickup, and Rory drove it off so I could hook up mine in its place."

"Ahh . . . I kinda figured it was somethin' like that. Him and Price got into it earlier. They hate each other, anyway. What did you do with him?"

"Who?"

"Rory."

"I took him home."

"Yours or his?" Her throaty chuckle came again.

"His, of course."

Jada gave an elaborate sigh. "I do wonder about you. I really do. I could sure think of better things to do with Rory Breen than takin' him home."

Zoe sat up. "Then you should do them. As for me, I am not in the habit of takin' home men I've just met. Especially men I've met in a tavern parking lot. I've got two babies to raise, and I'm not interested in another cowboy. I'm not interested in another man, period."

"Well, that's a sentiment every woman has had at least once in her life. But don't put Rory Breen into the same category as your husband, honey. He's nothin' like Dusty. He has a few problems, sure, but don't we all? Rory's always had a wild streak, but it was his wife who drove him to drinkin'. She really liked to party, had him to clubs every weekend. And she ran around on him, then left him flat. Deep inside he's a good, solid man who has temporarily lost his way. What he needs is the love of a good woman to straighten him out."

Zoe chuckled dryly. "That a woman can straighten out a man is a fantasy. Can't be done, and I'm certainly not fool enough to try that again. I have enough to deal with."

She thought of her mother and father, of herself and Dusty. Humans were an odd species. Her grandmother had always said that people themselves want to prove that God had a sense of humor—He'd created them in the first place.

"Honey, your heart won't stay broken forever," Jada said softly.

"And you're one to give advice on men and heartache," Zoe returned.

"Well, don't follow my example, follow my advice. Changing the subject just a mite—am I to assume Blue is still in business to take care of the ladies?"

"Yes, he's still got all his working parts," Zoe said and gave silent thanks to the powers that be. "I guess Price figured he'd be better off tryin' to sell Blue for his blood line than for his training. Plenty of people are gonna remember his mama was a champion cutter—and he's her only son, even if he hasn't ever done much to prove out.''

"So, what are you gonna do with him? Think you can sell him? Or would you do better to put him to stud?''

Zoe sighed. "I'll keep him for now. I may need the money, but I just can't sell him. I remember when he was born and how much hope Daddy had for him. He's a link to Daddy, you know," she added softly. "If Daddy hadn't had to sell off his stock, he would have trained Blue, had him showing by now. Besides, it galls me to let him go for a couple of thousand, when with some training and experience he could be worth triple that at least. As for putting him to stud—maybe I could get three hundred a pop, but breeding season is all but over this year.'' She thought how crazy it was, her desire for this stud who would require money for feed and time for training. A streak of her father running through her, no doubt.

Jada's yawn came across the line. Horses were not of great interest to her. "How many appointments do you have tomorrow?'' she asked. Hair design, manicures and clothes were of profound interest.

"Just three, but maybe I'll get some walk-ins. My first appointment—at eight-thirty, no less—is Eldoree Winslow, who wants a perm *and* a facial.'' Facing Eldoree first thing in the morning was trying to a person's sanity.

Jada said, laughing, "It's gonna take a heck of a lot more than a facial to help Eldoree. She needs a New York City plastic surgeon and a lot of prayer.'' Jada laughed easily and a lot, which was what Zoe liked about her. What everyone liked about Jada. "Well, I hope you can squeeze me in sometime. My color needs freshenin', and I believe I'd like a facial, too. I have a date with Frank Vargas. He's takin' me to dinner in Raton.''

"Frank Vargas? The guy you met through the *Lonely Hearts Newsletter?*'' Zoe went to chuckling. "He's coming down from Colorado Springs?''

"Yes, ma'am, he is, and I intend to make it worth his while.''

"Well, for such an occasion, I'll have to make time for you. Does eleven o'clock suit you?" Zoe said. Her heart swelled; she knew Jada came in twice as much as she needed just to help Zoe out financially.

After hanging up, Zoe sat there, noticing the extreme quiet. Gloom seemed to seep like a mist from the corners and fill the room, wrapping around her, threatening to suffocate her. Her eyes strayed to the folded papers propped against the portable radio. She reached for them—her divorce decree. Two weeks ago the judge had granted her a divorce, but she'd never filed the paper at the courthouse. Oh, the lawyer could have done it, but she'd said she would. It seemed only fitting—*her* marriage, *her* divorce, so she should file the paper, not some stranger.

Sharp pain sliced through her chest. With shaking hands, she refolded the papers and set them back beside the cheap little radio.

She was alone. The thought echoed through her mind, growing louder, more frightening. She was the one who had to provide her daughters with a home and food. She was the one who had to hold it all together. And then she thought how it had always been that way, even when she'd been with Dusty. Even years before, when she'd lived with her father.

Her gaze ran around the room. She'd painted the entire house, trying to make everything cheery and clean, but underneath, the dirty truth was there—underneath the modern latex paint that covered the old, hazardous lead-based kind, underneath the windowsills with cracks so large that snow seeped in during the winter, underneath the lights that flickered occasionally because of poor wiring.

She had to get herself and the girls out of here. Inside her head twirled pictures, ideas of going to the city. Albuquerque, maybe. She knew that city. She would work in a classy salon and maybe one day have her own. They would live in a nice little house, with a fenced yard, all of it clean and safe. She saw the girls with ribbons in their hair, playing.

Money. It all came down to that. She'd been saving, but it seemed to add up so slowly. Just when she had a little put by, something came along to suck it up, lately the dentist for her, before that the doctor for the girls. Perhaps Blue... Oh,

Lord, she was thinking of long shots, like her daddy had done.

Quickly she reached over and turned on the portable radio. Randy Travis's latest tune came to her, tinny sounding through the cheap speaker. She curled up on the bed, drew up her legs, wrapped her arms around them, rested her chin on her knees and lost herself in the music, leaving all the pain and uncertainties behind.

Chapter Four

Rory was awakened by a flood of water cascading over his face.

"What the..." He sat up, choked and gasped for breath.

With blurred vision he saw Matt three feet away, legs splayed, a metal bucket dangling from his hand. He looked like the wrath of God pointed right at Rory. "Time to wake up, brother. Mornin's half over."

"By damn, Matt..." Rory scrambled to his feet, slinging back his wet hair and struggling to focus. "There wasn't any call for that."

"We have cattle to attend to and can't be waitin' for you to fight off a hangover." Matt's tone echoed with contempt. He had a rather strong righteous streak. He wrinkled his nose. "You stink like rancid whiskey."

"Then don't get so close." Shaking, Rory lowered himself to a hay bale.

"You're sure a pretty sight." That was from Oren, who stood over by the corral entrance. "When you weren't in your bed this mornin', we all figured you'd stayed the night with Zoe Yarberry."

That brought Rory's head up. "Don't go makin' up rumors about Zoe Yarberry." His head throbbed, and he inwardly cursed his brothers for disturbing him.

"Sorry. I wasn't slandering her. I just meant everyone at Kelly's saw you drive off with her—and then you weren't in the house when I got home."

"I barely know Zoe Yarberry—I just gave the girl a helpin' hand. Satisfied? Now, you two go on and let me throw up in peace."

"I believe, Matt, what our brother here needs is a cool bath." Oren grinned with mischief, which wasn't anything new for him.

Pained by the bright light of day, Rory squeezed his eyes closed.

"I sure hate for Annie and Little Jesse to see you like this, brother," Matt said reproachfully.

Rory thought he did, too, and wished he could get his head to quit spinning. "Just leave me alone—the both of you." Why wouldn't anyone leave him alone? If people would just leave him alone, he'd leave them alone, too. His head felt as if it were filled with greasy cream gravy. He just wanted to go back to sleep.

Suddenly Matt and Oren were both there, taking hold of him.

"We're gonna help you get a bath," Matt said, his eyes sparking like the devil.

"And you won't even have to go through the house to do it," Oren added with great glee.

And then they were dragging him out of the barn and into the corral, toward the big round water tank.

Rory came to life. With a surge of energy, he got his arm loose and managed a clumsy swing at Oren, who ducked neatly.

"You're no good the mornin' after, big brother," Oren shouted. "Any woman ever tell you that?"

Rory struggled, his spirit rising valiantly to the challenge. His first movements were sluggish and heavy, but quickly his blood began to pump. He wasn't going peacefully. No, sir—he wasn't having it! "You hombres just give it a try, if you think you're man enough!"

He grabbed a hay bale, and Oren bit his hand to make him let loose. He formed a fist and rapped Oren in the teeth, and was rewarded by a yowl. He pushed Matt down, but Matt just clutched him and rolled toward the tank. They were all near in size and strength—but there were two of them against one of him. With grunts and curses and yells, they got to the edge of the tank. Suddenly Rory found he'd broken free. He scrambled to get some distance, but Oren flew over and tackled him around the legs, throwing them both beneath the feet of one of the three colts who were looking on. Rory instinctively hunkered protectively over Oren's head and ducked his own against flying hooves. A second later he had Matt on him again. Oren took his shoulders.

Rory kicked fiercely, heedless of the damage he might do to one of them. "Damn you two! My boots!" He caught Matt in the stomach and sent him stumbling.

But Matt came back in a flash and latched on to a flailing leg, taunting, "Take some of the money you spend on booze and buy a new pair."

"Little water won't hurt those boots," Oren said. "And it'll do you a world of good."

They had him on the edge, and Rory had just about spent all his fighting strength.

"Time to repent, sinner!" Laughing, Oren shoved.

"I ain't goin' alone!"

As he toppled over backward into the murky water, Rory managed to latch on to both of his brothers, pulling them with him in one great splash.

Their heads broke water at the same time, all three of them gasping from the exertion. Oren was laughing between spitting, and Matt was looking for all the world as if he'd been struck in the head by a two-by-four. Rory couldn't seem to get his breath.

Then a great, shocking yell sounded from over by the barn. Rory jerked his head around to see a figure—his father!—running toward the tank and yelling, "Ooooweee!"

They scrambled out of the way as, with one spring, their father jumped in with them. Water mixed with bits of green algae, slimy hay and rotting oats shot up, then fell down upon their heads once more.

Their father sat up, shaking his head. His corduroy sport coat billowed up. "Ooooweee, you boys been havin' this much fun without me? I've been missin' out on a lot down there in Amarillo."

Matt wiped an oat from his nose and made a face. "You gotta clean this tank, Rory," he said.

Rory sent him a mocking look. "It was all your idea, big brother. Enjoy."

As a surprise, Big Jesse, as Rory's father was called more and more these days, and his new wife Marnie had come home, bringing their baby daughter, who'd been born two weeks earlier.

Though the doctors had maintained that Marnie's health was excellent, Jesse had worried. Marnie was thirty-eight, and this was her first child. Jesse had taken a condo for them in Amarillo, within ten minutes of the hospital, and they had spent the previous two months there, awaiting the debut of the new baby. It turned out that Jesse had been right to be ready for anything, for the little one had decided to come almost three weeks early. However, little Mary Regina was wonderfully healthy. If anyone had any problems now it was Jesse, who had spent too long in the city to be comfortable.

"Your father is in great need of the wide open spaces," Marnie said. "He's been watching all the nature programs on television until he's about to go bug-eyed. And we're going to own the telephone company, Matt, for all the calls he's been making back here. For what we've been spending, he could just have hired a doctor to live with us here."

Big Jesse whacked her bottom. "Oh, you love this country boy, and you know it."

The two of them sent each other warm, intimate looks that made Rory both glad and uncomfortable. It was easy to accept Marnie, because she made their father very happy. But sometimes it was harder to see the man who'd always been his father as being a man in his own right. A very virile man, who had just produced a little sister for Rory. It wasn't easy to digest.

After the four men had cleaned up properly, the Breen clan enjoyed a picnic out beneath the trees down by the pond. It was Marnie's idea, even though everyone knew she wasn't a great lover of picnics. She was a city girl, and they all teased her about it.

Rory helped Matt haul a comfortable living room chair down from the house for Marnie and little Mary Regina, and tried to pretend his head wasn't about to crack open. He ate Annie's fried chicken, too, and willed his stomach to accept it. He pushed Little Jesse in the swing and on his tricycle. And then he held little Mary Regina. Marnie pushed the beginning-to-fuss baby into his arms. "They say you have the charm to quiet babies," she said with a grin and sparkling eyes. "And I promise, she is dry."

Rory swallowed and held the baby gingerly. He'd taken care of Little Jesse a lot; Rory had always been good with babies and did indeed have a sort of "touch." However, this was a *girl*.

He gazed down into her face. She looked back and became suddenly content. Rory thought that at least he had one talent—he settled babies.

She was beautiful. He tried to find a resemblance to his father but couldn't. He looked at his dad, who was looking at his wife. He looked back at his sister. Mary Regina. Rory's mother's name had been Regina. The name showed how much his father still remembered her—and how much Marnie loved his father.

Rory wondered if he would ever have children of his own. He held his sister a little closer; this might be the closest he ever got.

Later—courtesy of Oren, of course—the family all heard about the previous night's escapades, and Rory patiently put up with the ribbing about getting kicked out of Kelly's. And, when prodded, he told the tale of unhitching Mitchum's trailer and tossing his keys. He didn't admit to still having those keys and decided now, in the light of day, it would be best if no one ever knew. Price Mitchum was hot enough. Rory would mail the keys back to him—and from over in the Raton post office, too.

Mostly, on that balmy May afternoon, Rory lounged on a blanket, a little off to the side, listening to the others talk. He felt out of place, alone, right there in the midst of his family. He'd felt this way for so much of his life, he thought. There was a difference inside him that they couldn't understand. That he didn't understand. Yet he wanted so much to feel a part of them.

When Annie would have gone back up to the house for more ice, Rory volunteered to get it for her.

"Oh, you sweetie." She gave him an easy hug and handed him the empty ice bucket. "There's another bucket in the cabinet in the dining room. Fill it with ice, too, so we won't run out again."

He headed to the house in long strides, glad for an excuse to get off by himself for a few minutes. For some reason, he felt frustrated. He was struggling to appear like a contented old gelding out on grass, while inside he felt like a yearling colt kept in an eight-by-eight pen.

The quiet house was heaven. As he rinsed the ice bucket and filled it with ice, he mused over the idea of getting a place of his own. Perhaps that would help him. But where? The workings of the ranch required him to be *here*, and this house was the only one available. And this was his home; he didn't really want to leave it.

Pausing, he pulled a can of cream soda from the refrigerator, popped the lid and drank. Down at the picnic, they were drinking glasses of iced tea and cola, which was fine, but he preferred cream soda—and straight from the can. He was decadent, he thought with a sad chuckle.

Without hurrying, he went on to the dining room to find the second ice bucket. "In the cabinet" was all Annie had said, which sent him searching behind all the doors. He found formal glasses, Christmas china, crystal platters, neatly folded linen tablecloths. Just about twenty years of stuff. He opened a third door, stopped and stared. He'd come to the house's small liquor cabinet.

There were only four bottles: brandy, a red wine that Aunt Ina liked, tequila and a quart bottle of Jack D. No one in the house, except Rory, drank very much. These bottles were kept for New Year's and special occasions.

He sure would like a drink, he thought, and lifted out the bottle of Jack D. He gazed at it.

Not a good idea, buddy.

One little swig wouldn't hurt anything. No one would know.

Don't borrow trouble. Not now. Not while everyone is enjoying themselves.

Gingerly, Rory replaced the bottle.

"I should have known where to find you—at the damn liquor."

Rory jerked his head around to see Matt shoving through the swinging door, his face full of condemnation.

Rory stiffened, drawing into himself. "I was just getting the ice bucket for Annie," he said stiffly and reached for it behind the bottles.

But the next instant Matt took him by the collar and jerked him around. "A convenient excuse, that's for sure. Damn it, Rory. Couldn't you leave that stuff alone for one afternoon—today when Dad's finally come home?"

Rory exploded inside. He knocked away Matt's hand, then shoved him hard. "I *said* I came for the ice bucket!"

Matt, his eyes shooting fire, came back at him, grabbed him by the shirt and whirled him against the wall hard enough to rattle the pictures. Rory brought both arms up and broke his brother's grasp, drew back to punch him, then froze. Rory stared into his brother's fiery blue eyes, his pulse pounding in his ears.

"What's going on here?"

Their father stepped slowly through the swinging door. Rory looked at him, realized his hand was still poised and he lowered it. He glanced at Matt, then averted his gaze. He could feel his brother's fury and his father's concerned puzzlement, and wanted to get away from both before he started swinging and couldn't stop. Without a word, he snatched the ice bucket from where it had landed on the floor, skirted his father and left the room.

* * *

Jesse put his arm out to stop Matt from going after Rory. "Let him alone."

Matt lashed out in his frustration. "Someone has to talk some sense into him. I caught him at the liquor cabinet. He started this last month after Krystal called, and he's gotten so bad, he can't leave the stuff alone for a whole afternoon. He's way out of hand, Dad."

Jesse sighed, and memory brought a deep pain. He and his middle son were so much alike. Looking at Rory was like seeing a replica of himself at that age—wild as wind swirling around a mountain and just as lost. But when Jesse had been his son's age, he'd had his Gina to be a beacon for him. His son didn't have a special someone to help him understand himself. To *force* him to understand himself.

He spoke from experience when he said, "You can't get your brother in order, Matt, like you can your prize cattle or that computer in there. The harder you try, the more he's gonna back up, just like a stubborn mule."

"I just want to help him," Matt said, his anger slipping away into desperation. "We're losin' him, Dad."

"You can't help by *demanding* to help him. You can't live his life for him—every one of us has to figure out our own life, and no one can do it for us. Your part as Rory's brother is to be there when he *asks* for your help."

Matt looked unconvinced and frustrated. "And what if he's too stubborn and proud to ask?"

Jesse squeezed Matt's shoulder. "Rory's a good man, Matt. Remember that and take comfort from it."

He left Matt and went to find Rory. And to do exactly what he'd just told Matt not to do—butt in. But then, Jesse reasoned, he was Rory's father, and there had been a time when he'd walked in the boots Rory was walking in now. Besides, he was better at butting in than most people.

He found Rory in the barn, saddling up Walter. Rory's expression was thunderous. For an instant Jesse saw his son as he'd been at eight, when he'd come home, trying not to cry, and said the teacher had accused him of writing filthy words on the blackboard.

"I didn't do it, Dad," he'd said. "I told her I didn't do it, but Billy Dee said I did, and she wouldn't believe me."

The injustice of it had cut him to the core. Rory had never understood that his anger sprang from his deep passion. Rory cared very deeply—for other people, animals, justice and honor and truth. And because of that, he could easily be hurt.

Of course, back then Jesse had marched himself to school and set the teacher straight. He wished helping his son could be done as easily now.

Rory paused in tightening the cinch and gazed defiantly at Jesse. "I don't owe anyone an explanation for what I do. If I give it, I expect it to be accepted."

"I won't argue the point with you, son. And whatever disagreement you have with Matt is between you two."

Suspicion, then coolness, slipped across Rory's face. There was a wall there that pushing would only cause to go higher. Jesse backed off.

"Your brother is only worried about you," he said. Guilt was a powerful weapon for a parent.

Rory slapped the stirrup leather. "He doesn't need to be—he brings it on himself, because he thinks he can order the world to be perfect."

"And that's a bit of truth," Jesse allowed and saw a smile touch the corner of his son's hard mouth. He pulled out a cigar, bit off the end and tucked it between his lips. "Have some compassion for him. It's a rare brother who can love you the way Matt does. And put yourself in his place—you two are very much alike, you know."

"Thought you'd given up smoking. You have a daughter to think of now," Rory said, throwing guilt right back at Jesse.

Jesse chuckled inwardly over that. "I'm just chewing on it." He watched his son round the horse, checking the saddle rigging. Rory put the bridle on Walter, then turned.

"Well, are you gonna have your say? I'd like to go on my ride."

Jesse gazed at Rory's grim features. "Do you think you're drinkin' too much?"

Rory's eyes flickered; his face was a stoic mask. "I'm drinkin'. And I'm not ready to stop."

Gazing at him, Jesse almost asked if there was anything he could do for Rory, but he knew that was a useless question. Rory didn't have the answer, wouldn't want the question. A flash of frustration swept through Jesse, and he formed a fist, then unknotted it. "I love you, son. I'm here if you need anything."

Rory's eyes darkened, and he turned away. "I know, Dad." He mounted Walter.

Grasping at wanting to do more, Jesse said, "I do have some advice. Try not to fight yourself so hard. You don't have to be perfect, no matter how people like to press you to be. Pray some. And find someone else to focus your interest on beside yourself—preferably a woman."

Rory grinned thinly. "I already had a woman. It didn't work out so well."

"How many horses have thrown you?"

Rory gazed down at him.

His father winked. "Get my point? Gotta get up and get on again. Can't lie forever in the dirt. For one thing, as long as you're lyin' there, that horse is gonna come stomp all over you until you're so ground into the dirt, you become the dirt."

They gazed at each other for a long second.

Then Rory said, "Mind if I borrow your hat?"

His father swept it off and tossed it to Rory. "Keep it."

Jesse watched his son ride away. He wanted to believe this was just a phase, one that would pass as if it had never been. But sometimes a person's fight with his demons could drag on for years. Sometimes a person sank so far down in his inner hell that he couldn't get out. How well he knew, for his own father had been like that. Jesse rarely thought about his father or his years growing up with the mean drunkard of a man. *Lord, save my son,* he prayed and comforted himself with the hope that God listened especially to the prayers of fathers.

Then he thought of how he was starting all over again, this time with a girl. *A girl, by golly.* Maybe he would lock her in her room and not let her out until she was thirty.

* * *

Rory was at home on a horse. On a horse, he knew who he was, exactly what to do, how to handle himself and anything that came his way. He spurred Walter across the grass, flying, moving in perfect rhythm with the horse for two miles, then slowed to a trot, to a walk, then moved back to a run again. He knew where the fences sagged and jumped them. He knew where the arroyos were and avoided them—or jumped the ones he could and experienced an exciting rush. He lost himself in the land and the sky and the strength of the horse, until, after an hour, he stopped on a rise and gazed at the Ferguson place down a long slope from him.

It looked forlorn and alone, baking in the sun, with only one tree, a scraggly thing, out back by the tool shed. The house was small, shotgun-style, with peeling white paint. Zoe Yarberry's old '75 Chevy truck sat near the barn. There was a fenced area at the east side of the house, and the two little girls were playing in there, chasing each other.

Rory asked himself what he was doing there.

He didn't need to be going to see Zoe Yarberry, didn't need to be entertaining thoughts of her at all. He was in no shape to fool around with a girl—and *girl* was the right word. She was way too young for him to flirt with.

But he should make certain Price Mitchum hadn't been bothering her, he thought. It was the polite thing, since, after all, he'd helped goad Mitchum into a burning fury. If Mitchum took his anger out on her, it would all be Rory's fault.

Stupid rationalizing. Real stupid.

Yes, he thought, urging Walter forward. But he was very good at rationalizing.

As he rode slowly around the perimeter of the sagging fence that surrounded the buildings, he thought of how his father had tried several times in past years to buy the place from Otis Ferguson—at least the outlying three hundred acres that the old man leased out. But old Otis was tight as tree bark and had asked twice its worth.

He saw the corral outside the barn, but the horse he'd helped Zoe Yarberry retrieve last night wasn't in sight. He came around to the front of the house and saw Miss Loretta's red Toyota sitting in the curved drive. On a post was a blue sign, with black, flowing, hand-formed letters. Zoe's Beauty Room.

His gaze moved from the blue sign over the sandy ground, fading grass, paint-peeling house.

Then he saw the two little girls. They stood side by side within the fenced area and stared at him. The fence was made of chicken wire and thin stakes, and it appeared those little girls could have pushed it right over. Their faces were identical, their hair blond, straight and cut Buster Brownstyle. They were dressed differently, however, one in pink overalls, one in blue. They raised little hands and waved. Self-conscious, Rory returned the wave. They grinned, and his heart lifted a bit. There was always something nice about kids waving at you.

He left Walter tied to the old hitching post and went to the front porch. Low female voices and the smell of hair-fixing stuff came to him as he raised his hand hesitantly to knock on the screen door.

Though the knock on the door startled Zoe—she hadn't heard a car—she called, "Come in." The screen door squeaked, and footsteps and jingling spurs sounded lightly. And of all the possible people that it could be who flitted through her mind, Rory Breen was not one of them.

He seemed to fill the room. He wore a pale shirt, creased denims and a rodeo belt buckle. And spurs on dusty boots. The spurs jingled when he moved farther into the room. Politely he swept the brown hat from his head. Zoe stared so long at him that she like to have burnt Miss Loretta with the curling iron.

"Ooo, honey, that's hot," Miss Loretta said, pulling away.

"Oh! I'm sorry, Miss Loretta." Zoe fiddled with the curl, thankful to see that neither the hair nor the elderly lady's skin was singed. Her neck prickled with the sensation of Rory Breen's gaze.

Miss Loretta leaned forward to peer into the mirror. "Hello, Rory. Did you come for a haircut? I believe you could use one."

"Hello, Miss Loretta . . . Miss Yarberry. How are you ladies doin' today?"

Zoe wasn't used to being called by any form of address, not Mrs., which she was technically, nor Miss, which was a common form of courtesy given to women in this part of the country. Keeping her gaze on Miss Loretta's hair, she said, "Fine."

Miss Loretta said, "Don't be dropping your *g*'s, Rory. You must say do*ing,* not doin'."

"Yes, ma'am," he said, automatically, as if he was used to Miss Loretta's correction.

"How is Annie? Has she gotten pregnant again yet?" Miss Loretta was as blunt as an old table knife. She had been a schoolteacher and was now the postmistress, and felt herself in charge of the town.

"Not that I know of, ma'am." Grinning, he looked at Zoe. She quickly averted her eyes and felt silly for it.

"I'll have to drive out and take her some ginseng tea. I've told her that it will do the trick, but she obviously hasn't so much as tried it."

"I don't know about that, either, ma'am."

Zoe said, "How's that, Miss Loretta? Think you'll enjoy these curls?"

Miss Loretta turned her head this way and that, observing her snow-white hair in the mirror. Thin, the elderly woman's usually wild hair was pulled into a neater than normal bun, just as she'd worn it for the past fifty years, but Zoe had cut and curled bangs. They softened the woman's face considerably.

"It's a very nice change, Miss Loretta," Rory Breen said. Both his words and gentle tone were a surprise to Zoe.

Miss Loretta shot Rory a bland look. "You are a charmer, Rory Breen, and I don't believe a word you say." After half a minute, however, she pronounced, "I like it very much, though I suppose now I'll have to purchase me one of those hot irons. They're nothing new, you know. I grew up with the kind you heat on the stove. A wood stove." Her smile

came suddenly and unexpectedly brought loveliness to her
stern face. "I imagine I still have it somewhere. I'll give it a
try."

"Just don't burn yourself," Zoe cautioned.

"I'm no more likely to burn myself than you were to burn
me," she snapped, her stern expression once more in place
as she hopped from the chair like a woman half her age.

Miss Loretta paid and left. Zoe was alone with Rory
Breen, there in her front-room beauty shop. The two of
them alone, together. She thought he was more handsome,
in a rough sort of way, than had been her impression last
night, but there was evidence in his eyes of his heavy drinking.

"I thank you again for helping me last night." She
thought maybe that was what he was waiting for—to hash
over what had happened. Then it occurred to her. "You
aren't in trouble for helpin' me, are you?" She thought of
Miss Loretta's admonition about dropping g's.

He shook his head. "Not me. I came to see if you'd heard
anything further from Price Mitchum."

"He called, but just to ask me if I knew where my husband was." She didn't feel obligated to say that she had no
idea of her husband's whereabouts.

Rory Breen frowned. "He didn't get out of line or anything?"

"No. He cursed, but not really at me. Actually, he cursed
at you."

Rory Breen chuckled at that. "It surely isn't the first
time."

She tossed the hairdressing cape over the back of the chair
and began to tidy up. "I think it's like I said last night—he's
too mad at you to think a whole lot about me."

"He knows where to find me," he said, almost absently,
and she realized he was looking at her intently.

She glanced in the mirror and saw that her hair was falling loose. She'd pinned it off her neck, and now it resembled an old mop. She hadn't bothered with makeup and
looked dull as dishwater. Though that didn't matter one bit,
because she was working, not going to a dance, she thought

smartly and moved to check on the girls through the window. They were both sitting in the sandbox.

She unhooked the screen and poked her head out. "You two doin'—doing okay out there?" She would watch those g's, she thought, conscious of Miss Loretta's correction and what kind of influence she wanted to be on her daughters. And she didn't want Rory Breen to get the wrong idea about her being an uneducated bumpkin. "Would you like some apple juice?"

"Yeah!" the two chimed.

"Coming right up!"

She replaced the screen and straightened to face Rory Breen.

"Ah...could I get a haircut?" he asked.

Zoe certainly hadn't expected that, not at all.

"Miss Loretta's right," he said and ran a hand over his hair. "I do need one." He was looking at her intently again.

Blandly, Zoe said, "No problem. I have an opening right now. It's twelve dollars." And she turned the chair for him.

He backed up to the chair. "Only costs me eight where I regularly go over in Raton," he said as he sat. Men always braced themselves on the arms and lowered themselves gingerly into the chair as if they expected it to collapse underneath them.

"Then spend four dollars in gas to drive over there and get one," Zoe replied.

Their eyes met in the mirror, and a rush about the size of Niagara Falls swept over Zoe. He grinned all the way to his eyes, eyes blue as a summer sky and sparkling as crystals.

"No," he said, all full of himself. "This suits me just fine."

Zoe pushed away Niagara Falls, put her lips together and held back her grin. No, sir, she wasn't going to flirt with this cowboy, she thought. Sometimes men who got their hair cut thought a little bit of fun and games came with it. She'd let this one know immediately that wasn't the case. She'd let him know right off that she wasn't out for any hanky-panky.

She said with cool politeness, "Excuse me for a minute. I have to get my girls some juice."

Rory watched her disappear through the door and close it behind her. He mostly imagined how her slim-fitting jeans looked on her, because she wore a big loose smock that covered her from her neck to her thighs. She was as petite as he recalled, though, and even more attractive than he'd thought last night. Last night he hadn't been able to see her cocoa-brown eyes or satiny skin.

He looked around. He hadn't ever been in a beauty shop before, so he had nothing to compare this to, but he imagined that it was a far cry from one of the styling salons in the shopping malls down in Amarillo.

He had to admire the effort she'd put forth to make this place as nice as possible with limited means. A lot of it must have come from flea markets—the two waiting chairs, for example, chrome and green vinyl patched with black tape. In front of him was what resembled a woman's elaborate vanity, the top fifties' era pearl Formica, with a sink for washing hair planted in the middle. The big oval mirror had a beveled edge and looked fairly new and somehow hung there as if it were a highly prized possession. The woodwork was painted a dusky blue and the walls ivory. Posters of fashionable hairstyles were interspersed with classic trademark advertisements: Coca-Cola, Pond's Cold Cream, Bonner's Witch Hazel. Coat hangers hung on an antique oak coatrack, and a tall black fan purred from over in the corner. There was a big metal storage cabinet, painted the same color as the woodwork, and an odd-looking chair with a hair dryer attached. The window to the east, the one she'd talked to the girls through, had gingham curtains, and the west window held a room air conditioner that had seen many a summer and had been set into place crooked.

All in all, it was a friendly, comfortable place, he decided, and certainly adequate for Wings. There weren't too many fancy folks around.

The door opened, and Zoe Yarberry entered briskly. She seemed almost surprised to find him still there. "Now we can get to it," she said, rather as if she were planning surgery.

She took his hat from where he'd rested it on his knee and tossed it to the coatrack—where it settled neatly over a hook. The woman had tossed a hat or two before. Then she wrapped a strip of soft cotton around his neck. Her fingers were cool against his skin—and sent ripples down his back. He sat very still, almost afraid to breathe, and watched her face in the mirror. She didn't look him in the eyes, had no expression at all. Her eyebrows were thick, almost straight over her eyes, and she had long, silky lashes.

With a sharp snap she shook out the cape, then whisked it around him and fastened it tightly at his neck. She twirled the swivel chair, startling him, and, without warning, jerked the lever to recline it. His stiff back followed with a plop, his legs went out straight and he found himself trapped there on his back, with her bending over him.

"For twelve dollars, you get a shampoo," she said, turning on the faucet and pushing his head back into the sink.

Chapter Five

Lying there while she adjusted the water, Rory reflected that he hadn't felt so awkward since the age of twelve, when he'd had to bare his bottom for a female nurse to give him a shot.

A man went to a barber to get his hair cut, not *shampooed*. *Shampoo* was a woman's word. Sometimes a man got a shave at the barber's, but Rory hadn't ever done that, either. For at least twenty-eight years he'd done his own shaving and had *washed* his own hair. Not even Krystal had washed his hair. And now here was a woman, a comparative stranger, washing—*shampooing*—his hair. Touching him. She was close enough for her sweet feminine scent to swirl all around him. *Close enough for him to feel the life of her.*

"I never had anyone wash my hair before," he said.

Her eyes darted to his; they were dark and shiny, like thick drops of oil. "I promise not to drown you." She was cool and uppity, just like she'd been last night. He wondered what in the world had led him to ask for a haircut in the first place.

He gazed upward at her arm, only inches from his nose. A woman. He shifted his gaze to her chest, but he couldn't see the swells of her breasts beneath the smock she wore. He moved his gaze again and looked at her face. Her dark eyes were prominent against her fair complexion. She kept her gaze on his hair. But he *knew* she was as aware of him as he was of her.

The water was warm on his head as her fingers massaged, and he closed his eyes and breathed in her feminine scent. Being raised in a household of men, he noticed things like that. Her feminine fragrance had been one of the things he'd missed most about his mother; after she'd died, he'd taken one of her aprons and hidden it in his room, where he could smell it and take comfort. Of course, eventually the scent had gone away. Now he inhaled deeply, enjoying the sweet and tender feminine fragrance of Zoe Yarberry.

Abruptly, just as Rory was getting accustomed to, and even enjoying, having his hair *shampooed,* she turned off the water and plopped a towel over his head.

"That's it," she said.

Next thing Rory knew the chair shoved him upright, and she was attacking his hair with the towel. She was going at his head with the gusto his Aunt Ina used in kneading bread dough. Then she whipped the towel away, and he saw himself in the mirror, his hair standing on end.

The next instant she attacked his hair with a comb, ripping through the tangles with the intensity and ruthlessness of a surgeon.

Her lashes came up, and their eyes met in the big, beveled glass mirror.

"How do you want it?" she asked.

"I wouldn't mind if you left a few hairs in my head."

She blinked blandly. "Cut short, trimmed, what?"

"You're the expert. I'll trust you to do what you think would look best."

Her right eyebrow arched. "Are you always so trusting?"

"Nope." He didn't break the gaze. She did. He continued to stare at her and to think that she was about the prettiest, freshest thing he'd seen in a long time.

Zoe cut his hair. It was glossy, healthy hair, the color of dark walnut wood and with a natural wave. And thick, she thought. She'd rarely seen thicker. Many a woman would die for hair such as he had. She sectioned it off and played it, warm and silky, through her fingers. White strands were already starting at his temples, though she didn't think him terribly old. Early thirties, she mused. *And a rough one, if ever I saw one.*

Glancing in the mirror, she saw him looking at her. Studying her. Of course, she told herself, there wasn't much else for him to do.

"How long have you been in this line of work?" he asked.

"Almost four years officially. All my life unofficially."

She could feel the warmth coming off him. His scent came to her; it was a cologne she couldn't name, but it was about the best she'd ever smelled in her life. It stirred a familiar warmth deep in her abdomen, a familiar warmth she hadn't felt in a long, long time.

Clip, clip, clip. She trimmed at his neckline and saw a small white scar and wondered what had made it. The skin of his face was very tanned from years in the sun.

"You've been cuttin' Oren's hair for a while now, haven't you?" he asked.

"Uhmm . . . three months or so."

"And Annie's been here, too, she says. She's my sister-in-law. My brother Matt's wife."

"Umm . . ."

"Oren is very particular about his hair and doesn't let just anyone mess with it, so you must be pretty good."

"Guess you'll decide that when I'm done."

She tilted his head one way, then another, feeling absurdly odd about touching him. His eyelashes were almost obscenely thick, and she certainly hadn't expected that. Unless a person got as close to him as she was—trimming the hair over his ears—a person wouldn't notice those eyelashes on that rugged face. Nor would they see the small scar on his temple, as she did, because she was that close to him. She could lean over and put her tongue in that ear, and that notion shocked her into straightening right back to her senses.

"How's your horse?" he asked.

"What?" She only appeared to glance at him. "Oh, he's fine."

"I didn't see him out in the corral."

"He's probably in the barn. His hay's in there."

Her fingers didn't want to behave as she told them; she felt so clumsy. *She felt as aware of Rory Breen as she would have been of a piece of hay down her pants.*

"Did Dusty rope with him?"

Surprised, she met his gaze in the mirror.

"You know Dusty?"

"You could say we're acquainted—done a few of the same rodeos. He ropes some, doesn't he? He used to have a pretty fair paint horse he roped on."

"He still has him. He's roped some on Blue but never was happy with him."

"But he still took him when he lit out from here." His eyes were speculating, not at all shy about prying, and it was clear as sunrise that he was wondering about her and Dusty.

"Yes, he did." She didn't want to talk about Dusty.

While evening out his sideburns with the electric clippers, she leaned close. Her eyes collided with his bright blue ones, and she nicked into his hairline. But she didn't let on, simply refocused and trimmed an even line.

"How's that?" she asked when she'd finished and handed him a mirror so he could check his hair all the way around. She'd taken a lot off the top and sides but had left the back longer and had shaped it smoothly, where it had been ragged before.

He surveyed the job closely, ran his hands over it several times. She sure hoped he liked it, because she couldn't put it back on. Still, he wasn't saying anything, nor giving the least hint from his expression. She tightened inside.

"You did tell me to do what I thought best," she reminded him, then wished she'd kept her mouth shut.

His gaze flashed to hers. "I like it fine. Thanks." He grinned happily, and her heart gave an absurd little leap.

"You're welcome," she said, greatly relieved. She had to respond to his grin, but cut it off quickly enough. "Let me dust you off. If those little hairs get down your shirt, they'll drive you crazy all day, itching and pricking. Not much of anything worse." First she'd been bumbling, now she was blabbering. She pressed her lips together and passed the thick, soft brush over his neck, then removed the cape and cotton strip while trying not to touch him. "There you are."

He stood and paused and leaned close to the mirror, looking at his hair again, lifting his chin and turning his head this way and that. A lot of people didn't do that; a lot of people were too self-conscious to examine themselves for any great length of time in the mirror while someone stood there watching them. But apparently Rory Breen wasn't that sort. Zoe doubted Rory Breen was self-conscious about anything.

He turned to her and dug into his pocket, pulling out a wad of bills. "I don't believe I've ever had as fine a cut," he said, peeling off several bills. "I thank you very much, Zoe."

She jumped inwardly when he said her name. "I'm glad you feel that way. Tell your friends. I can always use the business." Without looking at it, she stuffed the money into the pocket of her smock.

He moved to the door. His boots scraped on the floor, and his spurs jingled. She followed to bid him goodbye.

"I'd like to see your horse," he said. "Do you have time to show him to me?"

Again he'd surprised her. She said, "Sure," because she couldn't think of a reason not to. As she hung up her smock, she realized that she *wanted* to show him Blue, which went again to prove the foolishness of the human species.

When she followed him out across the porch, she saw with great puzzlement that there was no vehicle parked in the driveway. The next instant she saw a horse tied to the post, a half-asleep bay with a well-used flat-seat saddle.

He'd ridden a horse here.

She looked at his tall frame, from his hat to his Wrangler jeans, faded in the seat, to his scuffed boots and spurs with silver initials and told herself it shouldn't come as any surprise.

* * *

Rory watched Zoe Yarberry open the rickety gate to the meshed chicken wire fence. The stiff west breeze tugged at her wavy hair, and she squinted in the bright sun. She'd taken off her smock, and underneath she wore a blue print, sleeveless cotton shirt tucked into faded jeans that conformed to her body shape. Her petiteness was deceptive on first glance, for she was sturdy, too, with clearly defined biceps, firm shoulders and sleek, taut thighs. Probably muscles built from trying to keep this place together, he thought.

She took each of her daughters by the hand, and they regarded him with large, curious eyes. Their eyes were pale, as was their hair. Rory recalled that Dusty Yarberry had pale hair, though he had no idea about his eyes. But these little ones were beautiful, like their mama. And Zoe Yarberry was indeed beautiful—in the way the morning sun shining across the grass was, all fresh and holding promise.

"Hi," he said to the little girls. He couldn't remember their names—except he knew they were odd ones.

"Mercy and Glory," Zoe said, lifting a hand in turn to identify them and sending them looks of pure, unadulterated adoration and pride. "Girls, this is Mr. Breen. Remember meetin' him last night?"

"Hi," said the little one named Glory. The other one looked away shyly.

The breeze sent wisps of dust ahead of them as they all trooped on to the barn—Rory and three females with odd names.

He heard his spurs jingle; subconsciously he always found the sound comforting, the way some men found smoking a cigarette comforting. The sound gave him a sense of keeping his feet on the ground. Walking beside the females, Rory felt unusually tall. And out of place—rather like an old ranch mustang walking beside three registered show fillies. But the feeling faded as they entered the barn and his eyes struggled to adjust to the dimness and to see the horse.

Rory was a horseman through and through, and as such he liked to look at horses, any horses, wild and rangy or highbred and registered, outstanding specimens or good-for-nothing pukes. No two were ever alike, all fascinated him and he loved nothing better than to enter into a discussion about a horse's attributes—or lack of them. He considered himself an expert judge of horseflesh, had never met a man better at this than himself, though he never professed this view aloud. For one thing, to do so would have gotten him into at least twice as many fights, because many a man, or woman, fancied themselves good judges of horses and all believed to their core that they were dead right in their estimations. For a second thing, his ability wasn't something he'd attained for himself, but a God-given talent, and therefore not something he should be bragging about.

The horse was inside his stall, but he came to stick his head over and sniff them. He was a coppery sorrel—and a stud, which surprised Rory. Zoe Yarberry was a woman, a petite one at that, and studs weren't always easy to handle. Few women he knew messed with them.

The little girls grabbed fistfuls of hay and stuck them through the tiny slits in the stall wall. Their mother allowed it, and the horse, while doing his normal stud sniffing and prancing, appeared gentle enough. Rory ran a quick, practiced eye over the animal, noting the thick muscle structure and rangy coat of a classic quarter horse of the old cow horse variety. Then he saw the marks across the stud's hip.

He raised an eyebrow to Zoe. "Were those on him last night?"

"I didn't put them there," she said.

He gazed at the marks. "I didn't think you did." He recalled the time he'd caught Mitchum whipping a horse. Someone needed to give Mitchum a taste of his own medicine.

"Can I go in and have a look at him?" Rory asked, as was only polite.

She hesitated, then got the halter. "I'll halter him for you. He's a little skittish yet."

She went ahead of him into the stall, and the stud backed up warily, snorting and quivering and raising his head aggressively. Rory tensed, ready to jump in and toss her out of harm's way.

However, very quietly and calmly, she went over and slipped on the halter and stood petting him. Rory watched her with surprise and respect. The woman knew horses.

He stepped forward with slow, quiet movements. "Hello, boy." He rubbed the animal's forehead and allowed him a good sniff, then softly exchanged breaths with him. "I don't guess anyone could accuse him of being a pretty boy," he said, as he ran a hand over the horse's strong shoulder.

Zoe Yarberry actually grinned. "No...I guess they couldn't." She looked at the horse in much the same way she had her daughters, with affection and pride, and totally unaffected by Rory's opinion.

The horse wasn't overly tall but boasted a good solid build. A plain sorrel, the color favoured by the cowboys of old because of how it held up in the sun. Rory had always favoured red ones like this. He'd never known one that didn't have good sense and stamina. This one looked rangy, which was deceptive, because he had good confirmation. Not great; Rory wouldn't go so far as to say great. But he had a deep heart girth and good, strong hips. Carefully he ran a hand down the stud's front leg. The animal had legs that would carry a man for days through heat or snow, over mountain or flatland and not give out. He went to pick up the hoof, and the stud gave it easily; the foot was big and healthy.

"He almost has a clubfoot there," Rory said, pointing to the left front hoof.

"Doesn't interfere with his movement," Zoe answered blandly, rubbing the horse's head. "He has everything he needs—strength and stamina and flexibility. And he's willing."

Rory inwardly debated the flexibility part. The stud appeared too thick to have that. Rory moved out of the stall, and Zoe removed the halter, then followed.

"What's his breeding?" Rory asked as she fastened the stall gate.

"Cutting horse on both sides—his mama was Diamond Bizniz, and he's her only son," Zoe answered, enjoying the surprise that bloomed on Rory Breen's face.

"Diamond Bizniz?" he echoed. "Joe Padilla's mare?"

She nodded and averted her eyes to the horse, stuffing her hands into her back pockets. She held her tongue about being Joe Padilla's daughter.

Rory gazed at the horse, too. "That mare was a great cutter. I rode her once in Belen—came in first on her, too. She was great, would almost lie right down in front of the cow."

"You rode her?"

He nodded. "I rode a couple of horses for Joe Padilla back after he had his new place down near Ruidoso."

She studied him. "Joe Padilla was my father."

His eyebrows rose, and he stared at her. "Well, I'll be darned." Then a slow grin spread his mustache, and he pushed his hat back. "No wonder you can handle this stud. Joe was about the best there was—except for me, of course."

"Oh, of course," Zoe returned sarcastically, feeling pleasantly relaxed. She inclined her head toward the horse. "Dad was very hopeful about Blue. He was just about ready to break him when he died. Then all of his stock was sold. Blue had three owners before I picked him up cheap down in Fort Worth last year. No one's paid him much attention. He's not the flashy sort."

"No, I wouldn't call him flashy," Rory agreed and knotted his brows. He looked from the horse to her. "You call him Blue?"

She nodded, grinning.

"Funny name for a red horse."

Zoe gazed fondly at Blue. "It's for his heart, not his color. He had a difficult birth, and the mare dropped him from a standing position. Daddy said he was born with a true-blue heart, and that's what he named him—True Blue Heart. He called him *Corazón*. He believed he had another champion on his hands."

Rory looked intently at the horse, then turned his gaze to her. Suddenly self-conscious, she stepped backward and glanced around, searching for the girls. They were chasing each other out the doors on the east side of the barn, and she started out that way.

Rory followed, asking, "How did he do as a roping horse for your husband?"

"Okay, but he never seemed fast enough for it." She let it go unsaid that she thought Blue simply didn't like being a roping horse—he was a cutter.

"So what are you gonna do with him?"

Zoe shrugged. "I'm not certain." She certainly wasn't going to speak of the idea that had been stirring around inside her mind. It would sound silly to him—to anyone. "Come on, girls. Let's go back to the house."

As they walked back past the horse, Rory Breen said, "You could probably sell him for a good ranch horse. He's solid and doesn't have to be fast as lightnin' to do normal ranch work."

"That's true," Zoe said simply. She didn't feel she had to justify herself to anyone, most especially to this man. She was on her own and didn't need a man to tell her she was whistling in the north wind, nor to give her permission to do so. She walked toward his horse. The girls chased the gray cat beneath the porch.

"He might be worth a little bit, to the right person, as breeding stock, too."

"He's worth that to me."

"But he doesn't have a great track record, or a lot of trainin' to get one, either. I doubt you'll get many people wanting to breed to him—and this season's almost over."

"That's true" was all she said and stopped near his horse.

He raised an eyebrow. "You're walkin' me to my horse."

"Yes, I am."

The cocky son-of-a-gun leaned lazily on the saddle. "I guess that means it's time for me to say goodbye." He didn't appear at all ready to do that.

His blue eyes twinkled brightly and beautifully in his tanned face, and Zoe felt a great rush to the pit of her stomach. They eyed each other for a long, very warm moment. It lay there between them, feelings dancing and spiraling like dust devils in August.

"Yes, Mr. Breen," Zoe said, not wavering her gaze. "Please excuse me. I have things to do."

And that was her answer to his unasked question, she thought as she started away. She was letting hot dust devils go on without her.

"I'll give you a thousand dollars for him."

She whirled, staring at him.

"That's more than butcher prices right now."

"He's worth more than butcher prices."

"Yes, ma'am, he is." He gazed steadily at her.

"Why would you want him?" It flashed across her mind that a thousand dollars would go a long way to getting her and the girls sent on better times.

"I like him. He's a good solid horse. I'd like to see what I could do with him."

This Zoe could understand. She gazed at Rory Breen and knew this part of him very well; he was just like her father had been, just like Dusty was.

"He's worth a lot more," she said.

"Okay—how about twelve hundred?"

She looked at him and thought herself a fool as she shook her head. "I think I'll wait. Goodbye, Mr. Breen."

He gazed at her for a moment, with a look that sent warmth swirling deep inside. Then a darkness slipped into his eyes. He touched the brim of his hat. "Adios, Zoe."

Again something jumped inside her when he said her name. She turned quickly away and went to chase down Glory and Mercy, who were crawling under the porch after the gray cat. She listened to his horse's hooves as he trotted away.

Whirling, she looked after him. Her gaze followed him, his straight back, the fluid movement of the horse, the spirals of dust they kicked up.

The only other man in her entire life to stir such a hot reaction in her had been Dusty. And look at the trouble that had gotten her into! She wasn't getting carried away this time. No, ma'am, she wasn't. She was not going to get involved with another cowboy—and she sure as double-H wasn't going to even think about him!

Then she cursed her foolishness in not selling Blue to him.

But she couldn't give up Blue, for all sorts of insane and sentimental reasons. She did have her father's heart.

* * *

Over the following week Rory stayed out at the ranch and kept to himself, away from Kelly's and away from his own family as much as possible. Days, he spent working harder than he had in months. He rode the fence line and repaired fence until Matt had to break down and compliment him. He moved cattle, doctored cattle, greased all the axle bearings on the stock trailer. He spent long hours training his yearlings and exercising the older horses, and he trimmed all the horses' hooves. He got kicked in the forehead in the process, too, and as he lay there in the dirt, wondering exactly what had happened to him, he thought he saw Zoe Yarberry coming out of a cloud.

While he worked he could keep his thoughts in line, but the nights were long and hard and lonely. He rode Walter in the moonlight, then would sit and sip from a pint bottle of Jack D. that he'd stashed in the veterinary supply chest. It being only a small bottle, and his only one, he paced himself and drank only enough to get mellow and to be able to sleep. But always the loneliness and confusion lingered in the recesses of his mind. And now thoughts of Zoe Yarberry plagued him, too.

He thought himself too old and worn for someone as young and fresh as she was. He certainly had nothing to offer her. And he most certainly didn't want to get involved with any woman! He wasn't ready to climb up on that sort of bucking bronc at this point. He might never be ready to do that again. His body could stand a pounding, but his heart had taken about all it could.

Practical sense told him all this, but his spirit didn't seem to listen. The demons continued to taunt him. And when he drove into Wings on Saturday, to get a prescription for Little Jesse, foolish hope lingered in his heart that he would see her. He was rewarded, or taunted, depending on the way he looked at it, when he found her sitting there at the lunch counter of Cobb's Drugstore.

It was a hot, lazy Saturday afternoon, and Zoe and her girls and Jada were the only ones in the drugstore. Zoe and the girls sat on the stools at the lunch counter; Jada leaned on her elbows on the other side. Zoe and Jada had been discussing the pros and cons of lightening Jada's hair, while the girls sipped ice-cream sodas and whirled on their stools. Fans stirred the air; Jada didn't think the customer traffic enough to put up with the noisy air conditioner.

When the bell above the door jingled, Zoe looked over to see a dark silhouette against the bright light from outside. It was Rory Breen. Her heartbeat picked up.

"Why, hello, Rory," Jada called merrily. "Haven't seen much of you this week."

"Been kept busy." His voice was deep as he came toward them, and his features became distinct.

It seemed stupid and rude not to acknowledge him, so Zoe cast him a nod and a pleasant expression. "Hello." Then she stirred the straw around in her ice-cream soda.

"Hello." He nodded and smiled slightly. His gaze was intense. Of all the stools left, he took the one next to Glory. He pushed back his hat and looked down at her. "What you're drinkin' there looks pretty good to me."

Both girls grinned up at him, and he grinned back and winked.

"But I think I'll just have a cream soda," he said.

Jada said, "Coming right up."

Zoe shifted her bottom on the stool and felt impatient with herself for feeling attracted.

Glory and Mercy whirled around again on their stools. Zoe stirred the straw around in her glass some more and watched the ice cream foam. Jada commented on the warm day, and Rory said they could use rain, despite all they'd had that spring.

"It's gonna be a hot summer," he said, his gaze skimming over Zoe.

He drank half his glass of cream soda in several big gulps. Zoe saw this out of the corner of her eye. She noticed, too, his large shoulder muscles that stretched his shirt as he leaned on the counter. And the way his jeans stretched over lean, tight hips. She grew warm in nether places and thought that she certainly had better thoughts to think than those.

Then he was looking at her. Hunger flickered in his pale blue eyes, quickly yet very plainly, before he blinked and it was gone.

"Have you considered about your horse?" he asked. "I'll up my offer to fourteen hundred."

Zoe shook her head and looked away to her glass, to her straw. "He's not for sale right now." She'd firmed this in her mind, crazy or not, and no matter what he offered—well, short of a million, at least.

"Well, you let me know if you change your mind."

"I will."

He finished his drink and tossed a dollar on the counter. "Thanks, Jada."

He grinned easily at Jada, and she grinned easily, sexily back at him. "You're more than welcome, darlin'. Come see me anytime."

They both chuckled over their private communication, and Zoe jabbed the straw up and down in her glass.

"Gotta pick up a prescription," Rory said and walked to the prescription counter at the back. Seconds later he passed back by on his way out and gave them a little wave, then left.

Zoe looked up to see one of Jada's carefully formed eyebrows raised in high speculation. "Okay—give. Rory Breen offered to buy your stud for fourteen hundred, and you *refused?* Why in heaven did you do that?"

"I just can't sell him, not yet. Besides, I think I'll get a lot more money for him down the line, if I'm just patient. His mother once sold for over forty thousand." She dug into her purse for money to pay her tab.

Jada leaned on the counter and grinned wickedly. "So you're keepin' your horse. What are you gonna do about Rory?"

Zoe shoved the money across the counter. "What do you mean, 'do about Rory?'"

Jada pushed the money back at her. "Your money's no good today. What are you gonna do about Rory looking at you like a boy staring at a big plate of hot chocolate-chip cookies?"

"It appeared to me that you and he were the two doing the heavy flirting." She left the money and rose.

"Honey, I've known Rory since he was a kid. We always carry on like that, just for fun. But it was you he was interested in, and I can't recall the last time I saw Rory really interested in a woman."

"Maybe," Zoe said. "And maybe you're just a big romantic sap. Girls—quit spinnin' that magazine rack. Come on, we have chores waitin'—wait*ing* at home."

She stepped out into the bright sunlight. Across the street she saw Rory Breen coming out of Kelly's Tavern with a small brown bag. A sadness swept over her. Suddenly she saw the image of her father, sprawled in the dust, bottle in hand.

Zoe drove home, fast. She pulled the Chevy up in front of the barn, helped the girls out, then slammed the door and strode into the barn. She went straight over to an object sitting in the corner, shrouded by an old quilt. Carefully she folded back the guilt and lifted it away, revealing a saddle on a rickety old stand. A handmade flat-seat cutter, the leather glossy, dark and supple. The faint indentation of her buttocks showed; she'd used this saddle well for a year, not so well since then. Her father had given it to her for her sixteenth birthday, the year she was showing in high school cutting.

Glory and Mercy stood side by side, staring curiously at her and then at the saddle.

She smiled. "Come on. Let's get Blue out, brush him up and have him stand tied for the afternoon to improve his patience.

"You gonna ride 'im, Mama?" Glory said, her eyes dancing.

"Guess I will this evening."

"Don't get kicked in the head," Mercy said, eyes wide.

"I'll be careful," Zoe promised.

It was crazy, she knew, the ideas she had stirring in her mind. She wasn't the trainer her father had been. She had no money, and cutting took money these days. But she'd just see the possibilities, she thought. Nothing wrong with that. And she needed a dream right now—desperately.

The coral rays of a setting sun painted the grass. Rory sat astride Walter and gazed down on the Ferguson place. In the small training pen, Zoe was riding the sorrel named Blue. She wore a battered straw hat, captured with strings beneath the chin, a sleeveless blue shirt, denims. The two little girls sat on the tailgate of the rusty gold pickup truck that was parked next to the corral.

Zoe rode the stud in circles and figure eights, first one way and then the other, again and again. Rory couldn't see from this distance, but he knew she was working to get the horse to respond to leg pressure. The stud was fractious, but in the minutes that Rory watched, he began to settle down. Atop him, the small woman rode well.

He wanted to go down to her. Longed to go and be with her like a thirsty man longs for water. And he was damn curious about the horse. It was a novel experience, being drawn by both the woman and her horse.

The next instant he spurred Walter to a run along the slope. He stopped quickly and watched to see if he'd drawn her attention. He had. She halted the stud and gazed in his direction. He waited for her to acknowledge him, to give him an invitation.

She didn't.

She turned away and began riding in circles again.

Rory turned Walter and spurred, sending the horse back up the slope and racing across the ground. He tried to lose himself in the wind in his face and the speed and the pounding of the horse's hooves.

He hadn't frequented Kelly's Tavern since the night he'd gotten into it with Price Mitchum and met Zoe Yarberry. He returned this night, looking for something or someone to fill the emptiness that ate at him. As it turned out, Mitchum was there, just waiting for Rory, waiting to even the score. Rory obliged. It was inevitable, and he might as well get it done.

They went out into the parking lot. He had only one drink first. He bloodied Mitchum's face and left him lying in the gravel, and suffered a busted chin and bruised ribs in return. Yet this time, for the first time he could recall, he'd felt no sweet anticipation at the fight and no sense of release afterward. If he felt anything, it was a sense of desolation.

Oren drove him home and taped his chin and his ribs and for once, blessedly, knew enough not to wisecrack or offer advice.

Chapter Six

It was a hot day. There had been no rain for three weeks. The air was unusually calm, so the dust remained around ankle level. Although it was only nine o'clock, sweat was beginning to dampen Rory's starched shirt beneath the arms and around his waist and the inner thighs of his jeans where they moved against his saddle. A good breeze would be most welcome by afternoon.

Rory looked out from beneath the shade of his hat and saw three more riders enter the arena, joining the four already exercising their horses. Seven riders and easily room for a dozen more, but Rory felt crowded. He almost wished he hadn't come, though he'd actually been looking forward to the day earlier that morning. He didn't seem to know what he wanted these days, he thought as he rode his horse—his best cow pony, a palomino—to the rail and dismounted.

Spurs jingling with every footstep, he loosened the cinch and led his horse out of the arena and over to his trailer, where he tied her.

A small crowd had gathered at Frank Quevedo's ranch for a day of cutting-horse fun and competition. George Collins had brought over his catering trailer to sell barbecue, burritos and soft drinks. He wanted to sell beer, too, but Frank wouldn't allow it. Frank was so straight, he cracked when he sat down, but he was still one of Rory's favorite people.

Rory bought a cola and burrito, then stood off to the side and looked at the scene—people milling, talking and riding and grooming horses. Wasn't a person he didn't know, at least by face, though for most he knew first, last and middle names. These were people he'd lived among all his life.

Trucks and horse trailers stretched out around the arena. Men balanced on the top rail; women positioned themselves in lawn chairs, and children played in the sand. Etta Quevedo and Corinne Hunsicker passed, smiling and saying hello. Corinne smiled sexily. Oren called her one hot tamale, but, even though he would have to admit Corinne was on the fiery side, Rory didn't like that kind of talk about her. He'd been smitten with her a couple of years ago, but she'd been only seventeen. She'd scared the daylights out of him by throwing herself on him one day in her father's barn, saying she wanted him to be the first. Rory had managed to get out of that one, had protected her from herself and him, and he still felt protective of her. She came over now and gave him a great, suggestive hug. Not wanting to hurt her feelings, Rory endured it, but he was glad when she released him and went sashaying away with swinging hips. He thought that she needed a good spanking, but with her angel face, that wasn't easy for her father, or anyone, to do.

Then he looked around to see That Jerk Price Mitchum coming toward the snack trailer. He drew in a deep breath and got all tight inside. He thought, as he watched Mitchum's bulk, that for the rest of their lives they would grate against each other, as they had for all the years that had gone before. It was a wearing thought.

"Well, hello, Breen." Mitchum's smile was cocky, extremely so for a man Rory had left lying in the dust. The telltale dark shadows of a broken nose lingered around his eyes.

"Hello, Mitchum." Rory watched him cautiously and felt the curious glances of others.

"Heard you provided the cattle for today."

"Yep."

"Gives you a good edge, doesn't it—usin' cattle you've practiced on?"

Rory gazed at his smirking face and wasn't about to answer the rude suggestions. He tipped his cup and drank deeply, then said, "If you don't like the cattle, don't bother havin' a go." He crushed the paper cup, tossed it into a nearby box and walked away to his trailer.

He jerked open the door to the combination tack and dressing room, stepped inside and rifled through a cabinet. He drew out a bottle of Jack D., unscrewed the cap and took a long, deep drink. He started to take another, then stopped and replaced the bottle in the cabinet, quietly closing the cabinet door.

As he stepped back out into the sunlight, he saw a familiar truck and trailer bumping across the grass. Zoe Yarberry.

Zoe's palms were damp on the steering wheel. Looking for a space to park, she wiped first one palm and then the other down her denim-covered thigh. Trucks and trailers were strung out across the grass, a number of them big fancy rigs, some more modest, some, like her own, downright haggard. She passed the fancy rig of the Breens—a bright white, six-passenger pickup with a long aluminum horse trailer that bore a *B* emblem in fancy script. Anticipation ran over her like a river as she wondered if it was Rory who had come. Farther on she saw Price Mitchum's red truck and matching trailer.

Her stomach churned. The urge to turn around and leave swept her, passing quickly. The desire to practice Blue on cattle, to see what he would do, was much stronger. She'd been working him every morning for two weeks on a moving flag, which wasn't at all the same as working a real cow. The cutting competition today was offering a free practice clinic in the morning, which gave Zoe the chance to try Blue on real cattle to see what she'd accomplished and what she needed to work on. It was a rare opportunity, and she wasn't about to let it pass by.

Involuntarily she glanced over to the empty space in the seat beside her. She'd left Mercy and Glory with Jada, and alone among so many strangers, she greatly missed their company. Somehow they gave her strength. When they were beside her, she didn't feel so much as if it were just her against the world. Her mind always kept thinking that she could do anything because she had to do it for them.

She pulled to a stop in an empty space on the grass, sat back and took a deep breath. Telling herself to get some starch in her backbone, she got out and stuck on her good summer hat. She checked on Blue, left him in the safety and shade of the trailer, and started off to find out where to register.

Then, leaning against a lamppost directly in her path, was Price Mitchum.

She slowed, and the idea of walking a wide circle around him presented itself, but her pride wouldn't let her. With him looking at her and smiling his slimy smile, there was little chance of ignoring him, either.

He spoke first. "Well, if it isn't the little lady who goes around stealin' horses and trailers."

Zoe had to cock her head in order to look up at him. "Are you in the habit of calling yourself a little lady, Price?"

His smile faded. "I did you a favor by not goin' to the sheriff, and you should appreciate that."

She sighed. "I would appreciate you droppin' the matter and leaving me alone. The horse and trailer are mine, and we both know it, and neither one of us wants to have to go to court to prove it."

"Naw—I don't want 'em anymore. I don't have any use for Dusty Yarberry's castoffs."

The remark cut deep. She said coolly, "Then we don't need to be talkin'." And she started on.

"Hey, I tracked Dusty down."

She turned around, then could have kicked herself for it. "I'm glad for you." She wanted to know where Dusty was, but she wasn't about to ask.

He gave her that slimy grin again. "Found him down in San Antone. He did right good at the rodeo there and had money to pay me what he owed. I imagine he owes you a few pennies, too. But that's all he has now—a few pennies.''

Zoe turned and walked away. Dusty was in San Antonio, she thought. So far away. And he hadn't sent her a dime or even called her in six weeks. Just like he'd forgotten she and the girls existed. Of course, to Dusty, only people touching his life at a given moment existed. He would go for months and not even contact his parents, who lived alone on a scrap of a farm down on the Llano. She really should file those divorce papers.

Forcing her thoughts back to the business at hand, she continued on toward a long table outside the west rail of the arena. Etta Quevedo, one of her customers, and a couple of men whose hair she cut regularly greeted her as she passed, and their friendliness felt good.

The long table had a bunch of men around it and others lined up waiting their turn to use it. There were two women, too, but one of them looked like a man and the other like a city hooker in heavy makeup, with a bright turquoise hat the exact shade of her bright turquoise jeans. In a pale pink shirt and her best blue jeans, Zoe felt short and insubstantial and as out of place as a cat in the midst of a pack of happy hound dogs. But she still wanted to ride Blue on cattle, so she waited her turn.

The gray-haired man sitting behind the table gave her a friendly smile and passed her a piece of paper. ''Sign in here.'' Zoe bent to fill out the form, and the man continued. ''Since you're here before ten, you're welcome to join in our practice clinic. A few of us will be giving pointers, though we don't claim to know everything,'' he said, grinning modestly. ''The contest events start at one o'clock—or thereabouts. We don't run strictly by the clock.''

Zoe finished writing and handed back the paper. She pulled several neatly folded bills from her jeans pocket.

The man scanned the form. ''You're enterin' one class— novice. Glad to have you—'' He peered again at her name.

''Zo*ee*,'' she said, ''and thank you.''

''Zoe. Why, that's a pretty name.'' He smiled, then looked at a sheet of paper. ''Let's see . . . entry fee for novice is thirty-five dollars, and the cattle charge for today is forty.'' He waited.

Zoe stood there. The money burned in her hand, and her heart dropped to her toes. She'd learned of the cutting from Cyrus Bird, and he'd said the total for the day would be fifty dollars, twenty-five for each fee. And she didn't have twenty-five more dollars. She had three, for soft drinks later in the day. Her lunch and snack sat in a brown paper sack on the seat of her truck. She hadn't even brought her checkbook, because the electric bill had taken all but twenty dollars from her account yesterday. She had gotten the money in her hand by scrimping and saving for two weeks, and it was all she had to spare.

Embarrassment and defeat stared her in the face.

''Hey, Frank, I'm sorry, I meant to tell you—I waived the cattle fee. They're my contribution for today.'' Zoe spun around to see Rory Breen sauntering forward. Her eyes met his, and her face burned. Then Rory grinned an easy grin at the man behind the table. ''Guess you'll have to give a lot of folks their money back, but I don't suppose they'll mind the mistake.''

The man raised his eyebrows at Rory for a second. ''Well, now, that's pretty generous of you,'' he drawled, clearly wondering.

Rory said, ''You lend your arena and facilities half the time. I guess I can match you once in a while.''

Frank chuckled. ''Guess you can—and I don't think anyone will mind gettin' their money back, either. You can forget the charge, Zoe.'' He took her money, then handed her back change and held out his hand. ''Nice to have you join us. I'm Frank Quevedo. If you need anything today, you let me—or Rory here—know. Hope you enjoy yourself.''

''Thank you. I'm sure I will.'' Her gaze came around and found Rory Breen's eyes intent upon her. ''Thank you, Mr. Breen,'' she said, her pride all beaten and battered, and walked away.

Rory Breen had just tossed away a thousand-plus dollars. And Zoe didn't believe he'd been planning to donate the use of those cattle; she didn't believe that for one minute. He'd done it for her. That thought revolved in her mind and wore her ragged.

Rory rode over to where Zoe was exercising her stud in the grass beyond the parked vehicles. She gave Rory no more than a quick glance. It could be possible that she might truly wish he *wasn't* there, but he wasn't convinced of it.

He leaned on his saddle horn and watched her.

She sat a horse well, which was what he would expect from a kid of Joe Padilla's. Still, as well as she handled the stud, he gave signs—a sharp swish of his tail, a twitch of his ears, a roll of his eyes—that betrayed the brimming power of him just itching to be off. She had to stay on guard every minute to keep control.

She wore her hat more in the vaquero style, with thinly braided horsehair strings that fastened beneath her chin to keep it held tight against the wind. In her pink blouse and blue denims and brown boots, she was as fresh and vibrant as the sun and as supple as a blade of grass.

Rory continued to watch, and she continued to ignore him. He noticed that the stud turned fluidly to the right, more stiffly to the left, not very quickly, but better than Rory had thought he could.

When the stud had broken a good sweat and was breathing hard, she slowed him, finally walking him over to where Rory sat. The stud gave a high-pitched nicker at the palomino; Zoe firmly silenced him. Her brown eyes were large, calm and steady. A man could lose himself in those eyes.

"That's a flashy animal you're sittin' on," she said.

"Thank you. She doesn't work quite as well as she looks, but she's a good mare." He inclined his head. "Your stud looks a lot better than the first time I saw him."

"Yes, he does."

He chuckled at her forthrightness.

She said, "You lost a great deal of money because of me today."

"I lost money? Now why would you think that?" he asked, amused at the pink blotches that bloomed on her cheeks.

"Did you suspect I was short the cattle charge?" she asked levelly.

It was a direct question, requiring a yes or no. And she knew the answer, so lying wasn't the thing to do. He said, "I thought there was a good possibility," because he couldn't bring himself to say an outright yes.

She gazed at him, and he saw suspicion in her eyes.

"If you have a mare you'd like to breed to Blue, I'll be glad to provide his service. Perhaps he isn't in the class with the high-bred performance horses you may have..." She said that as if she didn't believe it for an instant. "But even without a track record, his bloodline would make a foal worth at least a thousand the minute it popped out. And it would be a good ranch horse."

Irritation flashed inside him. "That's a lot to do for payment of a forty-dollar cattle charge—especially when losing it doesn't bother me any."

"There are only a few ways I can repay you." She paused, and he saw by the meaningful look in her eyes that she thought he was trying to get into her bed. "And offering Blue's services is one of them."

Her low opinion of him hurt. "Is it so hard for you to accept a little favor? I wanted to do it, or I wouldn't have done it. You don't owe when someone freely gives."

They gazed at each other for long seconds. Suspicion lingered in her brown eyes, but finally they softened. He ran his gaze over her pale skin, and it came over him like the rising breeze: he wanted her, and he knew she knew it, so he couldn't blame her for her suspicions.

He shifted his eyes to the stud. "Has he been on cattle before?"

She stroked the horse's neck. "Only doin' the bit of roping he did for Dusty. I don't know what experience he had before I bought him. I don't think it was much."

"You've been practicing him on a flag, haven't you?"

Her eyes met his, and he thought of seeing her ride in her corral. She nodded. "The girls move it for me. He's got the idea."

Rory turned his horse. "Well, we'd better get on over to the arena and let him have a go at the real thing."

* * *

Cutting as a competitive sport dated from the old days in West Texas before the turn of the century, when cowboys got together and had a high time showing off their horses and their own riding ability at doing what they had to do as daily work. For Zoe, growing up in southeast New Mexico, cutting had always been there; just as some kids grew up with a basketball hoop above the garage door, she had grown up with cutting horses being bred, born and trained out in the corrals. Of course, she didn't remember it, but her grandmother had said she'd done her first cutting at the age of two, when her father had set her in the saddle with him when he and his favorite horse of the time won a silver buckle for their efforts.

In recent years, the popularity of cutting had spread nationwide, with competitions taking place in such places as Columbus, Ohio, and even Madison Square Garden in New York City. It had evolved from dusty rural-arena fun to a big-money professional sport. Famous American personalities and wealthy foreigners—Italians, Australians, Brazilians, even Japanese—were buying and exhibiting cutting horses. Some said that what had begun as a cowboy's work had turned into not only a sport of rich businessmen but a lucrative business endeavor, too, squeezing out the opportunity for the common man.

But as Zoe sat there on Blue, feeling the sun on her back and smelling the warm earth, and as she ran her gaze from Rory Breen to the others sitting around on their horses, she thought she could hear her father say that the true, grassroots cutting contests, like this one today, would always exist. This was cutting's bedrock, with people and horses to whom working cattle wasn't some fancy razzle-dazzle sport to be exploited, but a talent, a craft, an experience, to be savored and enjoyed. For these people, cutting was a way of life.

Frank Quevedo quieted everyone and introduced the two people who'd be the judges, then requested Rory to give the first demonstration. Zoe riveted her eyes on Rory. If her father had let Rory ride his horses, he had to be awfully good.

He screwed his hat on tight. His manner was quiet, even unassuming, as he sat slouched on his horse in working-cowboy manner. From the instant he rode his horse into the small herd of cattle, it was obvious that this was something Rory loved doing.

Though cutting certainly wasn't complicated, it had to be understood to be appreciated. Basically all that was required was for a horse and rider to cut a cow from a herd of twenty or so and keep it from rejoining the herd for two and a half minutes. The horse and rider who did it best, in the eyes of the judges, won.

What had to be understood was that not just any horse could do this. It took horses that could be quiet, turn on a dime, sprint faster than an arrow, and read the cow like a man reads a book. It took a rider who could communicate with his horse by the movement of his body. The rider and horse became one in the endeavor.

Zoe knew she was seeing one of those riders when she watched Rory quietly, even lazily, enter the herd and cut away four young heifers. One thing about cutting was the quiet. There was only soft shushing from cattle moving against each other, occasionally blowing or bawling back in the pens, people moving on their horses, soft voices here and there, and the breeze. When the horse started to work, no sound was noticed at all.

Eager excitement rose in her as she watched Rory select the heifer he wanted, block it and let the others sprint back to their buddies. Selection of the cow wasn't made by chance, if a rider could help it. He specifically picked it because he thought it would give his horse a challenge and show to best advantage his horse's abilities. Cattle had a strong herding instinct and never wanted to be standing out alone. This one moved instantly to follow her herd mates, but Rory spurred his horse into motion to block the way. The heifer stopped and appeared to consider the situation. Rory, obviously a man who preferred working right in front of the herd, backed the palomino for several steps. Then the hand holding the reins dropped to the palomino's neck, and without any guidance—at least, none that could be seen—the horse took over. She focused on that cow like a magnet.

The heifer was fresh, agitated and intent on getting back to the safety of the herd. She swung to the horse's right, and the horse moved, too. She swung to the left, and the palomino swung to block her. Again and again the heifer moved, and again and again the mare matched her, drawing back and sinking down, almost like a playful puppy, but without the friendliness.

Rory hunkered slightly, his butt set as if glued to the saddle. In the days and months preceding this he had taught his horse what to do. Now his job was to stay in the saddle no matter how hard a turn the horse made, to keep centered, keep out of his horse's way and let her do what she'd been trained for.

Years seemed to flash through Zoe's mind, dragging her back to other sunny days, other arenas, other cuttings. She saw her father's face beaming up at her after she'd ridden; she saw him again atop a horse, handsome, cocksure, proud. The excitement of those times mingled with this one and bubbled up inside her. With envy and rising admiration she watched Rory Breen on his horse. The palomino moved with controlled power and grace. Its mane and tail flashed like spun strands of silver in the sun. The man sat atop the horse with the same power and grace, quiet, centered, a part of the horse and the moment.

When the buzzer sounded, indicating the end of the go, Zoe realized she'd been holding her breath and urging Rory and his horse on with every fiber of her body. It had always been like that for her. She sat back now, breathed deeply, and enjoyed the pleasure and excitement that washed over her. And she realized for certain that she had done the right thing in keeping Blue. For an instant she felt as if she'd come home.

Then she was looking at Rory. He was yards away, his face indistinct in the shade of his hat, and she felt the vibrancy coming from his pale eyes rather than saw it. The sharing of feelings passed between them. It wasn't wise. It connected her to him, if only for a moment, and she didn't want that. But it happened before she could do anything about it. And, though she coolly turned both her head and

Blue and pulled back into herself, she couldn't wipe out that electric moment.

More riders took practice runs on the cattle, some once, others two or three times, with Frank Quevedo, Rory and occasionally another person giving pointers. Zoe watched intently and filed everything that was said and done into her mind to join lessons from her father and her own experience. She hadn't ridden a cutting horse for nearly five years. She wondered if any ability would remain.

And then it was her turn. She'd never been comfortable with attention, no matter how slight, and her muscles tightened with the weight of everyone's gazes as she rode Blue forward. Rory and Frank took up the positions as "turnbacks"—one on either side of the herd to keep the cattle bunched together. She kept her gaze on the herd; she'd already decided on the heifer she wanted to single out, which was an edge she had after watching others cut for a while.

Blue quivered upon entering the herd, though he responded to her control, if just barely. She directed him with leg pressure; she used her legs much more than her reins. Driving three head from the herd was easy, but singling out the heifer she wanted wasn't. The one she'd wanted slipped past to rejoin its buddies, and Blue was left staring at a curious white-faced cow more by accident than anything else. He quivered beneath her, filling with excitement like a balloon filled with air.

When the cow moved, he focused on it, as if relating it to the flag Zoe had been working him on. With Rory and Frank calling commands to her—"Spur him now!" "Pull back!" "Turn, turn, turn!" "Straighten up, don't fall in the hole!"—Zoe directed Blue to stick to that cow and used all she had to stay in the saddle. When the heifer slipped past Blue and rejoined the herd, she sat back, her mind racing with all the things she'd done wrong, several she'd done right, and every cell rushing with an incredible high.

"Give it another try," Rory called.

Their eyes met, she saw him grin, and a grin came naturally to her own lips. She quickly averted her face.

She and Blue took two more practice tries. With each one he grew a little more tired but moved as if he more fully understood what was required of him. Deliberately, Zoe chose cows that were more listless, slower. She wanted Blue to get the idea and the moves; swiftness would come later. She was pleased with him when they finished. He showed promise, and that was all she was hoping for.

At the break between the practice clinic and the actual events, Zoe left Blue tied in the shade and accepted Etta Quevedo's invitation to join her family and some others for lunch. Rory joined them, too. Zoe made a point of sitting on the opposite side of the picnic table and conversed mostly with Etta and Frank. From where she sat, it appeared that Rory Breen and the heavily made-up woman in the turquoise hat, Stella MacGuire, were well acquainted—and that the woman was intent on knowing Rory Breen even better.

Which went to show she was correct in wanting nothing to do with him, Zoe thought. He was a cowboy with an eye for a flashy woman.

Shortly after lunch the cutting contests began. The sun was hot, the breeze thankfully stiff. While Zoe awaited her turn in the novice class, which would come later in the afternoon, using well-seasoned cattle, she sat on Blue and watched each rider as he took his turn, mentally assessing their performances. And she noticed several admiring glances directed at Blue.

A middle-aged man with a strong Mexican heritage and *rancher* stamped all over him came by and introduced himself as W. Jones, asking particulars about Blue, his breeding, age, experience. Then he made an offer of twelve hundred for the horse. Pleased as a woman complimented her on her dress, Zoe politely said Blue wasn't for sale—yet. She would, however, remember Mr. Jones's offer should she decide to sell later. Then Etta Quevedo called her to the arena rail and brought her a soft drink in a paper cup, with plenty of ice. Zoe pledged a discount on Etta's next hair styling.

A couple of times Price Mitchum rode past, making certain he got her attention. Price was rather like a big, obnoxious bulldog who liked to go around getting everyone's attention. He had a big, sturdy bay gelding. He rode the horse hard, pulling on his mouth, spurring with force. Every time Price came close, Blue tensed and his eyes widened aggressively. Once Price rode very quietly behind Zoe, coming up beside her before she noticed, and smacked Blue on the hip. Blue jerked, brought up his front feet and danced to the side, and Zoe came within a hairbreadth of ending up in the dust.

Price just cackled, as if he'd never seen anything so funny. "Have to learn to handle that horse in all situations, little lady."

Zoe looked steadily at him, deliberately filling her eyes with quiet malice. "I owe you one, Price." And her voice was a promise.

A sliver of surprise registered in his glimmering eyes. He laughed, though with a hint of uncertainty. "Hey, I was just havin' a little fun. Didn't mean anything by it," he said and rode away.

Zoe thought he probably hadn't truly meant anything; Price Mitchum was stricken with obnoxiousness as some people were stricken with disease.

Across the arena she saw Rory look her way. She felt him waiting for her to give him a sign. An invitation.

She wasn't going to do it. She wasn't about to play with fire. She had two daughters who were relying on her. She had plans that didn't include getting involved with a man. She wasn't getting herself all twisted into knots again.

Dusk was coming when the novice class finished. Zoe loaded Blue into the trailer to head home. She wanted to pick up her girls from Jada's. She was tired, and her weak knee was aching; it had been a long time since she'd stayed so many hours atop a horse. But her heart was full with satisfaction, too. Out of the five people entered in the novice division, Zoe and Blue had come in dead last. But Zoe wasn't disappointed. On every go with the cattle, Blue had shown potential. Zoe couldn't have pointed out why she believed this; it was something she felt in the way he moved beneath her. Blue had heart, just as her father had said. It was enough.

Forcing her throbbing knee to work, she pushed in the clutch and then directed the pickup truck slowly over the bumps of grass, wiping perspiration and grit from her temples. As she passed Rory Breen's rig, she saw him stepping out of the trailer. He had his hat in his hand, and the golden rays of the setting sun touched his thick, wavy brown hair. He paused and gazed intently at her.

With a casual nod, she turned her face forward. Her cheeks burned, and warmth stole up from her belly. Involuntarily her eyes cut to her side-view mirror. He was still standing there, staring after her, a cowboy, tall and hard, with that foolish hint of innocence a cowboy never lost and that misled a woman every time.

That night, after Zoe had the girls in bed and the first cool of night was finally whispering through the screens, Dusty called, collect of course. She accepted. He might be in trouble. And she needed to hear him.

"Hi, little darlin'." His familiar drawl woke a bitterness within her.

"Hi, Dusty." She voiced no emotion. She plopped on the edge of the bed, there in the circle of yellow light cast by the lamp, and stared at the faded roses on her cotton gown. Her eyes burned, and her throat swelled.

"So, how ya doin'?"

"Oh, we're doin' okay, I guess."

"The girls all right?"

"They're all right."

"Your shop still in business?"

"I'm still fixin' hair." She thought about the *g*'s again. "We have to eat."

There was what she'd always heard of as a pregnant pause, and then Dusty said, "Price Mitchum was down here a couple of days ago—oh, I'm down in San Antone. I came down for the stock show and rodeo. Well, Mitchum was down here and told me you got Blue and the trailer off him." Irritation laced his tone, and that provoked Zoe no end.

"Yes, I did. They're mine, and you never should have taken them."

"I had to have a trailer to haul my horse in, didn't I?"

"I suppose you did, but you shouldn't have taken mine—you could at least have paid me for it. And you shouldn't have taken Blue. I'm the one who bought Blue—and he was Daddy's. And you had no right to be payin' debts with my property."

"Well, I figured I was the only one that needed the trailer or that dang stud, not that he was doin' me any good. I'm the one who rides the rodeo. At least with me havin' the stud, you didn't have to buy feed for him. As for paying with your property, I figured, since we were married and all, that it was my property, too. Anyway, I left you a lot of my stuff."

"What stuff?" Zoe said.

He couldn't answer right away, and Zoe knew darn well it was because all he'd ever contributed to their marriage had been so little as to be easily forgotten.

"My television," he said then, and Zoe thought how it hardly worked. "And my tools—the drill and stuff. And I helped you make that beauty shop, too."

Zoe shut her mouth tight. There wasn't any use arguing with Dusty; he saw things as he saw them, to benefit himself, and she was just wasting her breath. "What are you hauling your horse in now?" she asked, offering a truce with her voice.

"Me and Willy Gordon have teamed up, usin' his trailer and my camper. Willy's a good guy, and sharin' the expenses like that helps out. I had money saved to send you, but I had to give most of it to Mitchum when he come after me. I just wanted you to know that—that I was gonna send you some money."

"Nice of you to think of us," Zoe said acidly. She hated it when she sounded like a shrew. For no reason on this earth should a woman sink to sounding like a shrew.

"I think of you, darlin'. I was layin' here thinkin' of you and the good times we used to have." His voice grew soft and cajoling, and she pictured his green eyes all sad and like a little boy's. Dusty had never grown up, never would. That was his charm and his curse. And that was why she always felt so responsible for him. "I miss you, Zoe. I'm tryin' to get myself straightened out."

A hollow the size of the Grand Canyon opened inside her. She said nothing; there wasn't anything for her to say. She knew he meant what he said, in his way, and that seemed to make it all the more pitiful and hopeless.

Dusty mentioned some of his successes in roping and bull riding and that he wished she'd seen him. He was suddenly as jovial as if he were just phoning her from a weekend away and would soon be coming home. He promised to send Glory and Mercy birthday gifts. For some reason he seemed to think their birthday was in August. It was in November. Zoe didn't correct him.

Then he said, "So—your shop is doin' good?"

Her caution raised a red flag. "It's putting food on our table."

"Sounds better than I'm doin' right now. I got enough money for a hamburger, but not enough to get me down to El Paso." A chuckle traced his voice; then he said, "I don't suppose you would consider loanin' me fifty?"

Zoe breathed deeply. Tears blurred her vision. "No...I can't do that. I just don't have the extra."

"Well, I wouldn't want to make you strapped," he said quickly. "I'll make out. Fella down at the stockyards said he had work for me for a few days. I can take that. I'll miss the rodeo at El Paso, but there's one up in Oklahoma in a couple of weeks. We have a good shot at takin' that one, too. I'll send you money from there...."

Zoe listened to his voice but didn't pay much attention. He'd said similar things a million times. She thought of breaking in and talking about how Blue had done at cutting that afternoon. But the words stuck in her throat. She knew he wouldn't have an encouraging word to say, though as long as she didn't mention it, she didn't have to know for sure that he wouldn't. He could always surprise her.

"*Damn him!*" she whispered between her teeth after she'd hung up. She glared at the phone and wiped her eyes, sniffing back foolish tears.

He'd called her because tonight he was alone, and Dusty hated to be alone. He was like a drop of water sizzling on a frying pan when he was alone, popping around and looking for relief. She'd been his relief for a few minutes. He'd used her again, and left her empty.

A person couldn't be used unless they let themselves, she thought as she grabbed a brush and raked it through her hair. She'd read that bit of wisdom somewhere—it was a quote from Eleanor Roosevelt, maybe, maybe not. Anyway, if Eleanor hadn't said it, she should have.

Why in the world did she feel so responsible for Dusty Dean Yarberry? she wondered. The question echoed all the way to her marrow, where she whispered the question: Why had she felt the same way about her daddy?

Suddenly lights shone out across the grass. She saw them through her window—headlights—and tires crunched on the gravel of the drive.

Who could that be at... eleven o'clock? She padded barefoot through the shop to the front door, thinking of Jada. She peered through one of the small square windowpanes in the door.

It was a pickup truck. A white truck. Rory Breen's truck, she thought, her heart leaping into her throat as she saw him coming around the hood.

She clutched her thin gown and jumped back into her bedroom, then ran to her closet to get her robe. It was stuck on the hook beneath a shirt and another gown, because she hardly ever wore a robe, didn't have need of one.

The truck horn blasted and caused her to jump nearly out of her skin. By heaven, but she'd had enough of male shenanigans!

She stomped to the front door and whipped it open, then pushed through the screen door. She saw Rory in the dim light of the cab of his truck, reaching to press the horn again.

"Shush!" she said.

He pulled himself out of the truck and slammed the door and stood there in the bit of silvery light cast by a sliver of moon. Clutching her robe together, Zoe pulled the door closed behind her. She didn't switch on the porch light, because she preferred to remain in the dark. She could tell by the way he again rounded the hood, with slow and deliberate steps, his hat cocked at an angle, that Rory Breen was about three sheets to the wind.

"What in the world do you think you're doing?" she demanded in a loud whisper. "Tryin' to wake the neighbors a mile down the road?"

Chapter Seven

"I was announcin' my arrival," he said. He sauntered toward her, listing a little to one side, though his speech was clear. "I didn't want to scare you by knockin' on the door."

"So you scared me by blowin' your horn."

His grin vanished. He was hatless, and the dim moonlight washed his face in dark shadows. "I really didn't mean to scare you," he said with extreme contrition. "And I forgot about the girls. I guess they're asleep. Wh-hoa...." he muttered as he stumbled over a tricycle. He caught himself, straightened and grinned a lopsided grin.

Zoe, suddenly quite aware of her bare feet on the rough wood, moved to the edge of the porch to keep him from stepping up on it. She didn't want him to do that; it would be too close. She had a sense of protecting her home, her castle. Her heart.

"What are you doing out here?" she asked in a low voice. "My shop is closed for the evening."

He stopped in front of her, and she gazed down at him. "I came out to see *you*." Again he gave a lopsided grin. The scent of whiskey came from him and mingled with the summer night breeze. His brown hair shone. She knew what it would feel like, all warm and silky. "I wanted to tell you that you did very good ridin' your horse today," he said, his voice low and sexy. "Your horse did good, too."

"Thank you. But that hardly seems important enough to drive all the way out here in the middle of the night." She stood with her legs together, her back straight and her arms wrapped tight around her middle.

"Horses are important to me," he said, as if they should be to everyone. His gaze drifted down her body, and she felt it. "You know, you could have a lot in that stud—you know that, don't you?"

"I know he has potential."

"Damn skippy he has potential." He chuckled and swayed as he pushed out his chest. "And I guarantee you, except maybe for old W. Jones and Frank, you and I were the only ones there today who knew how much. It's gonna take a lot of trainin', though. You have to know that. Joe Padilla said it all the time. A horse can't be any more than he's trained to be, and Joe was right."

She gazed at him. The night breeze slipped up under her robe and gown and teased her skin like fingers. She pressed her legs together, wrapped her right toes over her left foot and wondered exactly what to do. Wondered why in the world she felt like putting her arms around him. She thought of her bed inside, the chenille spread bathed golden in the glow of the small lamp. She thought about Rory laying her back on the cool sheets.

"I saw what Mitchum did today—smack your horse," he said sharply. "I warned him to leave you alone."

Her heart squeezed. "He was his obnoxious self. No more. You don't need to go around defendin' me. I can take care of myself."

"Guess you can. Yep, you sure seem to do a pretty good job of it." Again he flashed that charming, innocent grin. "Don't suppose you would ask me in to visit?"

"No. I don't have men visiting me at night. Especially ones who've had as much to drink as you have."

He looked wounded. His eyes held hers, then skittered away. "You don't cut an inch of slack, do you?" He breathed deeply, looked at the ground and peered back up at her. "You're a smart girl." He cocked his head. "How old are you, anyway?"

"Old enough to know not to be taken in by the charm of a cowboy."

He frowned. "And what have you got against cowboys?"

"Enough. I think you should be leavin' now, Rory."

He frowned. "Aren't you worried about bein' impolite?"

She didn't reply.

He cut his eyes to the porch swing. "You won't even let me sit in the swing with you?"

"No."

He gazed at her for several seconds. She met his gaze.

He said, "I think you're about the prettiest thing I've seen in a long time. And you try to act like you don't feel it, but I know you do." His eyes bore into her, and he spoke in a low drawl that crawled down her spine. "You react to me, darlin', just like I react to you—and that's hotter than fireworks on the Fourth of July."

Zoe's throat got tight, and her pulse pattered. "I want you to leave now."

He blinked, then drew a deep breath. "Okay. If you insist." He turned and took several steps, then paused. "You really should get yourself a guard dog. What if I wasn't some good-hearted guy? What if I was some low-down skunk who would rape and pillage? You and the girls need protection." He jutted his chin with certainty.

"I've been on my own a lot. I know how to take care of myself."

He nodded. "Yes, ma'am, I guess you do. Smart girl, like I said." He tipped his head, then walked, listing a little, back to his truck and drove off.

Zoe, standing there in her robe and bare feet, watched him disappear into the night. The darkness closed around her. The breeze rose and wafted up her legs and tugged at her hair, and clouds must have come across the moon, because it grew so dark she could see nothing beyond the light of the pole lamp. A loneliness dark as the night engulfed her.

* * *

"Rory?" It was Oren.

"Yeah—in here," Rory answered from the tack room. He was puttering, cleaning bridles now. He liked to putter by himself on Sunday afternoons, and irritation crawled over him at the interruption.

Oren poked his head around the door. "If you'd pick up the phone once in a while, you'd save us all a lot of trouble."

The telephone on the wall had just rung at least seven times, and four times before that, but Rory had ignored it, just as he always did. The only time Rory answered the telephone was when he was alone on the ranch. Otherwise, he relied on someone up at the house or out in the tractor barn to pick it up. He didn't much like speaking over a telephone.

Oren said, "Jada's tryin' to reach you. Something about Zoe Yarberry's horse being sick." The phone rang again, and he sprinted to answer it. "Yes, I got him, Jada." He passed the receiver to Rory and sat on a sawhorse, boldly listening to the conversation.

"Hello, beautiful," Rory said, his mind skittering from Jada to Zoe and her deep brown eyes. "What's up?"

"Rory, that horse of Zoe's is awfully sick, and she's worried to death. She doesn't have the money to call the vet—it would cost her at least sixty dollars just for Doc Lancaster to come out on a Sunday. I offered to lend it to her, but she's so darn proud and stubborn. I went ahead myself and called Doc, but he's way down south at the Madrigal ranch on an emergency, and no one knows how long he'll be there. I thought maybe you could run out to Zoe's now and see what you could do."

"What's wrong with the horse?"

"Flu symptoms—runny nose and stuff."

"I'll go over and have a look," he said.

"Right now?"

"Yes, right now."

And so he had an excuse to go to see her. A good, solid excuse, he thought as he hung up.

"What's wrong with Zoe's horse?" Oren asked, and Rory only then remembered his brother's presence.

"Seems to have the flu. Doc's out, so I'm gonna go over and have a look." Bending, he brought his medical kit from beneath the counter. It was a large blue fishing tackle box containing the basics: needles, syringes, surgical scissors, various wound sprays and ointments and suturing implements, colic remedy and several knives.

"Don't suppose you'd want me to go over and give you a hand?" Oren asked.

Every cell in Rory's body protested, but he wasn't about to reveal that. He shrugged as he opened the medicine box. "If you want—but I'm not pickin' you up when you pass out."

Oren put a hand on Rory's shoulder. "Guess I'd just be in the way at that." A chuckle laced his voice, and Rory glanced over to see a teasing light in his eyes. "You go help Zoe. And I'll help you by feedin' the horses tonight, so you don't have to hurry home, either." He headed for the door.

"Tell Annie I'm going," Rory called after him. One thing about Oren was his sensitivity to others—he could practically read minds, which made him a hell of a poker player. And made him disconcerting at times. Rory would just as soon not have people knowing how he felt about Zoe. Emotions always made him feel foolish. Vulnerable. And he sure felt that way about Zoe.

He reached into the small refrigerator on the counter and brought out a number of bottles of various medicines—antibiotics, analgesics, fever reducer, a little something for every need—and put them into his kit.

It seemed that, since his teens, Rory had taken over much of the animal doctoring. On a ranch the size of theirs, oftentimes cattle had to be treated out on the range, with little time to call in a vet. Matt preferred having nothing to do with the doctoring, and Oren's stomach could be unreliable, so Rory was usually elected. He'd learned a lot from his father, more from Doc Lancaster. He often helped Doc and many a neighbor. At one time he'd considered becoming a veterinarian, but he hadn't felt strongly enough about it to press on through the required schooling. Rory had been a fair student at best; his heart couldn't be bound with studies.

He tossed the medical kit onto the front seat of his truck, slipped behind the wheel and took off, anticipation rising in him. That anticipation was tempered quite a bit as he wondered what his reception would be, considering his behavior Saturday night a week ago.

It had rained earlier and was misty now, with low-hanging clouds and unusually cool temperatures. The house and other buildings looked dreary, like the last standing buildings of a ghost town. There was no other car in the drive, no noise or glimmer of lights from the beauty shop when Rory stepped up onto the porch. He knocked and listened. No one answered. He went to the edge of the porch and looked into the side yard, where he'd seen Zoe's truck parked. He stepped off the porch and headed for the barn.

Halfway there, he saw that the light was on and heard little voices. Little golden-haired figures in brown jumpers, giggling and shoving each other, appeared in the wide doorway. They saw Rory and stared with round eyes and small smiles, then disappeared into the interior of the barn. "Mama! Mama!"

Zoe stood at the horse's stall, a small figure in baggy, faded blue overalls and a white, long-sleeved shirt, her hair in a loose braid. He approached slowly. The eyes she turned to him were large, underlined by dark circles, and wary.

"Jada called me. She said your stud's sick."

Her chin came up. "Why'd she call you?"

"Because I do a lot of the animal doctorin' around here. She thought maybe I could give you a hand. But if you're sore about my late visit last week, or too proud to take another offer of help from me, I'll head on out." He hadn't meant to speak so gruffly. He waited, watched her pride do battle with her embarrassment and need.

"I'm not angry about the other night," she said in her quiet voice and with her eyes clearing. "I wasn't ever angry about it. And I'd appreciate you looking at Blue to see if there's anything you can do."

Rory stepped up and looked into the stall. The horse was lying down, his torso heaving with labored breaths and thick mucus running from his nose. "When did it start?"

Zoe pushed stray hairs from her face. "He came down with it Thursday night," she said, returning anxious eyes to the animal. "It seemed to hit so fast. He was fine when I checked on him before bed Thursday night—at least, he seemed okay—and then when I came out to feed him Friday morning, his nose was running." Anguish traced her voice. "He's just kept getting worse. He's been off his feed since Friday. He's been resting a lot, but he won't get up now, and he looks like he can hardly breathe."

Rory opened the stall gate. The stud gave him a weary, glassy-eyed look. Rory stepped inside, and Zoe followed, pushing back the girls, who wanted to come, too.

"I called the vet a little bit ago, but he's off on an emergency down south somewhere, and they don't know when he'll be free," she said, her voice shaking. "I started him on penicillin last night, but it hasn't seemed to do any good."

Rory crouched and rubbed the stud's forehead and assessed the animal. Heat simmered up from the horse as from a pot of boiling water. "Have you taken his temperature?"

"It was 104 an hour ago."

"What dosage of penicillin did you use?"

"Thirty-five c.c."

He breathed deeply. "He needs more. I'll get my stuff from the truck. You get a halter on him. We're gonna get him standing."

He strode out to his truck, got in and drove it into the barn. He brought out his medical kit and set it on the tailgate. The little girls watched him with wide, serious eyes.

He motioned to them. "Come here. You can stand in the truck, and then you can see everything." One of them—he still didn't know which was Glory and which was Mercy—came immediately, with arms upraised for him to lift her into the truck bed. The other one followed more slowly. The two crouched near his tackle box and watched him take out a needle and syringe.

"He won't get up," Zoe said from the stall.

Rory, putting together the needle and syringe, glanced over to see her tugging on the lead rope to no avail. "Just a second. I'll help." He tipped the antibiotic bottle, stuck in the needle and slowly filled the syringe. Suddenly he found two pairs of golden eyes barely two feet from his own. When they blinked it was like four window shades with long silky fringes going up and down.

"Are you gonna stick him wi' zat?" one of the twins said around the thumb in her mouth.

Rory nodded. "It's medicine."

"Are you gonna make him bet-tur?" the other one asked.

"I'm gonna try, darlin'."

"It'll hurt," pronounced the one with the thumb in her mouth. Her eyes were riveted on the needle.

"He won't hardly notice," Rory told her. "I promise."

"He might kick you in the head, and then you'll die," the other one said very seriously.

Those black words out of her little pink mouth gave him pause. "I won't put my head where he can kick it," he said. He put the cap on the needle and, with the little girls' eyes glued on him, went into the stall. The way they were looking at him made him feel more like evil Dr. Devil than the good Angel of Mercy. "Get up! Get up, boy!" He began vigorously kicking the horse in the buttocks. "Yah! Get up!" If his rough treatment bothered Zoe's sensibilities, she didn't protest. She tugged on the lead rope and coaxed in her softer voice.

Zoe pulled and Rory kicked. The horse got up, wheezing and coughing, standing on shaking legs. He was drawn up in the abdomen, obviously in pain from the effort of breathing. If he didn't have pneumonia, he was close enough. Rory uncapped the needle, stroked the horse and murmured to him, then mainlined the antibiotic into a vein in his throat. Finished, he looked up to see Zoe's eyes, startlingly dark in her pale face. He gave the horse a shot of painkiller. One of the medications he'd brought was to help bring down fever, but he wasn't certain of the dosage, so he put in a call to Doc Lancaster's office from the phone in his truck and left a message.

Rory had once treated a high fever in a horse with cool rubdowns, so he suggested that. Zoe brought a bucket of cool well water and cloths and began wiping the horse's body and legs. Rory figured it gave her something to do.

He sat on the tailgate of his truck, and the two little girls sat on either side of him, dangling their legs as he did his. The stud decided to lie back down, and Zoe kept putting the cool cloths on him there. Rory sincerely hoped the stud got well and didn't mention, and tried not to think about, the horse he'd had that had gone into meningitis from flu and had to be put down.

Aloud, he spoke of W. Jones having a horse come down with flu and speculated that the stud must have contracted the virus at the cutting. Zoe agreed. She hadn't had the horse anywhere else.

"I should have had him vaccinated before I took him anywhere. I really should have done that. But I thought, with it being so warm and all, his chances of catching anything were slim. I should have had him vaccinated," she repeated and looked so mournful, Rory wanted to say something to make her feel better.

"The chances of his catching anything were slim," he said. "It was just one of those things."

She just looked at him and blinked, then went back to wiping the horse. She rubbed that horse as if to impart her own health to him. The barn was quiet; raindrops drummed on the tin roof.

"You didn't get kicked in the head," the little girl on his right said as she gazed up at him. She had on a pink shirt and was the one who'd mentioned head-kicking before. Whether she was happy or sad he hadn't been kicked, he couldn't tell.

"He's too sick to kick," he said.

"No tellin' 'bout a horse," the other little girl said very matter-of-factly.

Rory's eyes strayed back to Zoe and saw her looking at them and chuckling.

"Yep," he said and that started him on telling them about a couple of his experiences with doctoring horses, all positive ones, leaving out the bad. In the middle of one of those stories it struck him that he was growing much like his father, a teller of tales, and that brought an unfamiliar, pleasing twinge of pride.

Zoe mentioned horses her father had owned. They talked about a couple of horses that had been at the cutting and went on to the change in the weather and what it would do next, all neutral subjects that passed the time.

After a while Rory noticed the little girls' repeated curious glances. Why, they were copying his movements! They swished their legs when he did, stretched their arms when he did. He scratched his thigh, and each one of them did, too. And when he saw one of them stroke a finger beneath her nose, he realized that he was stroking his mustache. He looked from one to the other, and they looked back, their golden eyes serious but with a hint of warm fun that flowed all over him. They liked him. And it seemed in that moment a singular phenomenon.

Zoe felt as if she'd been put in a terribly awkward position with Rory. She was at once greatly relieved he'd come and yet wished he hadn't, and not only because of having to owe him yet another debt. No, that was a small part of it. The bigger part was how she felt when she was around him, a feeling she didn't dare give name to.

This thing with Blue had her worn to a nub, weak, just ready to lean on a man's shoulder, ready to burst out crying, longing for comfort, and that was not a good state for her to be in around Rory Breen. Not a good state at all. She struggled to keep herself together and felt a lot as if she were being kept there by several twists of baling wire that any minute would spring apart, and then she would just crumple—and all over Rory Breen.

Doc Lancaster called on Rory's mobile phone and prescribed the dosage of fever medicine for Blue. After Rory had given Blue the injection, Zoe knew there wasn't anything else to be done. She hated it. She wished she could make Blue instantly well by her touch and imagined doing so with every caress. She imagined herself as a faith healer, pronouncing: *In the name of God, you are healed, dear horse.* Oh, my, but she'd grown very fond of him, and he'd been her father's, and it just didn't seem fair that they should lose him. What special thing would they have then? What special hope would she have to hold on to?

She kept all these thoughts to herself, though, and tried to be stoic. She didn't want to appear weak, and somehow worries seemed to take on more validity when admitted, almost like a curse.

So she went to the house and fixed dinner for them all. When anything upset her, she liked to do something with her hands. She made chili, with more beans than meat, and hot pepper corn bread—people always complimented her hot corn bread—and plain corn bread for the girls. The girls didn't eat much chili, preferring their corn bread mashed up in cups of milk, eaten with a spoon. Rory ate two big bowls of the chili, with slices of cheddar cheese on top, and half the pan of hot pepper bread, then complimented the meal, as was polite. He had very correct table manners, just as Zoe had been raised with. It had been her mother who'd first insisted on certain formalities at the table, so much so it had about driven her father crazy; he'd said it was because her mother was from Virginia—and though he never admitted it, he secretly thought Virginia people much more civilized and had loved his wife for being such a stickler about manners.

"He said we should call him Ror-ry," Mercy said, when Zoe corrected with Mr. Breen.

"Didn't you, Rorr-ry?" Glory added with grand satisfaction.

"Afraid I did, but Mom knows best."

"Make it *Mr.* Rory, then," Zoe said and felt things closing in around her.

The girls liked him; a blind person could see that. Most probably a man was a curious thing to them these days. Rory was the only man they'd been around for any length of time since Dusty had left. And he talked to the girls as though they were people, instead of simply kids and therefore unimportant.

When Rory commented on the girls' unusual names, Zoe explained that Glory was really Gloriana and Mercy was short for Mercedes. She'd decided on the names after the doctor's comment at their birth, which had been, "Twins! You're certainly going to need the glory and mercy of God to cope!"

Rory chuckled at that, just as everyone did, and then he told her about his middle name being Wilder and how his father had named him that because he'd predicted Rory would be as wild as a winter wind on a bare bottom. Then he said thoughtfully, "I've read of characters in books having the name Zoe but haven't known an actual woman with the name. What does it mean?"

The question came unexpectedly. "Life," she answered, and for some odd reason her cheeks burned.

Their gazes met and locked like two strong magnets. Zoe stared into Rory's eyes, blue as a clear winter sky, and thought they had to be the prettiest eyes she'd ever seen, stark as they were against his tanned face. And she felt the electricity to her core. There was no denying it, nor was there any mistaking that he knew she felt it.

Pushing back her chair, Zoe rose, took up her half-full bowl and the girls' small cups and carried them to the sink. She got a glass from the cabinet, filled it with milk and dunked in a tiny piece of corn bread, then mashed it with a spoon. She felt his gaze on her, but she didn't look up. She thought of his eyes, so blue in his tanned face, and of how hard she knew his muscles were beneath his shirt. And she thought of how one afternoon she'd met Dusty Dean Yarberry at a rodeo and been electrified from her hat to her boots, and of how she'd turned out pregnant four months later. And she thought, too, of how she'd stood in the yard on a cold winter's morning, with his two baby girls clinging to her pants legs, and watched Dusty drive away, with her horse and her trailer.

It was fully dark when they went out to the barn to check on Blue. Rory carried Glory, with a small quilt over her head, and Zoe carried Mercy, wrapped in her small quilt but with her head peeking out. The rain had stopped, but a thick mist partially obscured the barn. The doors had been shut, and inside, lit with the single yellow bulb, it was dry and cozy and smelled sweetly of hay.

Zoe thought Blue seemed to be breathing easier. He had drunk some water. She watched Rory's face as he examined the animal; his expression didn't reveal a thing.

He said, "He's no worse," and she thought he might have felt obligated to say something.

They left the stall, shut the gate and paused to gaze back at the horse. All that could be done for Blue had been done, and now they had to wait for the medicine to do its job. That the horse viewed her presence as comforting could be debated forever, but Zoe decided to stay with him awhile. It made her feel better to stay.

She looked up at Rory and realized it was time for him to bid good-night, and before he went, she knew she had to thank him.

"I really thank you for coming out today," she said, feeling as awkward as a chair with one short leg. "It seems like thanking you is getting to be a habit."

"You don't have to feel indebted. I wouldn't have come if I didn't want to." He gazed down at her, his eyes unwavering.

"I know...." She swallowed. She didn't want the link that indebtedness to this man brought—didn't want to be indebted to any man. "I'd like to pay you for the medicine, at least. I won't feel right if I don't."

He nodded thoughtfully. "A couple of your expensive haircuts ought to cover it," he said, with a hint of a grin.

She hadn't thought of that! "I owe you ten shampoos and cuts," she said, thoroughly pleased.

His grin widened. "If you think it will take that many, I won't say no." He threw the words over his shoulder as he walked away to the large stack of hay bales.

The thought struck Zoe that she'd just ensured that Rory Breen would be coming around her place regularly for several months. *She'd set her own bridge afire,* she thought with embarrassment and confusion.

And she watched, with much surprise, as Rory brought a hay bale over to where she stood, dropped it at her feet, then went back for another, set it beside the first, repeating this twice more until he'd formed a comfortable seat for each of them. Then he sat down and stretched out his legs.

He was clearly staying awhile.

Zoe thought she should bid him good-night. She should get the girls and say it was time she went inside.

But she didn't. She sat on her hay-chair. For just a while, she told herself.

Chapter Eight

The rain had started again, lightly, and the drops pattered on the barn roof. Inside, in the dim yellow glow from the single bulb, it was cozy, nice.

Rory thought, there he sat, in an old barn, with a warm woman. It seemed odd, but certainly not unpleasant, not at all.

Occasionally the horse in the stall would stir, and Zoe would turn anxious eyes to him or get up and give him a closer look. A couple of times she'd gone into the stall to caress him and talk to him, as if to will him back to health. Rory understood, just as he understood about sitting in the barn for all these hours. It was something a person did when their horse was ill—more than once he'd spent the night in the barn, doing nothing more than simply being there. And even though this stud didn't belong to him, Rory felt a sense of responsibility to the animal simply because he was a horse, and a good one—and he belonged to Zoe, someone Rory was beginning to care for.

The little girls spent a couple of hours of good fun on the stack of hay bales. They played hide-and-seek with the gray cat and jumped and climbed. When they tired of that, they climbed into the old wagon and pretended to travel. "Goin' to Cal-i-fornia," Glory told Rory when he asked. He could tell them apart now. Glory had on the blue shirt, Mercy the pink. Zoe said she let them choose the colors of their clothes, and Glory was passionate about blue, Mercy equally passionate about pink. Glory sucked her thumb, and Mercy's hair was just a shade lighter than Glory's, though it wasn't apparent until they stood side by side.

"Do they always get along so well together?" Rory asked, impressed. He and his brothers had fought often, and so did most of the siblings that he'd ever seen.

Zoe nodded and looked at her daughters with that enamored expression Rory had seen her give them a number of times. "They rarely even argue. Glory usually thinks she's in charge, but Mercy always gets her way."

She smiled a soft smile, one Rory was coming to look for. There was something about Zoe, a particular serenity, that made him feel at peace. And that drew him like a spring drew a thirsty man.

Once he realized he hadn't had a drink of whiskey all day—and that he had no desire for one. The tenseness that always seemed so much a part of him wasn't there at all. He felt unusually calm and settled inside. Filled. Except for his longing for Zoe, but even that was settled. He knew he wanted her and wasn't confused at all about it.

They fell naturally into talking about their lives, as two people will under such private circumstances. He spoke of his mother's death when he'd been fifteen and learned that Zoe's mother had left when Zoe had just turned eight.

"She wasn't uncaring," Zoe said. "She'd been charmed by a cowboy and fantasy of the romantic West, but it turned out that she missed her own home and ways too much. She hadn't been raised to do her own housework and figure out sixteen ways to serve hamburger, or to deal with a husband who put horses before her. Or a mother-in-law who couldn't quite accept her. In the end she figured we kids were more suited to our environment—I know I was—and she left. She died in a car crash the following year. Daddy never did remarry, and he kept her picture beside his bed."

"And you? Did you miss her?"

"Sometimes. Mostly when the other girls had their mother to shop with and stuff. But then, I'd always been my daddy's girl."

Remembering back, Rory smiled ruefully, then found himself admitting, "I guess I'd been my mother's boy. I know I missed her, seemed like a lot more than Matt or Oren. I spent a lot of time thinking of her face. It upset me that the memory seemed to fade around the edges. But not her scent . . . I still remember her scent." He'd never spoken of the hurt to anyone, not his father or brothers, or even to Krystal.

He found himself doing a lot of talking. That was a brand-new experience for him. He'd never before been much of a talker, not with the guys and especially not with a woman. He and Krystal hadn't ever carried on a conversation worth remembering. What Rory usually engaged in with a woman didn't require a lot of talk.

But here he sat, talking his head off to Zoe, bold enough to ask her about Dusty. She'd met him at a rodeo, of course, and he saw this soft light come into her eyes when she said his name. He hadn't expected that, hadn't expected her to still care for the guy, and it rubbed him like sandpaper.

"He married me because he got me pregnant," she said frankly. She blushed. "I was crazy about him, and I thought maybe we could make it, but Dusty never was one to hang his hat very long with one woman. An old, old story. And what about you? I understand you were married."

"And who told you that?"

"Jada."

"You've been talkin' about me with Jada?" he said, amused and enjoying the blush that came over her cheeks. He liked looking at Zoe a lot, and his hands fairly twitched to touch her. He pulled on a hay stem and worked it with his fingers to keep them occupied. He began to be certain that he was going to kiss her before he left.

"*She* was the one talkin' about you. I hear she knows you *very* well."

He inclined his head, and it was his turn to blush. "I've known Jada since I was a kid." He wasn't going to elaborate on that, but he did go on to tell her about Krystal, of how he'd met her up in Pueblo and dated her every weekend for six months before getting married.

"And what went wrong?" Zoe asked gently.

"Oh..." He looked down at the hay stem he was playing with. "Like you said... An old, old story. She couldn't handle being this far from the city." He paused, then said, "She liked lights and parties and the attentions of men. I guess somewhere we just didn't join."

He raised his eyes and found her gazing at him. Her eyes were dark and warm. And for that moment it was only the two of them, sharing an understanding too deep for words.

Then Zoe looked away. "I think I'll go to the house and make coffee. Would you keep an eye on the girls?" She rose, still not looking directly at him.

"Sure...no problem."

It was awkward, because neither one of them was thinking about coffee or watching the girls.

Zoe went to the house and returned with the coffee for them and juice for the girls. They sat there on the hay bales, inches from each other, and talked of everyday things, weather, horses, the remoteness of the area. There were long pauses between subjects, as if each of them was struggling to think of what to speak of next. Soon Glory and Mercy fell asleep on their quilts atop the hay. Rory kept thinking about leaving, but he didn't. He figured Zoe was going to tell him to leave any minute, but she didn't. And he knew it was about time to kiss her.

Zoe got up and petted on the stud again and observed that he felt cooler. Rory set aside his empty coffee cup and rose to stand outside the stall.

"I guess I should be heading on home," he said as she came out of the stall and closed the gate. "If anyone happens to find me here late like this, there'll be a lot of talk."

"Not much chance of anyone coming out here on a night like this... and people always talk." She looked up at him, and he knew in his bones that she was thinking along the same lines as he was.

He gazed at her mouth. "It isn't safe these days for you and the girls to be alone. People out here are generally trustworthy, but strangers do pass through. You *really* could use a dog." His eyes flicked back up to hers; a stray hair brushed her eyebrow.

"I'm careful. I look out for myself."

Her words came almost whispered. He reached for her. She came slowly, her eyes dark, hot pools that drew him.

He slipped his hand to the back of her neck; it was warm and damp. With the thumb of his other hand he caressed her cheek, carefully, fearful of scratching her with his rough skin. She closed her eyes, and pleasure swept her features and shimmied all over him. Her eyelashes were long and silky. Her skin was smooth as satin, just as he'd known it would be.

He kissed her, and she melted against him, wrapping all around him and kissing him in return. He came up for air, saw her eyes wide upon him and filled with heat, and he went back for more.

They kissed deeply, all out.

Everything inside Rory came alive. His pulse roared in his ears, and he experienced the rush he got when riding flat out across the high plain. He savored it, wrenching from the moment all it could give. Zoe was warm and pliable in his arms, and when she moaned, sweet hot desire flowed all through him.

At last they broke apart. Rory was throbbing. He saw the pulse beating in Zoe's neck, and her chest heaved rapidly. It flashed across his mind that he'd just kissed a woman in overalls. A darn passionate woman in overalls. And he wanted to do a whole lot more than that. He sucked in his breath and looked into her face, wondering if they were going to take another step. Her face was flushed, her eyes hot and luminous. Her lips were pink and moist from their kiss.

It was up to her where they went from here, because he knew what he wanted to do. His thoughts were bouncing all around from setting her down on the hay to taking her into her bedroom, or to simply getting onto the seat of his truck outside. He barely thought of the little girls.

He looked for the answer in her eyes. He saw it a fraction of a second before she turned her head and pulled from his arms. Her steps were unsteady. He ached like hell and wanted to pull her back to him. He knew he could; he felt her need as great as his own, and it was just further fuel to the burning fire inside him.

He let her go and did battle with raw disappointment.

Zoe wrapped her arms in front of her, trying to get herself all gathered back together. She shook, and the lonesome pocket inside her was wide and deep and black. She wanted this man.

He stood there, just waiting, the fire sparking in his pale eyes.

She said, "I have two children, a wayward ex-husband out there somewhere, and unfiled divorce papers still settin' on my nightstand, a sick horse, and more bills than glasses in my cabinet. I can't take on any more trouble."

The words poured out, not exactly a no. More a defining of herself. She wanted him to know where she stood.

His gaze sharpened, his expression turning hard. "And you think I'll be trouble?"

"I certainly think you can be for me. The only other man I've ever felt this way about was Dusty. He was the first man I ever slept with, and I got pregnant the very first time we slept together. I certainly can't take a chance on that happening again. I'm not in the market for a hot affair."

He seemed to digest that and to ponder his words. He was a man to speak carefully. "Are you in the market for a man at all?"

"I don't know about that."

They gazed at each other again, assessing, uncertain. For her part, Zoe was scared to death. Her heart pounded so loudly, she thought he must hear it.

He said, "I don't want to cause you any trouble. And you may be right about me being trouble. A lot of people sure think I am." He bent and got his hat, put it carefully on his head. "I've enjoyed being with you tonight. Thank you. I think you can safely relax about your stud now. He'll be a lot better by mornin'. Good night."

And he walked quietly away. The weathered door squeaked as he opened it and slipped outside.

Zoe stood staring at the rough boards of the door and listened to his truck pull from the yard.

* * *

In the tack room, Rory found his tucked-away bottle of Jack D. and took it with him to the far end of the barn, where he sat and watched the yearlings, and pondered. He took three swallows of the whiskey and suddenly lost his thirst for it. And he'd had enough of barns, so he went on into the house.

He stripped and lay on his bed, staring up into the darkness.

No doubt about it, Zoe Yarberry had surprised the socks off him. There was a big ball of fire inside that small woman. Her kiss had clean made him forget to breathe.

Or maybe it was just the combustion of him and her together.

That sat there loud and heavy in his mind . . . and in his loins.

He thought of what she'd said about having daughters and having divorce papers still on her nightstand. He pondered that and the expression he'd seen on her face when she'd said Dusty's name. In a part of her heart she was still Dusty's wife. That greatly disappointed Rory, but he figured it didn't change the way he felt about her. And as far as he could see, she was available. Dusty, fool that he was, had relinquished his claim.

However, she did have those two little girls, and he could see what she was saying about that. Her loyalty was to their welfare first. And she viewed a relationship with Rory as a possible threat to them.

She could be right.

He wondered what he wanted with Zoe Yarberry, beyond the first, very evident fact.

He wondered about that for a long time, there in the dark, and he came up with a few tentative ideas.

It was both Zoe and the horse. They were wrapped together in his mind. They gave him hope. Not anything big or tremendous, more like a little suspicious hope. Suspicion that maybe he, Rory Breen, was capable of feeling something for a woman again. Suspicion that maybe he could help her with the horse and, by doing so, help himself. That he even wanted to do something for her made him realize he was still alive, still held promise as a worthwhile man.

It certainly was a long shot, he thought, recalling Krystal and the last years and how he'd pretty well screwed up his life. He fell asleep with Zoe on his mind, and when he awoke, she was the first thing there again. He knew he was going back to her place. Her horse would need another injection of antibiotics, for one thing.

And Rory had to see what would happen between himself and Zoe.

It was nine o'clock, and the sun was shining brightly in the rain puddles left from the previous night, when Rory drove into Zoe's yard. Beside him on the seat was a thirteen-month-old black-and-white border collie, who was smearing the passenger door window with her eager, wet nose.

No one was in sight, but Zoe's old pickup truck was there. The big barn doors were open. When Glory, in a blue shirt, appeared in the doorway, Rory knew Zoe was there, too.

He grabbed up his medical box and spoke to the dog. "Come on, girl, we've got some women to charm." He silently hoped Zoe didn't take too great an offense to the dog.

She appeared beside Glory in the barn opening, arms crossed, staring at him. Mercy, in pink, came up and peeked around her mother's legs. All three of them stared first at him and then at the dog. Zoe's expression was unreadable—but the girls smiled eagerly. Glory ran forward. "Hi, Ro-ry! You brought your dog."

"Hi, pumpkin. I sure brought a dog, but she's not mine." He crouched to the level of the dog and the little girl, who immediately went to hugging the dog's neck. Mercy came lickety-split, not to be left out.

"Wha's her name?" they both asked at once.

"Fancy. And she needs a home."

The little ones' eyes popped wide, and their little mouths formed O's.

"She does?" Glory said and reverently stroked the dog's head.

And Rory plunged right ahead with, "Yep...and I thought you two might like her."

It was love at first sight, of course, just as Rory had figured. It wouldn't be easy to get the dog away now. The girls looked at him as if he were a grand hero, and he felt pretty darn high and mighty. He dared a glance at Zoe. He felt in deep trouble then.

She just stared at him, her face a stoic mask.

"How's the patient this morning?" he asked.

She gazed at him for several more seconds, and then a smile touched the corners of her lips, and a very small warmth lit her eyes. "Come on in and see for yourself."

The horse was indeed past the crisis. There was no need to bother Doc Lancaster. Rory gave the stud another injection of antibiotics, then instructed Zoe in how to orally administer the tablets he gave her for the next ten days.

"Now, don't try to work him for a week. And don't let him out in the big corral, where he's liable to get overheated."

"Yes, sir, Doctor," Zoe said. "Anything else?"

His eyes on hers, he shook his head. "That ought to do it."

They walked out to the yard, where the girls were playing chase with the dog.

"You are a mean piece of work, Rory Breen," Zoe said as she gazed at them.

"My dad needed a home for this dog, and you need a dog."

"I don't need you decidin' what I need."

"No, ma'am, I guess you don't."

She looked up at him with her big brown eyes. "I owe you ten haircuts."

His heart did a little flip, but he hid it well and casually tipped back his hat. "And shampoos. I'll come for the first one on Wednesday."

As he drove away, he saw the dog, the two little girls and the mother in his rearview mirror. The mother was standing there, looking after him. A young woman pretty as the grass in springtime.

It all scared the hell out of Rory. It was the same as when he climbed up on the back of a bucking bronc—he knew he was in for a wild ride, and maybe a lot of pain, maybe even death—but he couldn't resist the excitement and promise of sweet victory.

During the following days Zoe began to watch for Rory with anticipation pumping in her heart. She, Zoe Yarberry, a woman with good sense, did this.

He came Wednesday, as promised, and had to wait for her to finish with Eldoree Winslow. Eldoree eyed him the entire time, and she didn't hurry out, either.

"Your turn," Zoe said, when at last Eldoree was gone. She spun the chair around for him.

He sat gingerly, bracing himself on the arms.

"Do you want it the same as last time?" she asked.

"You do whatever you think should be done."

Their eyes met, and they both smiled; then Zoe looked quickly away and focused on the job. Her hands trembled, and she kept asking herself what she was doing letting her heart be turned by a cowboy.

The following day he came early in the morning. Zoe had been preparing coffee when she glanced out the window and saw him riding his big bay gelding down the slope behind the house. She almost dropped the pot of water into the sink. From the window, actually *hiding* behind the curtain, she watched his approach. Then she met him on the back stoop.

"Got mornin' coffee made?" he asked, his eyes sparking.

"You must get up awfully early," she said. She was very cool and proper.

"I'm a mornin' person. Actually, I'm a morning and a night person. Don't care much for what comes in between." He spoke with distinct sensuality and ran a seductive gaze over her body. "You look like a morning person, too."

"Yes, guess I am," she said, flirting despite her good intentions.

"Girls still asleep?" he asked and moved to step into the house.

Zoe pushed him back. "Yes...and I'll bring coffee *out-side*."

They sat on the concrete steps in the sunshine, close enough for their arms to touch, listening to the birds and watching day come into full bloom. Rory looked in on Blue before he left and pronounced him well enough to be let into the large corral.

"This horse has the makings of a grand cutter," he said. "What're your plans with him?"

Zoe hadn't formed any real plans for him and said so. "I may ride him in local jackpot cuttings, and I hope to be breeding him some next season. I certainly don't have money for anything more. Cutting's an expensive sport."

He'd looked thoughtful but said nothing more.

He didn't come again until Saturday afternoon. Zoe had begun rebuilding part of the large corral fence. She'd had to, because Blue had managed to knock a section with rotting posts almost completely to the ground. She'd done such work with her father and brother, so she knew what she was about—though she lacked the physical makeup to be doing it. Not only was she of small build, her weak knee protested the strain involved. While she struggled to whack off old railings and dig rotting posts from dirt turned hard as concrete, she entertained several fantasies—one of being rich enough to hire the job done, another of Rory Breen coming to help her. When Rory did appear, she sighed with relief and hope, and annoyance at herself for both feelings.

He sauntered over, grinning that charming, boyish grin of his that softened his hard face. "Are you gonna tell me you wouldn't like a hand?"

She wished he'd said anything but that. However, her intelligence overcame her pride. "No, I'm not."

He stepped to the post, shoved it one way, then the other, then lifted it clean out of the ground and tossed it aside with disgusting ease. Without a word he got a new post from the pile in her truck and plopped it into the old hole just about as easily as he would have a mop handle. He looked at her. "If you'll get the water hose, I'll dump in the concrete."

She went for the hose. A man was good for something, she thought, irritated at her womanly weakness—in more ways than one, for she felt weak inside when her gaze came up and her attention lit on his thick, manly muscles.

Together, with few words, they replaced twenty feet of fence. Afterward, Zoe offered him iced tea.

"Wouldn't suppose you'd have a beer or two?" Rory asked.

Zoe gazed at him. "I never have booze. I saw enough of that with my father to last me a lifetime."

His blue gaze studied her; she studied him, waiting.

He said, "I'd be glad for a glass of iced tea, thank you."

Zoe went off to get the tea and thought she should stop all this between them now. The last thing she needed was to get her heart all tangled up with a man who was battling drink.

But she did still owe him nine haircuts. And, by gum, she *liked* Rory Breen. And she simply couldn't turn away from the companionship he brought. The loneliness in her wouldn't allow it.

The next day Rory came in the evening, just after suppertime, when the sun was slipping toward the horizon, taking the heat of the day with it and bringing an intimate peace. And he came again the evening after that, and the next evening, too. He always played with the girls first for a few minutes, chase or ball or just teasing talk. One evening he brought a rope swing, with a wooden seat that had been carefully sanded smooth. She knew he'd made it. He hung it from a beam in the barn and began teaching them how to swing.

Later Zoe brought lemonade, sat on a bale of hay and watched the four of them—rough-tough man, girls and dog—laughing and being silly. She wondered who enjoyed being silly more, the girls or Rory.

"The dog is good for the girls," Rory said when he joined her. He sat stiffly, like a man who'd physically worn himself out, and took the cold glass of lemonade she offered. "Admit it. She's great to have around."

"She's great to have around," Zoe said. "Does that make you happy?" He beamed. "And you're good for the girls, too," she added softly, shyly, but she had to tell him. He should know of his own generosity, and the responsibility he was building.

Surprise flickered in his eyes; then he gazed off at the girls. "I like them, too. A person doesn't have to pretend anything with kids. They take a man just like he is."

Zoe stared at his hands, his fingers breaking a blade of dried grass into tiny pieces.

"Does Dusty come to see them?"

Her gaze flew to his. His blue eyes shimmered intently.

She shook her head. "Dusty hasn't been back since the day he drove away." And she looked down the road as if watching him driving away all over again. "I didn't know he wasn't coming back that day. He said he was going to a rodeo down in Fort Worth. We'd even talked about his returning a week later. He kissed the girls goodbye, waved at us just like always. Nothin' different. But that night I found he'd taken his best straw Stetson and all his summer shirts. Dusty never wears his straw hat until at least April, so I suspected he wasn't coming back. He called after four days to tell me." She shrugged. "He calls every once in a while."

They were both quiet for a long minute, watching the girls and the dog play tug-of-war with a red rag. Giggling so hard they fell down, the girls still held on.

"They don't miss him," Zoe said. "Dusty was sort of on the edges of their lives. They weren't children he planned for, and at times he found them an inconvenience."

"The divorce papers on your nightstand..." Rory again drew her gaze. "Unfiled, you said?"

She breathed deeply, looked at the ground and nodded. "Yes. I told the lawyer I'd file them. It seemed the correct thing, as it was *my* marriage and *my* divorce, not his. I just haven't done it yet."

His pale blue eyes searched hers. "Why not?"

She shrugged. "I don't really know. It didn't seem all that important, for one thing. Filing a piece of paper wasn't going to change my life any. And it's hard." She looked away from him and breathed deeply past the knot in her throat. "It's true we got married because I was pregnant, but I really loved Dusty very much. And I made those vows. They're not so easy to simply forget." She peered up at him, hoping for understanding. She found it in his eyes.

"No, they're not," he said, speaking clearly from his own experience. "Do you think he might come back?"

She gave a wry grin. "He probably will. I just don't know if it'll be too late then."

"But it isn't too late yet?"

"I don't know." It was an honest answer. And though she didn't say it, she let it show in her eyes: a lot of it being too late or not depended on what happened with him.

Slowly his hand came out and took hers. He rubbed his rough thumb over her palm, and a sensual charge shimmied up her arm.

Chapter Nine

Before a full week passed, Zoe began working Blue again, slowly the first few evenings. Rory, sitting on the corral rail, called instructions.

"Don't let him push you. You can't let him be in charge. Spur him and make him give to your leg."

She rode over to the rail. "Did I ask you for lessons?"

His gaze didn't waver. "No, but I won't charge you—unless you insist on paying, in which case I charge twenty dollars an hour."

"You're that good?"

"Oh, darlin', I'm that good," he said with a sexy grin.

Zoe's cheeks burned. "Well, I know how to ride," she said and turned the horse.

Rory called after her, "A truly intelligent person knows they don't know all there is to know." But he watched her without further comment.

The following morning Zoe rose early and rode Blue at first light—before the day's heat or Rory's appearance. She tested the stud with Rory's advice. The horse was pushing her, and he wasn't giving to her leg pressure as he should. She rode him in circles, made figure eights and swift turns, again and again, directing him with her body movements. She kept recalling lessons learned from her father and pointers Rory had given her. When Blue got impatient and tried to buck her off, she pulled his head into a circle and jabbed him with her spur, not fiercely, but sternly, so he knew he was getting a spanking. Then they tried again. She never actually forced the stud to her will but, with persistence, asked until he did it correctly. It was her aim to make them partners, to lead him into doing what he was naturally bred for.

Four evenings later, Zoe was practicing Blue on a moving flag that Rory shot back and forth by means of a pulley system. It was the first time since his illness that Zoe had pushed Blue to work hard. Done with the antibiotics, he appeared to have energy to spare. Again and again Zoe directed Blue to watch the flag and work it in the same manner he would a cow darting around in front of him. For those seconds Zoe forgot the heat and the dust, her frustrating attraction to Rory, and even her daughters. The girls were playing with their farm set in the sand. Fancy lay beside them. More and more, Zoe was relying on the dog, who'd set herself as guardian to her small human charges and herded and guarded them just as she would have sheep.

Even with the sun setting, it was hot. When sweat began to trickle into her eyes, Zoe stopped Blue; she didn't want to get him overheated. But she had the satisfaction of knowing the horse was looking good. Rory's critiques had been few, and his expression had revealed admiration.

"Your father was right to think this horse was a natural," he said when they were walking Blue to the barn.

Zoe stroked Blue's neck. "He's coming along."

"There's a cutting down in Dalhart a week from this Saturday," Rory said. "I'd be glad to take you and Blue down."

Her gaze skittered away from his as their attraction came again, washing all over her and bringing the image of herself sitting beside Rory all the way down to Dalhart. Spending the day with him. She shifted her mind to practical thought—money. A cutting meant entry fee money, and she had the electric bill to pay. She would be hard-pressed to come up with more cash. "Do you think he could do any good?" It didn't seem likely; there certainly wasn't much time to prepare, and she had no cattle to practice on.

Rory said, "He doesn't have to be perfect. And you've got to begin somewhere. It's just a small, friendly cutting. Entry fee and cattle charge together shouldn't be more than sixty dollars."

She stopped Blue at the tying post. "I don't think so. I'll have some appointments lined up by then, and I have to think about business first." Sixty dollars was almost three-fourths of her electric bill. But she didn't want to say that. It was embarrassing to admit to money being the cause. And she certainly didn't want to appear to be asking for a loan.

Rory unsaddled Blue, and Zoe brought a water hose and rinsed the heat from him, splashing a lot of water on herself in the process. Finished, she turned off the water and returned to find Rory leaning on Blue and gazing at her over the horse's back.

He said, "Sell me half interest in him."

She wiped her wet hands on her behind and shook her head. "No."

"No? Just like that?" Irritation traced his voice.

She focused on sluicing the water off Blue. "Yes . . . just like that. I don't want a partner."

"It'd be a good deal. I'll pay a thousand dollars and split all expenses. You can ride him in the non-pro divisions, and I'll ride him in the open or pro. We'll split fees and winnings."

"Providing there *are* any winnings," she said dryly.

"Oh, there'll be winnings with me trainin' him."

"No," she said flatly and took a brush to Blue's mane. "Hand me the conditioner, please." She pointed at the nearby shelf.

Rory handed her the spray bottle. "This horse has natural ability. He can be good enough by September to take to the Classic down in Fort Worth."

Zoe continued to brush. "And just what would be the entry fee for this Classic?" she asked sweetly.

Rory folded his arms across his chest. "Twelve hundred for entering the non-pro. But with us as partners, your part would be cut to six hundred. And for that you stand to win at least twenty thousand dollars—that's the payout in the non-pro division for five- and six-year-olds. And if all this stud did was come in second or third, you'd own a horse worth an easy thirty thousand—never mind that the day before he wouldn't bring a quarter of that. And you could sure be charging a good stud fee.''

She gazed at him over Blue's neck, then shook her head. "Come in second or third? Out of how many—a hundred entries? Now what could be the chance of that?" She shook the brush at him. "I grew up hearing talk like that. Going for the long shot. 'This horse is the one that'll do it, so go for broke.' And we always were broke, too. Well, sir, maybe you have the time and the money to waste doin' it, but I don't. I have two little girls to take care of, and I don't have six hundred plus dollars to throw away, nor time to get lost in crazy dreams."

Rory came around to her side of the horse. "There's a big difference in takin' a chance once or twice and makin' it a lifelong habit. And there's something to be said for answering when opportunity knocks. This horse is an opportunity beatin' down your door."

"Yes, he's an opportunity—not a golden goose from a fairy tale."

"So what are you gonna do with him?" Rory frowned. He was clearly angry.

"He'll bring in money . . . after he goes to some local cuttings. After he gets more experience." Which was solid reasoning that somehow sounded weak. Truth was, she'd been unconsciously dreaming along the lines of showing Blue big time, but it was nonsense now that she heard it said aloud.

Rory gazed at her in a deliberating fashion. "Maybe trying for a big pot is a crazy dream," he said quietly, "but people need big dreams. Sometimes they're all that make life tolerable, and what you hit while goin' for the big dream is more than you'd ever hoped."

Zoe saw that he was speaking as much to himself as to her. But she fled from all his idea implied. She shook her head. "That may be true. Maybe goin' to the Classic is even a good idea. But I don't want a partner."

"Damn, but you're a stubborn woman." He was furious now.

Zoe answered with deliberate calm. "That's your opinion. Mine is that I like being able to call my own shots." She led Blue into the barn.

"I'm helpin' you train, anyway. You got a head start right there."

That rankled good. "And who asked you?" She led Blue into his stall.

When she came out, Rory stood there, his arms hanging at his sides, his gaze challenging. "What do you think—that if we don't become partners in the horse, we're safe from becoming partners in bed?"

She looked him in the eye and repeated quietly, "I don't want a partner." And everything inside her jangled at the mere possibility. "Blue's mine, and I want to keep him that way." Their gazes held. She saw the hurt in his anger and regretted it. Still, by gum, she didn't intend to give. Her reasons were all knotted up inside herself, but they were her own, and she owed no one, not even Rory, an explanation.

The next instant he reached out, grabbed her to him and kissed her, hard and demanding. If it occurred to her at all to pull away, it was only for a split second before desire flamed.

Just as she lost her breath, he broke the kiss and gazed down at her. "If you think not becoming partners in your stud will keep what's happening between us from happening..." he said in a deep, sensual drawl "...then you're foolin' yourself, darlin'."

He let go and stomped away, leaving the truth of his words echoing in her ears. Movement caught her eye. Turning, she saw Glory and Mercy staring at her and giggling.

The following day Etta Quevedo came for a perm. Zoe held the question in until she'd finished and was walking Etta out to her car. Then it seemed to burst out of its own accord.

"Etta, do you know anything about the Classic cutting being held down in Fort Worth in September?"

"Uhmmm. I heard Frank talkin' about it the other day. His cousin Victor and his horse are entered in the open for four-year-olds."

Zoe followed Etta around to the driver's side of the car. "How would I get information?"

"The Cutting Association newsletter—or the *Quarter Horse News*. And I might have one of those right here. . . ." Etta slipped behind the wheel and twisted to look in the back seat. Etta's back seat looked like a junk closet—magazines, a bridle, a sweatshirt, ball caps. "Here it is. I imagine the ad for the Classic is in there, but if it isn't, someone at that magazine can tell you about it. Think you might take your stud?"

"Oh, I don't know. Someone just mentioned it."

"Well, your stud's good, honey. I saw old W. Jones's eyes light up every time he looked at him, and old W. knows cuttin' horses."

Zoe smiled. "Thanks for the magazine, Etta. I haven't seen one of these in a long time."

She folded the magazine and tucked it beneath her arm, stood back and waved goodbye. Then she walked around and got the girls from their play area and took them into the kitchen for lunch. As they ate, she opened the *Quarter Horse News* and paged through until she found the ad for the Classic. It took up a whole page. There it was in black and white—the five- and six-year-old non-pro division. Estimated purse: twenty thousand. And the total entry fee was twelve hundred dollars. It was amazing to think there were people out there who could plunk down that amount of money, ready to never see it again. For her it was as impossible to come up with as five thousand would have been.

Unless she accepted Rory's partnership offer, she thought in spite of herself.

Mercy wiggled into her lap, put her fingers at the corners of Zoe's mouth and pushed upward. "Put on a 'appy face."

Zoe laughed. "Yes, sugar."

Not to be left out, Glory wiggled up onto her, too. Zoe hugged them and thought how much she wanted for them. Dreams, she thought. Her dreams for her girls weren't much more outlandish than thinking Blue would have a chance at winning a place at a big cutting like this Classic. But she clung to the dreams for her girls, and, yes, for herself, too. She was going to have better for them all. Rory was right when he said that sometimes it was the crazy big dreams that got a person through, because she couldn't have stood another day if she thought this house, this ramshackle place, was all she was ever going to be able to afford.

She was in pretty high spirits that afternoon when she saw Rory's truck coming down the road in a cloud of dust. She walked out to greet him. To welcome him. But then, immediately, she noticed the unmistakable stamp of whiskey in his eyes and the scent of it about him.

"You look like somethin' the dog caught hold of underneath the porch," she said, and about as angrily as an old dog, too.

He grinned, though his eyes were pained. "And you look like a flower just waitin' to be picked." He stretched out a hand to her cheek, but she moved aside.

Folding her arms, she glared at him.

He straightened; his jaw got tight. "I came for a haircut."

She gazed at him, then said, "Chair's open," and pivoted, striding for the front door.

She did a quick job of trimming hair that didn't really need it. She barely touched him. She did well not to give in to bopping him upside the head. When she finished, she yanked the cape from around his neck and said, "Don't ever come around here when you've been drinkin' again."

She met his gaze in the mirror.

"Yes, ma'am," he said.

She turned to put away her things. Damn him for drinking!

"You gonna ride this evenin'?" he asked.

His question brought her whirling around. "I'd planned on it."

"I'll run the flag." He put on his hat and headed out the door, his steps slow but steady.

Rory spoke to the girls but kept his distance. He watched from the fence while Zoe warmed up Blue. Then, without a word, he went to work the flag.

He was clumsy, whiskey residue taking its toll. She was snippy, disappointment taking its toll. He stayed long after the sun had gone down, sitting in the balmy, starry night on the edge of the front porch with her and the girls and the dog, and drinking iced tea with a lemon wedge. She told him she thought she would take Blue down to the cutting in Dalhart, and he said he would drive her.

"You could ride him in the open class," she said at last.

But he shook his head. "You ride him. He's all yours."

And so their relationship continued with the summer days. Rory never asked her on a date—not out to a show or dinner, not even simply to go for pizza. Yet no more than a single day passed between his visits. And just as summer grew ever deeper and hotter, so did their relationship. Zoe found herself praying a lot.

Zoe and Blue took third place at the Dalhart cutting, out of only six entries, which wasn't worth a mention in the *County News,* but it was a respectable showing for his second time out. The following day Rory rounded up twenty heifers and drove them down to Zoe's place. When she caught sight of him, she shot out of the house like a bullet, just as he'd known she would.

"What in the world are you doin'?" One hand held her hair out of her face and the other gestured at the cows. She was hot as a prairie wildfire.

"Bringing you some cows to practice on." Keeping his cool, he whistled shrilly at Fancy and motioned for the dog to turn the cows down the fence line. The dog was born to herd and was as happy at it as a baby washing in ice cream. "You could open the gate. Fancy'll take 'em right in."

"And just what do you expect me to feed these cows?"

At that wonderfully appropriate time Oren pulled into the drive with a big round bale of hay on the back of the pickup truck. "Hi, Zoe!" he called and waved gaily.

Glory and Mercy had reached them and were calling eagerly, "Rory...Ror-ry!" Rory dismounted to lift them both up into his saddle.

Zoe got all red in the face and stomped down to the gate. Two cows got in her way, and she shoved them aside just as she would have a couple of skinny stray dogs, totally oblivious to them being big enough to run her down. She didn't open the gate, instead acting as if she were going to bar it, while the young cows crowded up.

With the girls on Walter beside him, rather like his team, he faced Zoe. "Your dad didn't have any money when he started showing Diamond Bizniz. He stuck his neck out and took a chance, and he wasn't too proud to take help from friends. And Diamond Bizniz made him enough to repay those friends and buy a ranch."

"A ranch that he immediately sunk into debt in tryin' the same thing with half a dozen other horses," she snapped.

"So...you're ahead of him. You don't own this place, so you can't lose it." By her expression, he immediately knew that that had been the wrong thing to say. "I want to help you," he said, injecting a certain humbleness into his tone. He wasn't going to get anywhere with Zoe by trying to browbeat her.

"I don't like you tryin' to call the shots for me, Rory. There isn't ever gonna be anyone who gets to do that—ever." There was a maddening vehemence in her tone.

Rory's temper flashed. "Don't place Dusty's sins on me, 'cause that's just what you're doin'!"

The words hung there between them. Her brown eyes searched his.

He said, "I guess I may be being a little high-handed, but I thought it would be fun to show up with these critters. I mean, it is a pretty good show." He tried for just a small grin.

He saw her weakening. And he knew she wanted the cows to practice on; she had the spirit in her blood. She looked at them, and then at Mercy and Glory atop the horse at his shoulder.

"What do you want from this?" she asked.

Fair question. "I want to help you with the horse, 'cause I think he has a chance of doing very well. I want a hand in turning him out. I want to see what we can do with him, Zoe. You and me together." It cost him to say that.

He saw the understanding in her eyes. Again she looked at the cows. At last she turned and opened the gate, then stood aside while Fancy drove the herd inside.

Zoe walked over to him. "I'll take your help with Blue, but I call the shots, decide about cuttings and pay the entry fees. I won't commit to taking him to the Classic, or any big cutting, until we see how he proves out. Then we'll go partners. You can have unlimited breedings, and if I sell him, you'll have first consideration at a good price."

Rory said, "That's more than fair."

She stuck out her hand, and he took it, but instead of a shake, he pulled her into his arms and kissed her until she'd melted against him and he'd lost a good deal of his senses.

On the first Saturday afternoon in August the town of Wings held its annual Founder's Day celebration. An enormous banner proclaiming the day was stretched from Cobb's Drugstore across the highway to a pole atop Kelly's. It was an event to bring people from all the outlying ranches, and those who had moved away to Clayton or Raton or even as far away as Amarillo often made a point of coming back to visit.

It was a true community effort. Several ranchers provided the ribs and cooked them in huge outdoor grills. There were chili-cooking enthusiasts, too, working up batches for the cook-off. Women brought savory covered dishes and delicious desserts and served them on the tables set up beneath awnings brought over from Talbot's Funeral Parlor. Kelly provided beer, Jada soft drinks and iced tea. There were booths: the dunking booth; a booth for selling kisses; Eldoree Winslow as a fortune-teller; tables for checkers and chess. There were horseshoe tossing and sack races, and horse races, too. Bright sunlight glimmered off shiny hair and straw hats, colorful dresses and shirts. People chatted, laughed and hollered; children ran and played.

Zoe dressed herself and the girls in their Sunday dresses, with matching ribbons in their hair. She brought two batches of her hot pepper corn bread and three dried peach pies, one for the auction, and dishes for herself and the girls, just as everyone did. She brought an extra place setting for Rory, just in case.

While Glory and Mercy played nearby with several of the Hunsicker children, Zoe joined Jada and Miss Loretta in the wooden booth complete with the fancy sunshade that Jada had made, serving cold drinks. Jada and Miss Loretta together were high entertainment, each trying to top the other with caustic insults.

Zoe kept looking for Rory. She'd worn her blue flowered Laura Ashley dress just for him, though she barely admitted this even to herself.

She caught a glimpse of him early on, walking with Oren and some other men, and later in the company of Corinne Hunsicker—who was draped over him like a silk table-cloth.

"Corinne comes on to all the fellas like that. It's nothin' on Rory's part," Jada whispered in her ear, and Zoe realized she was standing there staring at the two of them. Quickly she turned and busied herself with chopping ice in the cooler. Catching glimpses of Rory several times in the following hour, Zoe thought that he must have seen her, yet he didn't come over. It hurt.

The pie and cake auction was held in the shade of the cover above the gas pumps at Shatto's Garage; Joe Shatto was the auctioneer. The money raised was to go toward erecting a community building. The company of the cook was to go along with the purchase of the baked goods, and the cook's identity was to be a secret, but everyone knew who'd baked what—for certain women expected certain men to purchase their offerings.

Jada had bought a carrot cake from the bakery to auction off, and she'd identified it to Frank Vargas, so he would buy it—and therefore Jada's company. It turned out that Frank Vargas had to top Grandpa Hunsicker's bid of one hundred dollars for the honor. Zoe joined in the hooting and hollering at that. Jada preened.

Otto Hunsicker bought his wife's devil's food cake, Turley bought Miss Loretta's lemon meringue, two brothers bought Corinne Hunsicker's raisin pie, and on it went until Joe came to Zoe's pie. She stood with the girls and felt quite apprehensive about the possibility of having to keep company with a stranger while he ate a piece or two of her pie. She had counted on it being Rory who bid.

Joe started the bidding at ten dollars, and several bids brought it quickly to eighteen. And Rory was one of the bidders! Zoe blushed and felt a mixture of relief and high annoyance—after all, he hadn't approached her all afternoon.

And then, to her amazement, another bidder jumped in. Price Mitchum pushed himself forward with a bid of twenty-five dollars! Rory countered, and the war was on, while around them people watched with rabid curiosity and excitement. Zoe wanted to sink out of sight. To her further irritation, Mitchum and Rory seemed to be having a great time.

The two men kept bidding until they reached a hundred and fifty dollars. It appeared they were certainly doing their part for the community building. It was Rory's turn. He looked at Mitchum and said, "Two hundred."

"Two hundred! I have a bid of two hundred," Joe sang out.

Zoe wondered if she'd heard right.

Everyone looked from Zoe to Mitchum, though how everyone knew it was her pie, she didn't know. She held her breath, thinking that surely he would back out. But a wide grin came across his face, and he actually raised his hand. The next instant Rory lunged at him, and the two grappled. Then Oren and another man, who was obviously also a Breen—older brother Matt, Zoe guessed—appeared. While several men took hold of Rory, the Breen men took hold of Price Mitchum and dragged him, hollering, backward. The crowd parted for them, then closed again. Joe called, "Two hundred once . . . twice . . . sold!"

And Rory stepped forward, beaming. He took the pie from Joe, who called, "Pie baked by the Yarberry ladies!"

Rory, his eyes bright as diamonds, came up to Zoe, then included the girls in his gaze. "Ladies, may I have the honor of your company?" Glory immediately raised her arms to him, and he lifted her.

Her face burning, Zoe took up Mercy and walked away behind him.

The four of them filled lunch plates and joined Rory's family for their meal. For the first time, Zoe was formally introduced to Jesse Breen and his wife, Marnie, who was the most beautiful woman she'd ever seen. The two had a brand-new baby girl, who was the treasure of the family. She also met Annie's husband Matt, who had indeed been Oren's partner in capturing Price Mitchum, and their son Little Jesse. Oren and Matt refused comment as to what had transpired with Price Mitchum, except to assure the women they had not perpetrated any foul play. The men were highly pleased with themselves. And Zoe's pie was raved over. "We couldn't give up a pie like this!" Oren declared.

Zoe observed a family that was very close-knit. Though they physically favored each other, the brothers were distinctly different individuals—Matt quiet, Rory harder-edged and more outspoken, Oren happy-go-lucky and rarely quiet, certainly not shy. The brothers argued, too, over nearly everything from who forgot to bring a bottle opener to whose political opinion was the right one. Yet the love they had for each other was evident, mostly in the way they continually touched, no matter that they were big, tough men. Zoe thought this habit must have sprung from Jesse, for he often put a hand to one of his son's shoulders, hugged his wife, touched Annie's hair, kissed the babies. And that each of the Breens graciously included Zoe and her daughters in this time touched a deep lonely core inside of her that she hadn't known existed.

She and the girls spent the rest of the time with Rory. The four of them, no matter that Zoe was wearing her favorite dress, competed, after a fashion, in the sack races, then drank lemonade in the shade of Cobb's Drugstore. She and the girls stood in the crowd and cheered Rory on as he raced his palomino from the satellite dish behind Cobb's out to Miss Loretta's cottage, down by a big oak and around the cluster of red rocks and back to come in a close third. Several times they saw Price Mitchum in the distance, and he cast a dry grin their way, saluted Rory. He didn't have a black eye or anything, and Zoe wondered.

At dusk they went to sample Jesse Breen's chili. He took second in the cook-off, was quite insulted not to have taken first place, and thoroughly enjoyed the soothing attention Marnie gave him. The Breen family all gathered for a little rest, and afterward, when the western sky was crimson and stars were beginning to twinkle, there was dancing to a small country band on a wooden plank floor set up beneath colorful lights behind Kelly's. The children played around the perimeters; some slept on quilts.

Zoe was waiting for Rory, who'd gone to get them a couple of soft drinks, when Jesse came up beside her.

"May I have this dance? It's a slow one I can manage." He smiled and swept her into his arms and out onto the floor. His resemblance to his son was almost startling. "I'm sure glad to have had the chance to meet you, Zoe."

"I'm glad to meet you, too."

His grin, so much like his son's, could charm the spots from an Appaloosa. "I understand you have a stud that shows great promise as a cutter."

"We're hoping," Zoe said. She noticed his close study.

"Rory's very interested in him...." Jesse's eyes darkened. "It's been a long time since he's been interested in a horse. He's trained a number of winning cutters. Did you know that?"

"I knew he'd trained. He hasn't said much about it, though."

"He trained professionally for a couple of years. He had two top winners—one in the NCHA Futurity and one that took the Senior Cutting at the AQHA World Show. And there were a number of others that did well on the cutting circuit, too. That was about five years ago now—when he was in his twenties. One of the youngest trainers to ever succeed that well."

Zoe wasn't totally surprised, yet she was a bit mystified that Rory hadn't spoken of it. She studied Jesse, who was still studying her. "Why did he quit training?"

Jesse breathed deeply. "The problem with his wife just sort of knocked the wind out of him."

Zoe nodded, curious, but not about to ask anything about Krystal. What was there to ask? She knew the experience with his ex-wife had hurt Rory deeply—just as hers with Dusty had hurt her. An old story, as she and Rory had both said.

"I'm glad Rory met you," Jesse Breen said then, bringing her thoughts back to the moment. "You, your daughters and your horse are the first ones in a long, long time who my son has seemed to care about."

Zoe gazed into his blue eyes, eyes so much like Rory's, and didn't know what to say. He was telling her that Rory cared for her; he was saying he approved. She felt suddenly like she wanted to cry, and very frightened, too.

The next instant Rory was there beside them. Jesse released her with a smile and a small bow. "Thank you, Zoe." Rory took his place and whirled her around the floor. His hands were warm and damp, his blue eyes smoldering. Zoe found herself captured by those eyes. Her heart pattered. He smiled at her, a smile that went deep down to touch her heart and caused her to smile, too. She was being taken along by the dance, and in this moment she was glad.

Rory followed Zoe home and helped her carry Glory and Mercy, who'd fallen asleep, into the house.

"They sleep like the dead," Rory said with awe in his voice as he laid Mercy on the mattress.

"They always have. No, Fancy... you wait until I'm out of the room to sneak into bed. Rory, will you turn on the bathroom light? It'll give me enough light to get them into their pajamas."

He complied, then left her to the job. She got the girls settled, then stood staring at their cherub faces and thought of Rory waiting in the kitchen. Desire whispered through her veins.

He was leaning against the counter, staring at the floor, when she came into the room.

She closed the door behind her. "They're all settled." They gazed at each other, both thinking the same thing. Zoe said, "I had a very nice time today. Thank you. And it was nice meeting your family."

"They all like you."

"I like them. You're very fortunate."

"I know."

He reached out for her, took her by the arm and tugged her to him.

She melted into his embrace and savored his kiss. The whisper of desire turned quickly to a scream beating throughout her body. Breathless, she broke away and clung to him, feeling his hard shoulders beneath her palms, his heart beating against her. He nuzzled the tender skin of her neck.

"Rory..." Her voice came out a hoarse whisper. She started to pull away, but he captured her lips in another kiss, and it was too sweet to break.

At last he lifted his head, and she gazed into his questioning eyes while his hands continued to work upon her back and he pushed himself seductively against her.

Zoe fought for common sense and pulled from his embrace. "I'm not ready to go to bed with you."

"You felt pretty ready to me," he said sharp as a knife. "What are you holdin' out for—marriage? You think we got to have the sanctity of marriage to cover it?"

"I'm not *holding out* for anything," she shot right back. "I'm just not ready, and I'll be damned if I'll apologize for it or let you push me into it, either. If sex is your main reason for comin' around, then, buddy, there's the door."

He thought about that. "Sex isn't all I'm here for, and you know it."

She just looked at him.

"You know it, don't you? I sure as hell don't know anything more to do to show you that. And I don't see anything wrong with wantin' you. It comes with the territory."

At last she said, in a husky whisper, "I know. I want you, too."

And that hung there between them.

"Did Dusty push you into it?"

"Sometimes I blame him for it," she admitted. "But it wasn't his fault. It was my own doing. I could have said no."

"And you still can't let him go. Is that it?"

"Dusty doesn't have anything to do with it," she said with a small shake of her head. "I was so hot for Dusty that I gave no thought to consequences. Now two of those consequences are lying in that room, proof condoms aren't one hundred percent effective. And I'm allergic to every other type of birth control. You didn't know that, didn't think to ask, because it really isn't your problem." She gazed at him, though not in blame. "Those are reasons every bit as important as my feelings for Dusty. And I don't intend to make another mistake like I made with him, nor do I intend to be preoccupied by a dozen affairs while I have two little girls depending on me."

They stared at each other.

Rory took up his hat, plopped it on his head. "Good night."

Zoe watched the door close behind him, and her heart dropped to her toes. She wondered if she would see him again. She almost ran after him to ask, but pride kept her where she was. She would not humiliate either of them. And she couldn't change her mind. She was who she was, and she would make no apology for being exactly that.

And she thought how that applied to Rory as well.

Kelly placed a glass of Jack D. in front of Rory. Twisting the glass atop the shiny bar, Rory watched the glimmering of the liquid. *Booze,* Zoe had called it. She sure was a teetotaler; she acted as if even beer was sin itself. Rory thought about Joe Padilla and knew the reason lay there. Joe had been the sort to lace his morning coffee with tequila. Rory had gone honky-tonkin' with Joe a number of times; he'd carried Joe home more than once. That had been a few years ago, when Rory had still been in his twenties. When a man is in his twenties, he feels as if he will live forever and has time for everything he wants to do.

"You're in a thoughtful mood, amigo," Kelly said and leaned close from the opposite side of the bar.

"Thinking about women and life."

"Come up with any revelations?"

"How about that neither one of them makes a whole lot of sense and they're both excellent at irritatin' a man?"

Kelly laughed. "*Es verdad.* Very true on both counts. However, think of the alternative of doing without either."

"Do you still hanker after Jada, Kel?"

Kelly's long face got even longer. "Yep. Oh, I tried to give it up for six months, but that was all show."

"Ever sleep with her?" Rory asked in a whisper.

Kelly came back with, "That's a pretty personal question." Then he shook his head. "Jada says it would ruin our friendship—or somethin' like that."

Rory sighed. "How can you keep on hankerin' for her after all this time?"

"Love don't shut off like a faucet. Oh, it can be controlled to a certain extent by good sense, and a whole lot more by honor."

"You love her still?"

Kelly nodded. "I love her, and I want her to be happy. I guess I just take as much of Jada as she can give me, and I give her as much of myself as I can. We've reached what works for us. Probably wouldn't work for everyone. Everybody has to find a pattern of their own, and sometimes that takes a lot of cutting and pasting."

Rory thought about that and couldn't come up with anything that made sense. But suddenly he recalled how when Joe Padilla began training a horse in earnest, he would go down to the dry wash and pour out every single bottle of whiskey on the place.

Rory pushed the glass of Jack D. toward Kelly. "I don't suppose you'd have any cream soda back there, would ya?"

Kelly's mouth spread into a slow grin. "Sure do." He tossed his wiping cloth over his shoulder and took the glass of Jack D. away.

A figure slipped up next to Rory. A large figure—Price Mitchum, grinning like he'd just won the lottery on a ticket Rory had lost.

"Well, if it isn't Rory Breen—all by himself, without his brothers to back him up."

Rory sighed and thought, Here it comes again.

Mitchum turned his back to the bar and propped his elbows on it. "Two hundred dollars. Pie must have been awfully tasty—and the woman, too."

The hairs prickled on the back of Rory's neck. Kelly brought Rory's glass of cream soda. Rory lifted it to his lips.

"Money spent for a good cause. Or haven't you ever done that, Mitchum?"

Mitchum chuckled. "You're pretty good with a horse, but what about women? Think you can keep this one satisfied, Breen?"

Fury gushed through Rory like a powerful well. Slowly he lowered the glass. "If it's a fight you want, Mitchum, why not have the guts to just come out and say it? Better yet, why don't we just set up a monthly schedule for fightin'? Or maybe that would tax your brain too much."

A number of people around them heard, and the babble of voices lessened as eyes stared.

Mitchum went wide-eyed innocent. "What? What'd I say? I was just wishin' you luck with the hot little chickie. You know what they say about widows and divorcées." And he gave a sly, dirty grin. "Always ready."

Rory shoved his face close to Mitchum's. Looking upward at the taller man, he spoke low, for their ears alone. "Mitchum, you can't help being born no-account white trash, but you could stay home and spare the rest of us." He let the challenge sit there, then turned and walked away, expecting any moment to receive a blow from behind. He thought the least he could do for Kelly was carry this fight outside.

But when the blow came, it was verbal and said for all to hear. "You may call me no-account, but your wife sure didn't. No, sir, Krystal didn't. Not by a long shot."

Rory hesitated a second, then kept walking. It was time he quit giving Mitchum ammunition with which to shoot him, and Krystal had been gone a long time.

It was the sound of a blow and glass breaking that brought him whirling around, every muscle ready, his hands automatically flying upward. He was amazed to see it wasn't Mitchum coming for him—but that Kelly had thrown a punch right across the bar that sent Mitchum reeling. People tended to forget that Kelly had at one time been a professional fighter and known to bust up this very bar himself, before he'd tamed his temper.

Kelly motioned to Rory. "Come on back and finish your cream soda, Rory. This fella was just leavin'."

And of course there were a few whispered echoes. "Cream soda?"

Chapter Ten

Rory's favorite riding arena, next to his own, was at Robert Walker's place down near Glenrio. Walker's arena and pens had been carefully designed to provide the best, while echoing the old cowboy life of a hundred years ago, when cowboys had no money and their horses were worth five hundred, not fifty thousand. Of course, it had taken a hundred thousand bucks to do it.

There were a lot of people in attendance today. Pickup trucks and trailers sat alongside fancy Cadillacs and beat-up station wagons, people and horses meandered, kids and dogs played. These people were either friends of Robert Walker or people he owed favours to—Robert was always either in or seeking some political office—and this annual barbecue and cutting was his way of repaying. Rory fell in the "friend" category by way of his father.

"How much do you think the jackpot will be?" Zoe asked, scanning the vehicles as if mentally adding up entries. She was leading Blue, while Rory led Walter.

"I imagine there'll be near twenty-five entries in the non-pro. With the money Walker's adding, first'll probably pay out five hundred or more."

She cast him a hopeful glance, then shyly looked away. Rory rubbed his mustache and hid a smile. He walked along, his best silver spurs jingling, feeling quite satisfied with the day. The sun was shining, and he was about to spend the day riding and cutting—and with Zoe right beside him. And for once Zoe had left Glory and Mercy behind with Jada. For once they were alone. That was, if a person didn't count the several hundred other people milling around. And he expected Zoe and Blue to take first, which would make him proud and give Zoe some more money.

"He's about like a pilot light just waiting for the gas," Rory said of Blue. The stud kept jerking his head around. Excited, his ears were perked and his nostrils flared. There were a number of pretty and hot-to-trot fillies here. Rory was sometimes uneasy these days with Zoe, at one hundred pounds, one-ten at the most, handling the horse. The stud wasn't as mild-mannered as he'd once been, for now he was at his physical best and feeling his oats. He had a greater sense of pride, too, a hotshot horse who'd proven that he knew what cutting a cow was all about.

"It's the rich feed," Zoe said. "I told you we need to back off. There's such a thing as too much of a good thing."

"You want him at his peak." They stopped near the gate to the arena, where a number of people were already riding. "Why don't you let me warm him up?"

Zoe shook her head, just as Rory had known she would. She was possessive of the stud, as protective of him as she was of her girls. She didn't exactly see eye-to-eye with Rory about how to handle the horse—she thought Rory was way too overbearing. Rory had come to understand that her protectiveness sprang from her passion and responsibility for family; Blue was family to her. And it also had to do with losses in her life. He knew all this as he gazed down into her fresh and eager face. As always, a warmth washed over him.

Impulsively, before he knew what he was doing, he brought his hand to her neck, bent down, dodged her hat and kissed her. A swift kiss, but sweet as honey. More and more these days he was finding it hard to keep his hands off her.

He stepped back and took a deep breath. "I'll go get us registered and bring you back a Coke." He turned.

"Wait!" She dug into her jeans pocket. "Here's the entry fee."

Reluctantly he took it from her. For each of the small jackpot cuttings they attended, she paid, though he knew she had to scrimp to do it. He couldn't talk her out of it, though he'd flat-out refused to let her pay for gas on their excursions. "Either you let me haul you, or you go alone," he'd told her. She hadn't said another word about it.

She was perfectly capable of bringing herself to these wingdings, and it tickled him that she wanted him with her badly enough to accept his terms.

Their relationship was about like a dance, he mused as he tied Walter to the outside rail of the arena and then headed away for the registration table. A dance—two steps forward, a step backward and to the side. Just who led who changed from minute to minute, and their embrace was at best tentative and cautious. They caressed with their eyes and allowed an occasional light kiss, but their twirling was within a certain carefully marked area, and neither stepped over the line.

He'd gone all mushy a couple of times and brought her bouquets of wildflowers he'd picked himself. She kept cream soda and fresh lemon slices for iced tea for him in her refrigerator. Rory hadn't touched a drop of whiskey in weeks, and he had to say he didn't much miss it. He had indulged in a few beers—though not around Zoe.

This was the third cutting they'd entered. Blue had taken second place last time, taking home a hundred and fifty bucks. If he could take first this time, against some cutting horses that had points and money earned from official cuttings, Rory was going to press Zoe about going to the Classic. Out of mischief as much as anything, he hadn't brought up the subject of the Classic with her again, and out of stubbornness, Zoe wasn't about to mention it. But she was thinking about it. He knew that because he'd seen the ad for it lying on her kitchen table. Besides, she had horses and cutting in her blood, so there was no way she couldn't be thinking about it.

Rory had come to know that Zoe did very few things without careful consideration. She was considering the issue of the two of them, too. And until she decided one way or the other, she wasn't going to commit herself to sex. And, Rory mused, looking at it from her point of view—the threat of pregnancy—he certainly couldn't blame her. The thought tended to be like ice water thrown on his loins, too.

Rory wondered what in the world kept him after her. And he wondered what in the world he would do if he caught her. At the very back of his mind he knew he wanted for her to open herself to him, but he was having trouble doing likewise. He couldn't risk letting himself fall in love with Zoe, simply to lose her to Dusty. He couldn't do that.

There was a crowd at the registration table; Rory knew half of the people. He answered greetings, called his own and inched his way up to register. Stella MacGuire, looking like an ad for makeup just like always, was taking money; she came on to him, just like always, too, and he enjoyed it for several minutes. Actually, his response was about ten degrees hotter than normal, and he knew it was residue from wanting Zoe so much.

He left the registration table, stepped up on the old wooden bleachers and scanned the arena. He saw them— Zoe on the red horse called Blue. Quite a combination. His pulse raced as he watched the stud move. That horse promised great things.

His attention shifted to Zoe. The stud was pushing on the bit, but she handled him easily enough. She and the horse flowed. His eyes remained on her lithe body, and he experienced a warm rush and a whole lot of fantasies that circled around him and Zoe in bed.

He stepped from the bleachers and headed for the concession wagon, where he got a cold bottle of beer, drank it and had the powerful urge for another one. He ordered two colas. Just as the girl was bringing them, someone called his name in a way that brought him whirling around. W. Jones was waving to him from the arena rail. Etta and Frank and some others were hurrying that way, too.

Zoe! That was Blue's head bobbing around at the rail—and Zoe sitting on the ground!

Heart pounding, Rory lit out at a run. He didn't bother to go through the gate; he propelled himself to the top rail and over. The small gathering of people parted for him.

W. Jones had Zoe up and balancing on one leg when he got to her. Pain etched her features. Rory had the odd thought: Thank God she's alive.

"What happened?" he asked and took hold of her on the other side. Zoe, blinking back tears, felt his agitation, and he wasn't just agitated—he was angry. If the glance he shot Blue had been a bullet, it would have killed the horse on the spot.

"Horse spooked," W. Jones said.

And Rory's jaw hardened. His face was dark as a storm cloud, and Zoe would have bet anything he was thinking along the lines of shooting the horse. He always criticized Blue for being a spoiled horse and her for doing the spoiling. Zoe's opinion was that Rory, like ninety-nine percent of all men, had a propensity for needing to conquer an animal.

"He didn't throw me or anything, Rory," Zoe managed. "He just darted to the side. It was just one of those things, my mistake for not being ready. I'm fine. Nothing's broken. My knee's just popped out."

"What do you mean 'popped out'?" Rory leaned close. She caught the smell of beer. Their eyes met, and then his skittered away. Someone produced a box for her to sit on, and she stretched her leg, trying to find some relief for her knee. It hurt, but it had been worse than this. This was about a medium on the scale.

"I got off to tighten the cinch, and as I was gettin' back on, something startled Blue. I twisted my knee." She couldn't find a comfortable position for her leg. "The joint's popped out. . . . It happens sometimes."

"You mean this has happened before?" Rory's voice was sharp, though his hands were gentle as he tested her knee.

"Yes. Since I was a kid and got hit by Ulysses on his motorcycle."

He paused, stared at her. "Why didn't you ever tell me?" As if she'd been holding out secrets.

"Well, the subject simply hasn't ever come up," Zoe answered reasonably, with a tone very near sarcasm. "Now it has. My knee pops out of joint on occasion."

Rory's blue eyes smoldered, and Zoe realized that a crowd had gathered. She bit her lip as Rory again gently moved her leg. He studied her face, and she had pity on him. He really and truly was worried about her. Her heart squeezed.

"Just help me pop it back into place," she said softly.

His blue eyes skittered away from hers. "You take a look, W. You know more about this stuff." Rory moved aside for the old man. By the way W. moved her leg, Zoe assumed he did know a thing or two. Rory held one of her hands, and she helped W. snap her knee back into place. It didn't hurt as bad as it did sometimes.

W. and Rory helped her to stand; when she looked at Rory, she saw his face was as white as desert sand. When she limped with her first steps, he swept her up into his arms and carried her out of the arena. W. Jones followed, bringing the stud.

Rory carried her all the way to his pickup—and called to Zoe's mind John Wayne toting Maureen O'Hara. She would have laughed, except she was afraid she'd go to crying. His attention got to her. As gently as if she were an eggshell, he sat her in the pickup, her legs dangling out the open door. His face was knotted with worry. She just had to caress his cheek. "It's fine, really. I told you, this happens sometimes. It hurts, but it's certainly not in danger of amputation."

He smiled at that.

Etta Quevedo brought a couple of headache powder packets and two paper cups of Coca-Cola. Rory sprinted over to the concession wagon and brought back ice wrapped in plastic to put on her knee.

After an hour, though the pain was no worse, the knee had swollen twice in size. When Rory went for more soft drinks, Zoe hobbled around to the tack room in the trailer and found a leg wrap for horses. On second thought she returned it because it was red and chose a blue one instead.

She was wrapping her knee, on the outside of her jeans, when Rory got back.

"What in the world are you doin'?" he asked. He stood there, holding a full paper cup in each hand, glaring at her.

"Goin' mountain climbing," she said, unable to resist a stupid answer to a stupid question. She focused on wrapping the support bandage around her knee.

"You can't ride that stud with your knee like that. You won't be able to cue him—even if you can stay on."

She kept on wrapping. "He knows what to do. All I have to do is set him up."

"And stay on."

"I'll stay on."

She felt his gaze and refused to look at him. His blue eyes just might be her undoing. Oftentimes, she felt overpowered by Rory. She was too stubborn to admit she had to ride because she wasn't about to pass on this chance to win five hundred dollars—or at least her entry fee, which was what fourth place would bring. Because he was considered a pro, Rory couldn't take her place, so by golly, she was going to ride, and she was going to place.

"The joint is back in place. It even works...see? All I need is some added support."

He bent in front of her and set the soft drinks aside. "Let me do it. You don't have it tight enough."

The bandage proved to be hot as the dickens. Zoe thought it was good that she wore one so she could have an idea of how a horse felt with them on—after this she'd find some made of a natural material, ones that breathed. To make matters worse, she had to hide the fact that her knee ached or Rory would have dragged her out of there. She found that both touching and wearing.

When it came her and Blue's turn, she rode, and she stayed on, though twice she almost ate dirt and set Blue off balance. But as if to make up to her, he slunk back beneath her and kept her in the saddle. And in the heat of the two and a half minutes, focusing on keeping herself in the saddle and out of Blue's way, she clean forgot about her knee. But after the buzzer had sounded, she felt it plenty. Still, her ears heard the score called, and that score was the highest yet. But nine more entries were left to go after her.

At the trailer, Rory lifted his arms. "Let me help you."

Zoe practically fell on him. Involuntarily she relaxed against him, for a long minute leaning on his comfort and strength.

"I didn't fall off," she said.

"No, you didn't, darlin'." He held her to him; she buried her face in his neck. "How is it?"

"It's still in place, but it hurts like hell."

He carried her to the doorway of the tack compartment and set her there, then took care of the horses. She breathed deeply and tried to relax her leg. Rory slipped into the tack compartment, and she heard him rummaging. The next instant he was beside her and holding out a pint bottle of whiskey.

"Take a drink of this."

Anger flashed. "Have you been sippin' on this all the time—keepin' it handy when we're at these cuttings?"

"Now, what do you think? Do I appear to have been drinking?" His eyes sparked.

No, he didn't.

He urged, "Take a couple of swigs."

"Just get me some more aspirin."

"I'll do that, too. Come on. You won't go to hell or turn into a roarin' drunk on two swigs of whiskey."

It was the last taunt that got her. She knew Rory thought her something of a prude. Even Jada had mentioned it, and Zoe had seen a bit of it in herself. She took one drink, and it seared her throat, taking her breath. How in the world had her father managed to drink so much of this stuff? She saw Rory's lips twitch. She took two more small drinks and felt the warmth flow over her body. "Make you happy?" she said. "If you'll go twist your knee, I'll share."

"Watch yourself, Miss Smarty. Remember—I'm drivin'."

Blue took second place. He would have taken first, Zoe knew, except for her leg and the fact the first cow she'd cut out had been a deadhead. She laughed at those thoughts;

she sounded just like her father and all the other cutters—making excuses. No matter, for she was taking home over two hundred dollars.

She sat in the truck, in the last rays of the sun, while Rory loaded the horses into the trailer. In the arena, the lights were just coming on. Cutting would continue until the late hours. She counted and recounted the money in her hand and mentally added it to what she'd already saved. It was enough for her half of the entry fee for the Classic. She thought of the other expenses—stall fees and feed and motel and food. She would get them from somewhere.

Rory slipped behind the wheel. ''We're loaded and ready to go.'' He flopped his hat onto the rear seat, then ran his hands through his sweat-dampened hair.

Zoe's gaze lingered on his rich brown wavy hair, then met his eyes. They smiled at her, then dropped to the money in her hand.

She, too, looked at the money. ''I guess we can go to the Classic,'' she said.

They grinned at each other. Then Zoe leaned over and kissed him, hard and sound.

When they got into Clayton, Rory insisted on taking her to the hospital. Zoe argued; she didn't have money to be spending on a doctor. But Rory hauled her in, saying he would pay. She wasn't about to let him.

''Nothing's broken, and the joint is back in place,'' the medic told them. ''I don't think you've torn any ligaments, but you could have a problem with the cartilage. Here's some pain medication and an extra wrap. Stay off it—and if I were you, I'd see a specialist. Oh—that medication will make you pretty sleepy,'' he told her when they were leaving.

Zoe took half the prescribed dose and felt better by the time they pulled into Wings.

''Where's Zoe?'' Jada asked, when Rory went up to her apartment over the drugstore to get the girls.

''She's in the truck. She hurt her knee.''

"How bad?" But before he said a word, Jada, in a thin white robe, pushed past him on the landing and hurried down the stairs to the truck.

Zoe opened the door to show her the knee, which seemed silly to Rory, because there wasn't anything to see but jeans. He stayed where he was on the landing. The women's voices drifted up to him in the still evening air. He heard Zoe tell Jada about Blue taking second place and had to grin. She was as excited as a child. He heard Jada try to persuade Zoe to let the girls spend the night, but Zoe was having none of it.

When Jada came back up the stairs, she said, "Sorry, Rory. I tried."

"Much obliged, Jada," Rory said as he followed her inside.

"Zoe just can't stand to have her darlings out of her sight, and to tell you the truth, I don't much blame her. Those girls will grow up and be gone soon enough."

Rory didn't say anything to that. Jada carried Glory, and he carried Mercy, and put them in the rear seat of the big pickup truck. The little ones never woke.

When they got to Zoe's, he came around to carry her into the house first.

"Oh, for heaven's sake, I can walk," she said. "Hi, Fancy."

"But you don't need to," he said. "Get out of the way, Fancy."

"You get out of the way. No, just hold my arm."

"Come here."

"I told you . . . oh, Rory Breen!"

He swept her up in his arms. It made him feel pretty smart to do so. And he liked having her body against his. "If you don't be still—quit giggling—I'll throw you over my shoulder." Then he tripped over Fancy.

"Aaaahhh . . ." She grabbed his neck as he stumbled around, struggling for balance with rubber legs.

"Quit chokin' me!"

"Well, don't drop me. That's all I need—a *broken* something."

Rory grunted. "I'm closer to gettin' strangled."

"I never saw John Wayne stumblin' around with Maureen O'Hara."

"They had the benefit of retakes and editing."

He set her on her feet in the kitchen, allowing his hands to slip down the contours of her body and rest there, encircling her. He felt the dampness of her skin through her cotton blouse. They gazed at each other for a long, hot moment. He thought that this certainly wasn't the best time.

"The girls need to be put to bed," Zoe said at last.

"They're sleepin'," he said.

"The horse needs to be put in his stall."

"He ain't hurtin', and neither is Walter."

She stared at him. He turned and went to the sink, getting her a glass of water. Before he went back outside to the truck, he made certain she took the rest of her pain medication.

One at a time, he brought the girls into their room, laying them on the mattress on the floor. He thought they looked like little cherubs. He touched each one on the head. Zoe switched on the small window fan, and cool night air blew gently into the hot room. At Zoe's direction, he found the girls' nightgowns, then left her to get them settled, while he attended to the horses. He put Blue in his stall, and fed and watered Walter in the trailer. He spent some time doing it, taking comfort in the familiar actions, something he knew all about. He felt unsettled inside, uncertain, as if he didn't even know himself.

When he returned, he found Zoe in the kitchen, digging through her purse. "I have to get my lotion," she said and cast him a crooked smile. She held the tube up in triumph, but her eyes were heavy. As she stepped away from the table, she began to sink to the floor.

Rory caught her just in time. "Zoe? Are you okay?"

She giggled. "Well, my leg doesn't hurt anymore." Her full weight melted against him.

The pain pills, he thought. "I imagine nothing hurts about now. Come on. I'll help you into bed." He lifted her into his arms.

She went to giggling again, then put her fingers to her lips. "Shh. Don't wake the girls."

"A bawlin' bull outside the window wouldn't wake those girls." He set her to the floor in the brightly lit bathroom. "Think you'll be all right?"

"Yes...I do *not* need your assistance." And she laughed.

"I'll wait in here, just in case," he said firmly and stepped through to her bedroom.

By the bit of light shining from the bathroom, he located the lamp beside the bed and switched it on. It was the first glimpse he'd had of Zoe's bedroom—the bedspread was blue, her favorite. Both windows were open, but little air stirred. In the corner stood an old, gray metal fan on a stand, the army surplus sort built forty years ago. He moved it near one of the windows and switched it on. It helped. The room was neat; Zoe was a neat person. There were a lot of books, stacked on the floor, because there weren't any bookshelves. There was an assortment of colored bottles on top of the dresser. The small television had crimped aluminum foil sticking off the end of the antenna rods. Looked like some machine from Mars.

He was pulling down the bedspread when the telephone on the small bedside table rang. He glanced at the bathroom door, then answered the phone.

"Hello."

"Is this Zoe Yarberry's?" came a sharp male voice.

"Yes," Rory replied slowly, a coolness slipping over his shoulders. He looked again at the bathroom door; the sound of water still came from inside. "She's busy right now. Can I take a message?"

"Who's this?"

"This is Rory Breen. Who's this?"

"This is Zoe's *husband,* and I want to talk to her. Put her on."

"Sorry. Like I said, she's busy. I'll tell her you called." And Rory pressed his finger to disconnect the call. High-handed, maybe, but by virtue of the past weeks, he had some rights, he figured—and he laid the receiver beside the phone.

His eyes lit on some folded papers propped against the small radio. The divorce papers, he thought.

He lifted the papers, unfolded them. They were the divorce papers, all right, still there after all these months. He looked for a filing date and county stamp. There was neither. He refolded them and put them back.

The door creaked, and Zoe stood there. Her hair was loose and falling around her shoulders. She wore a sleeveless cotton nightgown, and her jeans and boots. It took Rory's gaze a second to get down to the jeans and boots.

She swayed and leaned against the doorframe. "I can't get my boots off." And she giggled. "You know, those pills are pretty good. My leg doesn't hurt at all."

Rory had to grin. "I doubt you feel any pain."

"Uh-huh. I feel great." She stepped out and sank toward the floor.

Rory caught her. "Sit down. I'll get your boots off."

"And my pants. Can't get them off, either."

Rory removed her boots and socks, then massaged her feet and watched the effect take hold in her eyes.

"That's nice," she drawled, looking sexy as hell. "You have wonderful hands."

"I do?"

She nodded. Then she closed her eyes. "My head is spinnin' like a merry-go-round."

"We have to get you into bed."

"Oh, I've heard that before," she drawled.

With her giggling and wiggling, he helped get her injured leg out of her jeans. He was a helpful kind of guy, he thought, as he inspected her swollen knee and enjoyed a great view of her creamy legs. He cupped her calf and rubbed downward. He wouldn't have been human if his pulse hadn't started thrumming.

"We had a great day," she said, with a silly smile.

"Yes, we did." He tossed her jeans onto the floor.

"Blue sure has fooled people, hasn't he? He doesn't look like all that much . . . but Daddy knew. Daddy always knew 'bout horses. It was just he couldn't figure out how to work life."

"Come on, get into bed." Rory shifted her up onto the pillows.

"Do you think he can do it, Rory?" she asked, her brows furrowed. "Do you think he can win at the Classic?"

"He has a good chance." He settled the cool sheet over her warm body.

She sat back up. "He's my chance to do better by Glory and Mercy. Oh, Rory, I love them so much. I'm a good mother, I really am." She spoke softly and with great pleasure. Then she cocked her head and peered at him with those warm, liquid brown eyes. "You could be a great father."

Rory backed up at that. "Well, there's some doubt there."

"No... there's no doubt. But you couldn't be drinkin'. No."

She lay back on the pillows, and her hair fanned out across them and down her arms. "I feel so funny. Is this what it's like to be drunk?"

"If you're lucky." He again pulled the sheet up.

She grabbed his arm and held his hand at her waist. "Stay with me awhile, Rory." And she scooted over.

He swallowed. "Okay."

He propped his back against the pillows and stretched out at the edge of the bed. Zoe snuggled against him, her head pillowed on his chest. All warm and womanly.

"Isn't this nice?" she murmured, rubbing her cheek against him.

He kissed the top of her head. "Yeah..." He began massaging her back; it felt small but hard beneath his hand. She moved against his body and made a small moan of pleasure. Just as he was getting ready to find her mouth, he felt her go heavy against him. "Zoe?" he whispered.

She'd fallen asleep.

With a heavy sigh, he thought of what might have been.

He continued to lie there with her in his arms. The fan made a rhythmic hum, as did the refrigerator from way in the kitchen, and he could feel Zoe's heart beating against his side. Her scent was all around him. He thought about Glory and Mercy and what Zoe had said about him being a good father. Odd, but now that she was the one bringing it up, he found the prospect unnerving.

To be a father would mean being a husband again.

And he'd messed up in that department pretty good already.

He gazed at Zoe and thought about staying the night, anticipating the morning, before the girls awoke, when they could finish what they'd started. Then his gaze strayed over to the papers lying there in the glow of the lamp.

What if he let himself go all-out in loving Zoe, giving his life to her, and she decided to return to Dusty?

The following morning Zoe found Rory had left a note. *Here's my half of the entry fee. It's up to you. Rory.* Then below that he'd added, *Dusty called last night and said he'd call back. Don't ride today.* He'd underlined the command.

The note was penned on a scrap torn from a brown paper bag. It and six one-hundred-dollar bills and the entry form for the Classic, with a circle around the registration deadline—which was next week—had been inserted into the folds of the divorce papers on the beside table. It stuck up like a brown flag.

Zoe knew that Rory had looked at the papers.

The girls remained asleep. Zoe made coffee and brought a cup back to her bed, which was something of a challenge, limping as she was. The swelling of her knee had receded a bit, though, and the ache was dull. It throbbed only when she tried to put weight on it.

Using a book as a desk, Zoe filled out the entry form for the Classic. She wrote carefully and thought how she had to be crazy—yet this craziness felt great. It was hope for the future, a daring to expect good things. A daring that she could handle what came.

Life, she thought, was to be lived...and one couldn't live by being afraid of taking chances. And that applied to her relationship with Rory, too, she thought.

Rory didn't return to Zoe's until Wednesday evening. It was the first time in weeks that he'd stayed away from her for three whole days. He'd spent the time alone, thinking, though he still hadn't figured out how he felt about things between them, things inside himself.

As he pulled his truck in front of the barn, Mercy and Glory and the dog came racing forward. The girls threw themselves at him, and the dog pranced around his feet. Feeling as welcome as Santa Claus, he lifted both girls. He felt their tiny hands around his neck, and his heart swelled to nearly bursting. He was struck by how deep he'd gotten in here.

Glory furrowed her little eyebrows. "Where you been, Ror-ry?"

"Oh, I had things to do, squirt."

"You been biz-zy," Mercy said seriously.

"Yeah, I was a little busy. But I'm sure glad to see you now. What have you two been up to?"

"Playin'," Glory said.

"We went t' town and got new shoes," Mercy said and stuck out her foot, showing off pink-and-white tennis shoes.

"Well, now, those sure are mighty pretty."

"We went t' the courthouse," Glory said.

That caught Rory's attention. "You did? And what did you do there?"

"Saw a la-dy with big hair." Laughing, Glory waved her hands around her head. Mercy copied her.

"So, where's your mama?" Rory asked as he set the girls to the ground. He wondered why Zoe hadn't come to greet him.

"In here!" the girls said in unison. Taking him by the hands, they pulled him toward the barn. "Mama! Mama! Ror-ry's here!"

Zoe was cleaning Blue's stall. She looked at him briefly, coolly, said, "Hello," then went back to work.

Rory thought, Ohh boy. She certainly wasn't as warm as she had been the last time they were together. Wary, he stopped by the stall door. As if sensing the fun was over, the girls went to play on the hay bales. Rory watched Zoe and noted that she still limped some.

"How's the knee?" he asked.

"It's better." She was as cool as a January wind.

Irritation rising, he came into the stall, reached for the cleaning fork. "Not better enough to be cleanin' a stall."

She held tight to the fork. "It has to be done."

"You could leave it for me. A couple of days wouldn't hurt anything."

"I left it a couple of days." She yanked the fork from his grasp and set it aside. "But I didn't know when you were comin'."

And suddenly he knew. "I just needed a couple of days to myself. I need that sometimes. I was comin' back, Zoe."

She shrugged. "That's your business. You certainly don't owe me anything."

He felt tight and angry himself. "Did you think I wasn't comin' back? Why in the world would you think that?"

She turned those brown eyes to him then. "How would I know if you were or not?"

She bent again to lift the wheelbarrow. He edged her aside, took it from her hands and, pushing it hard and fast, bumped it out of the stall and through to the manure pile outside, where he dumped it with a swift jerk. He could understand how she would have thought that about him, but it still didn't go down easy. Though the thought did occur to him that at least she cared. She cared a great deal. He wondered about this courthouse business.

Zoe was brushing Blue when he returned.

He said, "I'm sorry I didn't call or anything. I don't much care for using a telephone. But that's still no reason for you to think I wouldn't come back."

"You don't have to feel sorry. You don't owe me an explanation. Except, I really was wondering, since I sent in Blue's registration for the Classic." She looked at him, then returned her gaze to the stud and brushed him with a vengeance.

"Okay," he said slowly. "And what did you do at the courthouse?"

She went very still and at last turned to face him. "I filed my divorce papers."

Rory swallowed. He stood there gazing at her, into her deep brown eyes. She'd made a step, a big one for her, and it seemed it was his turn now. Turning, he strode over and grabbed the saddle and pad from the rack, brought them over and flung them atop Blue. "We've got a lot of practicing to do, partner."

They grinned at each other across the back of the horse. Her eyes were warm. And filled with something that touched a place deep inside him. He knew then, suddenly, that he was in love with Zoe Yarberry. It scared him to death, because he didn't know if he could be all she needed him to be.

He rode Blue that evening. He rode him hard, trying to lose himself in something he knew and understood. And when Zoe got up on the stud, Rory cut her no slack, making her repeat turns and maneuvers until she and the horse did them perfectly. He felt her eyes on him. He felt her questions, and he had some of his own.

As they put Blue away, he found his gaze lingering long on where Zoe's neckline disappeared into her blouse. She caught him once, and she grinned a shy grin, but her eyes were warm and steady.

Just before he left, when dusk was deepening and the girls were chasing moths in the glow of the porch light, he kissed her, the kind of kiss that gets the head to spinning and things to rising. She responded fully, molding her body against his. But when they broke apart, she backed up and said goodnight.

When he opened his truck door, he remembered and turned to call to her, "I'll be here tomorrow evening, round about six."

"Come for dinner. I'll make enchiladas," she called back.

As he drove away, Rory considered that maybe tomorrow evening he would bring her flowers. And maybe he would be staying with her.

Only, when tomorrow evening came around, so did Dusty Yarberry.

Chapter Eleven

Rory rode Blue over to where she sat on a hay bale. "What do you think?"

Zoe gazed up into his sparkling blue eyes. "I think you're spurrin' him too much, and he still dips that left shoulder."

"Yeah, he's droppin' that shoulder, but not every time." He averted his eyes to Blue and stroked the horse's neck. "And if I spur him good, he'll move better for you."

His eyes came back to her. For a second his gaze, sultry as an August afternoon, skimmed downward and lingered on her breasts. Immediately Zoe felt her breasts swell, her nipples harden. He turned the horse and rode back to the small herd of cattle.

The sun was far to the west, and the heat was lifting. The wind was still up and blowing the dust from Blue's hooves away from her. Zoe watched Rory ride. She thought that perhaps Rory was even better than her father, who'd been one of the best. She thought he was too strict with the horse, as were most men. She thought mostly about making love with him.

She watched the way his thighs hugged the horse, squeezing only ever so slightly to direct the animal. His back was slightly curved, his thick shoulders straight. His shoulders barely seemed to move, while his lower arms and hands moved the reins easily and quickly.

As she sat there, her breasts tingled, as if he'd touched her. She throbbed. She wanted him badly, and all her sane reasons against it were melting before her heat.

Did he know? Oh, yes. She could see it in the way he looked at her. Just as she could see that he felt the same. Yet, as their desire had seemed to spiral in the past few days, so had their caution. She, because of her experiences with her father and Dusty, and he, because of Krystal. It didn't take a psychologist to figure it out; it was perfectly logical. Experience was a thorough teacher. What they both had learned was that love could hurt very badly.

And still she wanted him.

She saw Rory look to the road before she heard the vehicle arriving. Twisting, she saw a truck and horse trailer pulling into the drive. The horn honked gaily. The golden sun was in her eyes, and she couldn't clearly see. Her first thought was of a customer. She took drop-ins, even at night, and she would book appointments until seven or eight. She would have booked an appointment at midnight, should a customer require it. Heaven knew she needed all the money she could make. What she would need for going to Fort Worth in a month nagged at her. Though tonight she was torn between her need of money and her need of being with Rory.

She walked to the corral gate, favoring her knee only slightly. Once she got the knee to moving, it quit catching. As she opened the gate, she shaded her eyes, squinting. A man was coming around the hood of the truck. And it came to her at once, with a cool shimmy up her spine—the red-and-white truck, the tall, slim man wearing tall, red-and-white boots.

Dusty. Good God, it was Dusty Dean. And he still had those damn custom-made boots he'd bought with the money she'd saved to pay the hospital for the babies' delivery.

He lifted his arm and waved. "Hey, Zoe!" His voice came faintly, whipped away by the wind.

She stood there. Her first clear thought was, *I should have known.* Things had been going along too smoothly. She'd been getting herself all straight, and now here he was.

She looked over at Glory and Mercy. They'd stopped playing in the sand and were standing and watching, not running forward. Fancy, her tail swishing hesitantly, stood in front of them. Zoe glanced back at Rory. He sat atop Blue, watching, too. Inhaling deeply, she continued on, walking slowly. Her heart pounded, and she felt caught in swirling anger and dismay and eagerness. Her eyes skimmed Dusty. He moved stiffly, and his left arm was in a cast and sling. He'd been hurt—so of course he'd headed here.

They met near the tie rail. Dusty grinned at her from beneath his summer straw Stetson. Dusty Dean Yarberry had the looks of a pinup calendar cowboy. That hadn't changed. His green eyes sparkled, but with a hint of wariness. Dusty was childish but not totally dense.

"Hi, Zo." His familiar warm voice washed over her. When Dusty wanted, he could melt a rock with his voice.

"Hello, Dusty."

He stepped forward as if to embrace her, but, looking in her eyes, he stopped. He grinned again. "You're lookin' good, darlin'," he said with that warm voice. His eyes moved over her like the caress of the breeze.

"You're lookin' busted up."

"Yeah..." He jiggled his injured arm. "I took one hell of a spill Sunday. Horse reared comin' out of the gate and then stomped the prunes out of me. Broken collarbone, broken wrist and three cracked ribs. Spent a day and a half in the hospital."

Zoe didn't know what in the world to say. A lump choked her throat. She wanted to smack him, and a small part of her wanted to hug him. He *was* pitiful with his arm all bandaged and in that rumpled shirt that had been washed, stored in a ball in his duffel bag, then pulled out that day to wear. She knew that was how he operated.

Zoe turned her attention to the shiny red four-horse trailer hooked to his truck. "Other than that, you appear to be doin' nicely. Does that belong to you?"

"Yeah. Man offered me a deal on it I couldn't pass up. I didn't have one, you know," he said pointedly.

What Zoe knew was that trailer would have cost thirty-five hundred dollars at the very least. And the most he'd given her in the past six months was two hundred dollars.

Then his gaze, bright and intent, moved beyond her. "Well, good golly Miss Molly... are these my little girls?"

Zoe felt Mercy's and Glory's hands slip around her legs as they took hold on each side.

Dusty crouched to their level, moving stiffly. "Ain't you two growed. Hey... you don't need to be shy of me—I'm your daddy."

He reached a hand out to touch Glory, but she shrank back and stuck her thumb in her mouth. Both girls' arms tightened around Zoe's legs. She put a hand to each of their heads. She said very quietly, "What do you want, Dusty?" Oh, she had a good idea of exactly what he wanted.

He straightened, and his grin slipped. He looked at her, then to the corral behind her. "Is that Rory Breen out there on Blue?"

"Uh-huh."

He looked into her eyes. "Do you suppose we could talk a bit, Zoe? I'd sure like some of your iced tea. I drove all the way up from Alamogordo today, and I ache all over."

Suddenly he looked very tired, and there was pain in his eyes, too. However reluctantly, Zoe's heart melted. She nodded. "Come on into the kitchen."

She felt Rory's gaze, but she didn't go over and tell him anything, because she had no idea of what to tell him. Dusty sat at the table, in the same place Rory always took—the place that had been Dusty's before he left. He stretched out his legs and those red-and-white boots. They'd been freshly shined. Lifting off his hat, he laid it, sweaty, on the table; she hated that. She picked it up and put it on top the refrigerator, just like she used to do. Glancing beneath her upraised arm, she saw Dusty's gaze, his eyes sultry and suggestive on her breasts.

He grinned. "Like I said—you look damn good, Zoe."

While she put frozen cubes of grape juice into cups, he tried again with the girls. "Come here, Glory...let me get a look at you."

"That's Mercy," Zoe said.

The girls giggled but remained shyly distant, not saying a word. After she'd settled them with their cups on the back steps, he asked her, "What have you been tellin' them about me—that I'm some kind of devil?"

"I haven't talked about you since the last time Glory asked when you were coming home—when I said you weren't. Wasn't anything to say. And they're shy because I've taught them not to talk to strangers."

She made two glasses of iced tea. She set one in front of Dusty and held hers and stood with her back to the sink.

He took a vial from his pocket, shook out a pill and swallowed it with his tea.

"Was it Skipper—" she motioned as if to the horse out in the trailer "—who threw you?"

He shook his head. "No. I'd borrowed Monte Braco's gelding. I was about to win the durn jackpot, too."

Zoe thought she'd heard that before.

She said, "I filed our divorce papers. I had them send your notice to your parents'. I didn't know any other address."

His eyebrows came up in surprise, and he stared at her. Then pure sadness filled his eyes, and he stared at his glass. "I certainly understand."

They were quiet for a long minute. Zoe gazed at his pale hair, felt guilty and rejected it. By damn, she'd waited.

Then Dusty said, "I'm sure glad to see you, Zo. And the girls...man, they're somethin', aren't they?"

She had to smile. "Yes, they're something."

"You're a good mama, Zo."

She looked at him. "What do you want, Dusty? I don't have any money to spare. The girls and I are just gettin' along."

"I don't want your money." He acted hurt. "I want to see you and the girls."

She wondered, and stared at him with unspoken skepticism.

Dusty rose and cleared his throat. "Excuse me a minute. Gotta see a man about a horse." And he went through to the bathroom. He moved slowly, stiffly.

Zoe went to the open back door and looked out through the screen of the porch. The girls were several yards away in the grass, letting Fancy lick the sticky juice from their fingers. Rory was working turns on Blue. The horse was lathered, and Rory was turning him swiftly. Along with the flush of the toilet in the bathroom, Zoe heard the opening and closing of the medicine cabinet. She knew Dusty was checking to see if Rory was staying here, had no doubt that he'd checked her bedroom, too.

Dusty came back into the room. "Hard job with just one hand," he said, grinning and gently lifting his injured arm. He eased himself again to the chair. "Mercy me, can't take these stompin's like I used to."

"You're not eighteen anymore," Zoe pointed out with more righteousness than she should have. She took up the pitcher and poured him more iced tea.

He reached out and took her hand. She looked down into his green eyes.

"Zoe . . . I need a place to stay."

She shook her head and tugged herself away. "I only have two beds here—and we're divorced, remember?"

"Just barely."

"Just barely?" Her voice rose. "Is that like being just barely pregnant? Well, let me tell you, our marriage is just as over as it was the day last winter when you left."

He looked at the floor for a long second, then peered at her. "After payin' the hospital, I'm just about broke, Zoe. Linda and the kids are staying at Mom's, so there's no way I can go there." He paused, and his eyes got all deep. "Just because we're divorced doesn't mean we cut off all our feelin's. A piece of paper can't wipe out all we've had. We still mean something to each other."

Zoe gazed into his pleading, boyish, cowboy eyes and thought of how much she'd loved him, of how their naked bodies had found ecstasy, of how he'd held her hand at the hospital when she'd had the girls. She owed him something for all that, she guessed. Still, she might have said no, except that he added one more thing.

"And I'd really like to spend some time with my daughters, Zo. I don't want to be a stranger they're afraid of. They're my flesh and blood."

Oh, boy.

At last she sighed. "Okay. You can have our—*my* bed, and I'll sleep with the girls."

He jumped up and came over to embrace her with his one good arm. "Thanks, Zo," he said huskily and buried his head in her hair.

Gently, mindful of his injuries, she pushed away. "I have to check on the girls—and see how Rory's doing." She was shaking when she went out the door. Dusty came right after her.

Rory saw Zoe and Dusty Yarberry coming and knew in his bones what was going on here. Dusty was banged up; he was like a wounded wolf coming back to the den.

The two approached the corral fence, and Rory walked Blue over to them. He'd ridden Blue hard and was having to walk him extensively to allow him to cool down slowly.

"Hi there, Breen," Yarberry said.

Cocky little bastard, Rory thought. "Hello" was all he said.

Neither of them extended his hand. Yarberry looked at Blue. "Are ya tryin' to make a cutter out of him?" His expression said he thought it doubtful.

"We *have* made a cutter out of him—and it seems the logical thing," Rory replied, "since his mother was a damn good one."

"Yeah . . . well, Zoe always did have a thing about workin' those cows."

The guy grinned warmly at Zoe. Intimately. Rory itched to punch him. Dismounting, he looked at Mercy and Glory, who were climbing up on the corral rails. "Want to ride a bit?"

They came eagerly into his arms to be plopped atop a very tired and docile Blue. In his mind Rory thought, *See there, Yarberry? This is mine.*

"Don't you two look fine," Yarberry said to the girls. "Real cowgirls, just like your mama...and daddy," he added with a cocky grin. Glory and Mercy beamed at him. He tapped the rail. "Guess I'd better be seein' to my horse and gettin' my stuff unloaded." He walked away, slowly, bent slightly.

Rory looked at Zoe. Her gaze was level and unreadable.

"Ride, Ror-ry," Glory urged, kicking her feet.

Rory walked away from Zoe, leading Blue by the reins. While the golden light slipped into dark, he walked the girls around on the stud. Zoe stood beside the fence, watching, until Yarberry hollered at her for something. She disappeared with the guy into the barn. Rory didn't head for the barn until he saw Yarberry carry his bag into the house. Zoe followed, her arms loaded.

The single light bulb glowed in the barn. Rory set Glory and Mercy onto the ground and told them to go into the house. They acted as if they weren't going, and he stamped his feet at them. "Get goin'!" he said in something near a bellow. Their golden eyes popped wide, and they scurried away.

Rory felt a twinge of guilt, but he figured he'd startled them enough that they would tell Zoe—and she would come out to speak to him. The childishness of it irritated him.

He unsaddled Blue and took him back outside to rinse him down, all the while waiting for Zoe. He felt tight as a bow string ready to let fly.

Just as he shut Blue into his stall, Zoe entered the barn. He heard her soft footfalls and felt her eyes on him. Her scent came to him. Slowly he looked at her. "I gave Blue some extra alfalfa. I worked him pretty hard this evenin'."

"Yes, you did."

She approached slowly, and her eyes assessed him. He didn't want to show his anger.

"Dusty needs a place to stay," she said.

"It's your call," Rory replied and watched Blue and Yarberry's paint gelding biting at each other over the stall rails. Blue was angry at the intrusion into his domain, and he was showing the gelding who was boss. Rory wanted to do the same thing. He wanted badly to hit something—preferably Dusty Yarberry.

"He doesn't have enough money to rent a place," Zoe said in a patient voice that irritated the hell out of him. "His sister is staying with their parents, so there's no room for him there. And he wants to spend some time with Mercy and Glory. They *are* his daughters."

"Sounds reasonable to me. But, like I said, it's your call. You don't owe me an explanation." He took up the bridle from the nail and slung it over his shoulder.

"No, I don't," she said sharply. "But I wanted to give you one."

They gazed at each other for a moment. Her eyes shot fire. Wispy curls had escaped her braid and hung at her cheeks. She jutted her chin, held her shoulders very square. Her breasts pushed at her shirt. She looked like a ripe peach. The heat whispered and swirled around them, taunting. Rory let it show in his eyes. Then he looked away, picked up his saddle and headed for the door, leaving her there beneath the swaying light bulb.

As he threw his saddle into the back of his truck, his gaze strayed to the house. The light was on in Zoe's room. Dusty Yarberry was silhouetted in the window.

Zoe leaned in the bedroom doorway. Dusty was propped against the pillows on the bed, his legs stretched out. The girls leaned against his legs, one on either side of him. They'd had their bath and were fresh and beautiful in matching flower-sprigged gowns. The sight brought to Zoe bittersweet thoughts of what might have been. She'd spoken to Glory and Mercy about Dusty and told them he would be staying for a while, until his injuries healed. In the course of the conversation she learned that Glory and Mercy indeed remembered their father, and fondly, though they remained shy for the first hours. However, between their natural curiosity for new people and broken bones and Dusty's cowboy charm for animals, women and little girls, they were soon pressing close to him.

"Does it hur-rt?" Glory asked about Dusty's arm.

"Not so much now," Dusty said. "But it sure does itch."

"Ror-ry could fix it," Mercy said.

Dusty's eyebrows rose. "He could, huh?"

Mercy nodded, and Glory said, "He fix-ed Blue. He gave 'im a big shot."

"And he didn' get kicked and die," Mercy added.

Zoe hid a smile. "Come on, girls. Time for bed."

Dusty came to tuck them in and listen to their prayers. He switched their names, too, still not telling them apart. Afterward, he went to take a shower and Zoe went to clean the dishes. Two minutes later he came into the kitchen.

"Could you help me get out of my shirt?" he asked, looking helpless.

She stepped over to help. He stretched out his good arm, and she slipped off the sleeve. Then she had to work the shirt carefully over his injured arm in its cast. Several inches of thick gauze wrapped his chest.

Dusty ran a hand over the gauze. "This stuff is hot. Would you take it off, too?"

"What about your ribs?"

"I'll be careful, but I can't stand much more itchin'. Really, Zoe...this place needs air-conditioning. How about if I turn on the one in the shop window? It'll cool into the bedroom, won't it?"

"Turn it on—if you want to give me fifty dollars for the electric bill." Carefully she unfastened and removed the wrapping around his chest. She noted several bruises on his bare back.

"Just like the old days," Dusty said, and she looked up to find him gazing sensually at her. He put a hand to her neck. "I sure always loved the way you smell," he said in an intimate tone.

She stepped backward and thrust out his shirt. "Go get your shower. I want in there next."

"I might need help. I'm not supposed to get this thing wet."

"You just do the best you can." She turned her back and willed her body to behave. It embarrassed and flustered her to be having a sexual reaction. *It was because of Rory,* she thought. Because of what she'd thought would be happening with him that evening—*instead of this!*

Zoe busied herself in the kitchen until Dusty had finished. Coming back through the bathroom, she mopped up the water he'd splattered with the two towels he'd left on the floor and picked up the empty bottle of shampoo he'd tossed there, too. She'd forgotten how messy he was. Though once he'd told her, "I never ask you to pick up after me, Zoe. You just do it." And he was right. She'd always felt so responsible for him.

She knocked on the bedroom door, which was ajar. "I need to come through to the shop."

"Hey...no need to knock. This is your room." He straightened from the bed, where he'd been lying in the breeze of the fan. He stretched, so that she clearly saw his handsome chest and the unfastened button of his jeans.

She turned her head so as not to laugh at his teenage stunt and went on to the shop to get another bottle of shampoo. It *was* flattering to have him paying her such attention.

Dusty was fiddling with the television when she returned. "Boy, this thing has about had it," he said. "How do you watch it?"

"I don't much. I'm usually too busy." She went on into the bathroom but out of habit neglected to close the door. The room remained cooler with the circulation of air from bedroom windows, too.

Dusty appeared and leaned against the doorframe. She was taking her hair from her braid and met his gaze in the mirror.

"The girls are beautiful," he said. "Just like their mama." His eyes were filled with sex.

Zoe averted her gaze and reached for the hairbrush, saying, "They look a lot like my sister."

"They look like *you*." He came up behind her and slipped an arm around her waist, splaying his hand on her belly. Through the thin fabric of her blouse, she felt both the cotton sling and his bare chest against her back. His chest was hot. He nuzzled her neck. "God, I love how you smell."

"You'd better watch your ribs," she cautioned and twisted away.

"We could be careful."

She faced him. "There's no sense to this, Dusty. You need a place to stay, and you want to get to know the girls. That's it. That's all I agreed to. If you think I'm lettin' you back in my bed, you're crazy."

He looked hurt. "I just saw you there, and all the old feelin's came back. Can you say you didn't feel something?"

His gaze slipped downward, lingered on her breasts, then moved lower. "God, we were hot together, Zoe. Remember?" he asked in a throaty whisper.

She said, "I'm not goin' down that road with you again, Dusty. You might as well get that out of your head now. I allowed you to stay for the girls—not for me."

He stared at her. "Are you sleepin' with Breen?" His voice was sharp.

"I don't think that's any of your business."

"It makes me jealous—if that makes you happy."

"I don't care if you're jealous or not."

He sighed and ran a hand through his hair. "I've changed a lot these last months, Zoe. I've learned a lot about myself."

"Good. I'm happy for you. But we're divorced now." He seemed to need that repeated.

He gave a cockeyed grin. "People get remarried all the time." She looked skeptical. He said, "I know I let you down when I left, Zo. I know I've sowed wild oats in the past. But that's over. I know what I threw away, and I know what I want now."

"So do I. I want to take a bath. Will you please get out?"

"It isn't like I never saw you naked." He grinned.

Hand on her hip, she said, "Just leave, Dusty. Now."

His grin slipped, and his eyes dulled with sadness. He gave a reluctant nod and backed from the room.

Feeling about like the big ogre who'd just jerked a lollipop from a little boy, Zoe stepped over and closed the door, hard. She had one foot in the tub when the door squeaked and Dusty's head peeked around it.

"Just wanted to let you know the television picture is comin' in real good now." His eyes took their pleasure, and he grinned seductively. "In case you want to come in and watch it with me."

She threw the soap at him. It hit the door as he closed it.

Zoe padded with wet feet over to the door and clicked the lock. Then she lay back in the old tub, closed her eyes and felt the water caressing her breasts and lapping between her thighs.

Dusty's attentions touched her. She felt flattered and even a little bit turned on, which seemed awfully stupid. How could that be? She *knew* Dusty Dean and how charming she—or any woman—was a pastime for him. By damn, she'd divorced him! She didn't love him anymore.

She thought of his smiling eyes. Rarely did those eyes hold anger. Dusty had such a good heart, always trying to please, in his way. She did feel something for him, she thought quietly, not understanding.

A good heart Dusty might have, but he wasn't husband material. He was still a boy. How could she still, after all she knew about him, all that had happened, have any feelings for him? Did that mean she didn't care for Rory like she thought she did?

She was aroused, she thought, because she'd been celibate for months and months. And for the past months she'd been tempted by Rory Breen. And this night she'd been toying, seriously, with sleeping with Rory, no matter how big a bite of trouble that could prove to be, and instead, here she was in the bathtub, with her ex-husband sleeping in her bed.

Good grief, she was a fool on all counts.

Rory came earlier than normal the next day, in plenty of time for dinner. Zoe greeted him at the back screen door. Relief washed across her face, followed by a sensual, welcoming warmth, which did a lot to massage his bruised pride.

She said, "Did you come for dinner? I made chili and hot pepper bread and a dried peach pie." And he knew she'd made it all for him. And that she'd worn that ruffled blouse and those tight denims just for him, too. She was enough to set him afire right there on the stoop.

He said with bold delight, "Yes, ma'am. I did."

He was bending down to kiss her when Dusty Yarberry came in, Glory and Mercy tugging him by the pant legs. They were giggling and obviously not shy of him anymore. He appeared to have just awakened; his shirt was hanging open, and he was stretching and yawning. He cut both short on sight of Rory.

"Well, hi, Breen," Yarberry said with a grating friendliness.

"Hello."

The girls beamed up at him. Glory said, "'Lo, Breen."

Rory had to smile at her. "'Lo, pumpkin," he said and ruffled her hair, while she smiled up at him.

Zoe told everyone to sit, and Yarberry took the chair Rory usually sat in. Rory moved around the table and sat in a chair opposite Zoe. She dished his chili first. Knowing how the girls liked their corn bread, Rory began to fix their glasses with milk and pieces of the bread.

Quite satisfied by Yarberry's curious expression, he said, "They like it mixed so they can eat it with a spoon."

"No kiddin'?" Yarberry grinned at the girls. "I used to do the same thing when I was a kid. Like father, like daughters."

Rory told himself that Yarberry being the girls' father was a fact of life and that it wouldn't do any good to punch the guy, anyway. He really had no reason to, except on the general principle that jerks like Dusty Yarberry *should* be punched.

Yarberry milked his injuries to the hilt. In between mentioning how his ribs and collarbone were hurting, he very gratefully and humbly had Zoe pouring his iced tea and buttering his bread. All that was left, Rory thought, was for her to feed him. Rory thought how *he'd* like to feed the guy—the whole hot pan of chili in his lap.

Zoe worked Blue that evening, and Rory sat on the fence, giving instructions. After a while Yarberry came out and lifted himself up beside him, without all the painful grimacing the guy put on in Zoe's presence.

"She's always been a good rider," Yarberry said. "Her daddy had her on a horse before she could walk."

"So she's said." Rory really didn't want to hold a conversation with the man. He focused his attention on Zoe and the stud. Blue definitely held a preference for her, moving easily wherever she guided him. Out of the corner of his eye, he saw Yarberry watching closely; Rory knew he was impressed.

"Zoe says you two are takin' the stud down to the Classic," Yarberry said.

"That's the plan."

Yarberry shook his head. "That one draws some mighty high-powered horses. Costs a hell of a lot just to enter."

"There's some that cost more."

"Lot of money wasted, if he doesn't even place. You think he really has a chance?"

"I wouldn't be doin' it if I didn't think so."

"Oh, I don't know. Fillin' Zoe with a fancy idea like that gives you a reason to keep comin' around here and actin' like the big trainer man. And promises of pots of gold tend to warm up a woman. Don't they?"

Rory turned his head and looked Yarberry in the eye. "I don't need to make up reasons to come around. And I damn sure don't need promises to warm a woman. And one more thing. A guy with his arm in a sling shouldn't be sittin' on the top rail of a rickety fence."

With those final words, Rory jumped to the ground, shaking the fence good in the process. The jarring sent Yarberry jumping down, too. Rory left him stumbling around for his balance. No, he told his conscience, he didn't care one bit if Yarberry fell on his damn arm.

Over the following days Dusty Yarberry was a giant, festering thorn in Rory's side. Yarberry was there every minute Rory and Zoe were working Blue. He appeared out the front door when Rory was bidding Zoe good-night on the porch. He poked his presence into every damn minute!

Deliberately coming during the girls' naptime one afternoon, Rory waited his turn behind Joe Shatto to have a haircut, which he didn't need, but which gave him an excuse to have Zoe touch him. He'd just sat down, and Zoe was fastening the cape around him, when Dusty, his shirt open, feet bare, appeared in the doorway from the bedroom.

"Well, hello there, Breen."

Rory nodded. He had a glimpse of the bed behind Dusty, rumpled, and the television was on.

Dusty walked forward and held out a jar. "You're a man with two good hands. How about openin' this jar of peanut butter for me?"

How about stuffin' it? Rory thought, but he reached up to take the jar.

"You know, Zoe, I could sure use a cut when you finish with Rory," Dusty said, running a hand over his pale hair. "I'm shaggy as a winter bear. Makes me hot."

He went back through to the kitchen, but left the door open and returned in five minutes with a sandwich in hand. Like a pushy fat cat, he sat himself in one of the waiting chairs.

Rory showed up at Zoe's early on Sunday morning and volunteered to take her to church. He knew she often took the girls to the church down the road from her house, which held services every other Sunday. He figured this would give him some quiet time with her away from her customers and Yarberry.

Then, just as they were getting into the truck to leave, there came Yarberry, white shirt, dark ribbon tie and proper black boots. All duded up and ready to go along.

"I didn't invite you," Rory said.

"Didn't know I had to have an invitation to church," Yarberry quipped. "Here, girls, you can sit on Daddy's lap."

There wasn't anything to do but take him along. And they made quite a picture moving down the aisle to a pew—Zoe and her girls, her ex-husband, and Rory bringing up the rear. Zoe went into the pew where Miss Loretta sat alone. The girls sat next to her, and then Yarberry sat, beaming with great satisfaction at Rory.

Rory sat, then got up and went around and inserted himself between Miss Loretta and Zoe.

"I'll pray for you, Rory," Miss Loretta said.

"I'll appreciate it, Miss Loretta."

Rory figured it wasn't quite fitting for him to be sitting there in the Lord's house with the preacher talking about forgiveness, all the while wishing Dusty Yarberry would drop dead.

However, the following evening it seemed he had been blessed by the Lord, when he happened to discover that Yarberry's broken collarbone had somehow miraculously mended.

Chapter Twelve

Rory had shut Dusty's horse outside in his run and was cleaning the horse's stall when Dusty came into the barn. He ambled over like some lean, yellow tomcat and leaned in the stall doorway.

"Zoe sent me to tell you she's dishin' up peaches and cream. How 'bout I tell her you decided to go on home tonight? You should be concerned about wearin' out your welcome, you know."

Rory gazed at him with amused satisfaction. "I wouldn't dream of passin' up peaches an' cream."

He and Dusty dueled with their eyes for three long seconds.

Then Dusty inclined his head and said, "As long as you're wearin' out your welcome, it sure is neighborly of you to clean my horse's stall. Yes, sir, mighty neighborly."

"Your horse has to put up with you," Rory said. "That's enough for the poor critter without him havin' to sleep in it, I guess."

Dusty just smirked, and Rory thought how he wouldn't have been cleaning the stall, but he'd taken over for Zoe.

"Why don't you do us all a favor and leave?" Rory said. He forked a pile of wet manure and tossed it at the wheelbarrow, strategically overshooting and hitting Dusty's boots.

Dusty shook his boots clean, first one, then the other, as best he could. "Zoe hasn't asked me to leave," he said quietly.

"Zoe would take in any busted-up, dumb animal that showed up at her door—even a skunk."

Dusty crossed one leg over the other. "Yeah, Zoe is soft-hearted that way. But, you know, it's hard to get over your first love." He gazed confidently at Rory. "There's some fires that just don't die."

Rory gripped the rake handle to keep from punching the handsome, smirking face. He said, "I can grant that's so. But there's a lot of fires that blow clean out with the second puff of wind." Stepping forward, he smacked the rake at Dusty, who automatically reached out to keep the handle from hitting him in the nose. "I guess, if you're feelin' up to romancin' a woman, you can manage to put your own horse away—and see to his water, too." Taking up the wheelbarrow, Rory pushed it through the barn and out the back door.

He dumped the contents into the big pile and thought again about punching Yarberry, thought about a good stiff shot of Jack D., then thought about Zoe. He thought how he was pretty poor to have let a skinny jerk like Yarberry get under his skin, and then he itched to punch the guy again. He lingered out behind the barn long enough to get control of his temper, and maybe that lingering was what put Dusty off guard. Perhaps he thought that Rory had gone on to the house. Because certainly Dusty wouldn't have taken his arm out of the sling and been using it to lift the stall gate into place if he'd thought Rory would have been coming back to catch him at it.

And that was exactly what Rory saw when he reentered the barn.

Dusty hadn't heard Rory's footsteps in the sandy dirt. Rory stood right there and watched him lifting the wooden gate with his forearm. The gate hung on its hinges and had to be lifted slightly in order for the latch to hook. Made of hard one-by-sixes, doubled in places, it couldn't be considered lightweight, and setting it in place wasn't a thing a man could do one-handed. Rory had helped Zoe with the gate on occasion; he'd forgotten about that.

Yes, watching Dusty strain that arm was an enlightening experience. Apparently the boy didn't have full use of his hand—it did seem like a bona fide cast on the wrist—but if that boy's collarbone had been broken, it had since healed, and Rory was greatly in doubt about the cracked ribs.

After he'd latched the door, Dusty straightened and began to tuck his arm back in its sling. It was then that he saw Rory.

The two stared at each other.

"The wrist *is* broken," Dusty said as he finished settling his arm in the sling.

"But you didn't think a broken wrist would be enough to get you in the house," Rory said matter-of-factly.

Dusty shrugged. "A man does crazy things when he's in love."

"Yeah...*some* men do." Rory looked at him another second, then stepped around him and headed for the kitchen door.

"My word against yours," Dusty called softly after him.

They all sat around the table and ate peaches and fresh cream. Mercy sat on Rory's knee, and Glory sat on Dusty's. Glory fed her daddy a sliced peach from her spoon and laughed when he sucked it through pursed lips. Then Mercy wanted to do the same thing with Rory. He joined in because it pleased her. Each girl appeared quite taken with having her own male attention. But watching them, Rory wondered if the little ones might not possess some age-old wisdom as to how to make peace. It was as if they had divided up in order to spread equal attention over two men who were vying for the love of the three females.

It made Rory feel low.

"Uhmm-um," Dusty said and beamed at Zoe. "No one can put together peaches and cream like you."

"W. Jones grew the peaches, and the cows provided the cream. It takes no special talent to cut peaches and spoon cream," Zoe said, but she was obviously pleased.

Again and again Dusty's eyes met Rory's, at first questioning, then daring, and finally satisfied. Triumphant.

"Can I get you more?" Zoe asked Rory, bringing his eyes swinging over to hers. She smiled, and her gaze was warm.

He shook his head. "I believe I've had enough." He watched her dish Dusty another helping and wondered what she felt for him. He knew she sure didn't hate Dusty. She didn't even dislike the fella.

When they'd finished and Zoe began to clear the dishes, Rory rose to help her. The next instant, Dusty, who normally would have sat there until the cows came home, jumped up to help, too. Then Glory and Mercy joined in to "help." In five seconds it was a lot like a clown show at the circus. In the confusion, Rory took the opportunity to slip several good shakes of salt into the fresh glass of iced tea that Zoe had poured for Dusty. Monumental satisfaction flowed over him as he watched Dusty take a swallow. He looked all fish-eyed and went to coughing.

"Dusty?" Zoe hovered. "Are you all right?"

Dusty looked at Rory. Rory gazed placidly back at him. Dusty sniffed, then croaked, "I'm okay. I just doubled the sugar in the tea by mistake."

Rory grabbed Zoe by the arm and drew her to the back door. "Me and Zoe are goin' for a breath of fresh air."

"Hey..." Dusty protested.

"Take care of your daughters," Rory said and lit out into the night, tugging Zoe, chuckling, after him.

With her hand still in his, they walked out into the middle of the backyard, where they were well away from any light spilling from the house. The night air was sweetly cooler than the hot kitchen. Rory drew his first good breath of the evening.

Zoe sighed. "There's nowhere else that the stars look so close—as if we could just reach up and grab a handful." And she reached high with her hand.

"I didn't come out here to look at the stars," Rory said and pulled her into his arms. She was surprised and stiff for several seconds. She relaxed as he gazed down at her. He felt her heart beating. Her eyes were no more than deep black shadows, but in his mind he saw them as they were by day, cocoa brown, clear and warm.

Slowly he kissed her. It was hesitant, testing, for each of them.

When they broke apart, they stared into each other's faces. Rory ran his hands up and down the curve of her back. She quivered against him. He could feel the dampness of her skin beneath her cotton shirt. The fire grew hotter between them, rising up to simmer and taunt.

He lowered his head again, and she lifted hers to meet him. This time they kissed fully, all out, each giving and eagerly taking. Heat flickered through him, seemed to wrap all around him.

When at last they broke apart, they were both gasping for breath, hearts pounding. Rory gazed down at her and thought that surely she couldn't have kissed him like that and been thinking of Dusty.

But Krystal had kissed him passionately, too.

"Ror-ry. . .Ror-ry!" The little voice came to him.

He and Zoe broke apart like errant teenagers and turned their heads toward the back door. The dim porch light shone through the screen. Dusty's tall, thin figure was silhouetted in the doorway, and a smaller figure came out into the night across the grass.

"Hey!" Dusty called. "Mercy needs you, Zoe."

Of course. That was the way to interrupt. As Zoe pulled from his embrace, Rory thought with irritation that if Dusty Yarberry would put as much thought into earning a living as he put into getting under Rory's skin, the fella could be a millionaire.

"Ror-ry!" It was Glory, not Mercy, and, evading her mother, she came to Rory. She held a dark object up to him, something with appendages. "Fix it."

Rory hefted her up into his arms and walked toward the back door with Zoe alongside. "What's the problem, little mite?"

"Sis-tur pulled her arm off."

Rory could see the doll and arm that Glory held toward him in the light spilling out from the house—what light that wasn't blocked by Dusty still standing in the doorway.

"I tried," Dusty said. "Needed another hand."

And, by damn, Rory almost spilled it then. Dusty must have sensed he was treading on thin ice, because he quickly retreated into the house. In the murky porch light, Rory fixed the doll, a none-too-easy job. He wondered how Mercy could have jerked the arm out of the hole when he had such a time getting it back in.

"It's the law with dolls," Zoe said. "Easy to break, hard to fix."

However, if it took all night, Rory damn well intended to fix it. He wasn't about to let Glory down. His reward was her beautiful little smile when he handed it back to her. *There. He'd done what Dusty couldn't.* Which was a pretty juvenile reaction, he thought.

"Thank you," Zoe said quietly.

They gazed at each other. Rory nodded. "Good night. Thanks for the meal." He was curt, and if she didn't know why, she should have. He started away.

"Rory..."

He turned back to her.

"The girls and I...we sure do enjoy your friendship very much."

That word *friendship* echoed. Again he nodded. "I'll be here tomorrow."

He didn't look back, but he heard the screen door bang as she went into the house. Where she'd be with Dusty all night. His strides lengthened, and the ground took the pounding of his boots as his spurs jingled loudly. The mixed scents of night and dirt wafted up to him. Just as he opened the door of his truck, Dusty's voice stopped him.

"Why didn't you tell her?"

Rory looked over to see the dark figure of the tall, thin man come forward from the shadows of the front porch.

"I didn't do it for you," Rory said, then got into his truck and drove away.

Rory couldn't tell Zoe about Dusty because he wasn't a snitch. And because he didn't want to be the one to hurt her, and he was pretty certain this, yet another betrayal by Dusty, someone she had once loved, someone she obviously still cared for, would hurt her. And mostly he couldn't tell her because Zoe had to come to know Dusty Yarberry's true nature all by herself. Though it did seem like she should already know it.

They said love was blind. Was that why she had blinders on where Dusty was concerned? Because she still loved him and couldn't see the truth of the man?

Rory's stunt with the salt in Dusty's tea had been just the start of a secret war. Always careful to be cordial to each other in front of Zoe and the girls, Rory and Dusty gave vent to their rivalry with small pranks.

Dusty's first retaliation was to shake Rory's can of cream soda. When Rory popped the top, cream soda spewed up with the force of a fire hydrant broken off at ground level soaking his face, hair and hat. His favorite work hat. Mercy and Glory thought it was very funny.

Rory "accidentally" sat on Dusty's hat. Dusty "accidentally" spilled chocolate pudding down Rory's back. Rory fixed the leg of the old wooden chair that Dusty sat in out by the corral so that it would break when Dusty leaned it back, as was his habit. The chair collapsed, sending Dusty's lanky body into the dirt—on his injured arm. Dusty put horse apples on the seat of Rory's truck seat, and Rory sat on them when going home in the dark. Rory found a garter snake and hid it in a cloth sack in the barn until the perfect time to slip it down Dusty's shirt. The result was greater than Rory had anticipated, because it turned out that Dusty had an excessive phobia about snakes. He went to screaming and jerking, so the snake tried to hide deeper by burrowing into where the shirt tucked in at the back of Dusty's waist. At one point, when he had to have Zoe sit on Dusty in order to get the snake out, Rory began to worry that the fella might have a heart attack. And Zoe gave Rory a thorough, thoughtful survey over that one.

While the pranks were mostly innocuous in nature, however, they were not in any way lighthearted. Both men meant them to take the place of the punches and bullets they would rather have exchanged. The pranks helped alleviate Rory's rising impatience with Dusty's presence but certainly didn't erase it. As far as he could see, Zoe wasn't growing one bit tired of her ex-husband sponging off her. In fact, it began to look like Dusty Yarberry had returned to stay.

Eldoree Winslow was totally pleased with the rinse Zoe had put on her hair. Eldoree being totally pleased with what was done with her hair was a first, and her tipping Zoe five dollars was almost beyond belief.

Zoe saw Eldoree out the door, then stood on the porch and watched Eldoree's stately Crown Victoria depart. Eldoree had a habit of going from zero to sixty in five seconds, even on dirt roads. Dust billowed up behind the car like a jet trail.

As if summer was throwing its last good punch, it was hot enough to fry an egg on the concrete steps and heavy now with the promise of rain. They needed rain badly. Studying the sky, Zoe thought how they needed rain but not the tornadoes that could come with it.

She went back inside, closing the door because she had the window air-conditioning unit going. The gray, rusty thing rattled ominously—but it had sounded like that from the first of the summer and was still going. No need to harbor pessimistic thoughts about it giving out. She cooled the back of her neck in front of it for a minute.

From the roomy pocket of her duster, she pulled the money she'd earned from Eldoree. Half of the money went into her purse and the other half into the antique Nestlé Rinse tin, where she kept the money she was saving for the trip to Fort Worth. With planning a lot of meals around peanut butter and jelly on whole wheat and staying at a cheap but clean motel she knew of, Zoe figured she could just manage. Rory probably wouldn't be happy that she wasn't staying in the same hotel he did, but she didn't have a prayer of being able to afford a room where he would stay—and she wasn't allowing him to foot her bills, either.

She'd just closed the lid of the tin when the door from the bedroom opened and Dusty stepped through. Wearing only his jeans, he rubbed a towel over his wet hair with his one good hand. "Whew! Had to take a shower to cool off."

As Zoe shoved the tin back into a drawer, Dusty went to stand in front of the air conditioner.

"Man, that feels great! Umm . . . you know, Zo, the water pressure is really poor."

"Why don't you have a look at the pressure tank?"

"Yeah . . . maybe I'll do that later. When it's cooler. Don't know that much about them, though." He held out his sling. "Would you do this for me?"

Nodding, she positioned it and stepped behind him to fasten it at his neck. His skin was sleek and cool, and the sweet scent of baby shampoo emanated from him. "How's your collarbone feeling?" she asked. He hadn't appeared to be in any pain these past few days.

"Lots better. I probably don't even need this thing—but I thought I should wear it a few more days, just to be safe."

"There . . . you're set."

He turned toward her, and she found her face only inches from his chest. She stared for a moment at his sleek, golden tanned skin. She looked upward to the darker tan line at his neck, to his slightly grinning lips, and then into his eyes. They were warm . . . flickering with fire.

Memories swirled in her mind, and emotions rose in her heart.

His hand came up to her cheek, and he bent toward her, his lips parting for a kiss.

She turned her head and stepped away. "I'm not getting into that," she said.

"But you wanted to, honey."

She looked over her shoulder to see his pale eyes intent upon her. "There are a hundred miles between a bit of wanting and the actual doing." And she left the room.

Rory sat on Walter and watched Zoe slowly walk Blue into the small herd of cattle. The stud knew his business and remained quiet; it was all old hat to him now. His sharp instincts picked up on Zoe's choice, and with little direction, he cut the calf from the others. Zoe directed him until the calf stood alone, a good working distance from the herd behind Blue. Rory quietly moved Walter forward, pressing the calf from behind.

Then Zoe lowered her hand, resting the reins on Blue's neck. This was the signal for Blue to take over—and he did. The calf darted to the left, and Blue moved to block him. Then it was to the right, and the calf ran, trying to get around the horse. Rory and Oren had brought these cattle over just two days ago, and they were fresh and wild as plains turkeys.

But Blue, enjoying the game, ran, too, breaking into a lope with one stride. The calf stopped and decided to retreat, and it was Rory's time to join in. He and Walter blocked the cow and sent it back toward Blue. The calf and stud met head to head. By damn, the horse crouched in front of the calf, pulling back to draw the calf to him. The calf darted, and so did the stud. And Zoe stayed right in the middle of the seat.

At last the calf turned around, quit challenging the stud and ran off. Rory let it go, and Zoe lifted the reins to signal Blue that the game was over. She walked the stud over to Rory. Her face was flushed; her eyes danced, and she was grinning, as she always was after a go on the cattle.

"His left shoulder still dips down," Rory said.

"Doesn't bother him much." She stroked the stud's neck.

"He can't turn as fast when he lets that happen."

"He gets the job done. Just because he doesn't do it to the current rule of fashion doesn't mean it isn't right."

"His way, there will be cows that can beat him."

She smiled at him. "He did good tonight."

"He did good, and we should stop him on that note." Rory lifted Walter's reins, starting him slowly toward the barn.

Zoe came alongside. She leaned forward and petted the stud's neck, speaking soft words that Rory couldn't distinguish. Women always talked to horses. Rory didn't much understand that. Oh, he talked to his horse when he was alone out on the grassland, but he did it simply to speak his thoughts aloud. He could as well say, he supposed, that he was talking to the sky and the air, because the talking was for himself. He didn't much think a horse cared whether a person talked to it or not. Of course, he had learned over the years not to voice this opinion to a woman, because they sure as shooting would argue him down about it. And as he looked at Zoe and Blue, he grudgingly admitted that the horse did relate better to her than he did to him. This horse had a preference for Zoe, and that was a fact.

When they rode into the barn, the setting sun cast its last golden rays through the wide front opening. Dusty was there, reclining on the hay bales, drinking a can of the cream soda Rory had brought over that evening and listening to country music from a boom box. Rory rarely saw the guy do much of anything else. He still wore that stupid sling, though Rory had heard him profess to Zoe that he was about healed. On sight of him, the mellow mood Rory had felt while riding with Zoe fizzled.

Rory allowed Dusty no more than a glance. He had no fondness for the sight, the sound or the smell of Dusty Yarberry. He dismounted and led Walter over for a drink of water.

"You sure are lookin' good on him, darlin'," Dusty said to Zoe.

"He's doing well," she said. "Where are the girls?"

"Oh, they're just outside the door, playin' in the sand."

"Are you sure?" Zoe walked over to look. "Oh, Dusty—they've gone over to the front porch. You know I don't like them to play under there. They're liable to come upon a snake or a brown spider." She hurried away toward them.

"They're fine. The dog's with 'em," Dusty called after her, stirring himself to rise from the hay bales. "Least it's shady there."

Rory tied Walter and moved to take Zoe's saddle off of Blue. Both horses were coated with sweat, though they hadn't been ridden hard or long. Dusty sauntered over and put his hand on Blue's rump. The proprietary action made Rory's teeth grate.

"Horse looks good," Dusty said.

Rory said nothing and kept his attention on uncinching Zoe's saddle.

"Yep. You're quite a man with horses, Breen." Dusty slapped Blue's hip twice, hard enough to cause the horse to prance against Rory and barely miss stepping on Rory's feet.

"You do that one more time and you're gonna be eatin' dirt," Rory said.

Dusty cast him a crooked grin. "Now, Zoe wouldn't like that—you pickin' on me with my broken bones and all."

"At least when I got finished, you wouldn't have to pretend." Rory gazed levelly at Dusty and saw the hesitant flicker in his pale eyes.

Dusty said, "So, how'd it go tonight? Do we have us a winner or not?"

Rory swept the saddle and pad from Blue and paused. "As far as I know, *you* don't have anything. And I don't like you and don't feel I need to carry on friendly conversation with you. Bug off." He hauled the saddle to its rack.

"You know, Breen, you're a real grouchy fella. You need to lighten up. You'd find life a lot more friendly that way."

Rory turned around, but Dusty was sauntering away, so Rory let him go. For an instant Dusty's words echoed in his mind and he heard the bit of truth in them. Then he angrily rejected that. Maybe he was a bit touchy these days, but the reason was the tall, thin man walking outside into the sunlight. Rory looked around him, wondering what prank Dusty had prepared. Seeing no possibilities, he led Blue outside to wash him off.

Once the sun hovered at the western horizon it dropped like a rock. It was doing that when Zoe came through the barn, looking for Rory. He was there, bending to clean Walter's front hoof. She found herself gazing at his trim hips, and sensual thoughts flickered through her mind.

"I'm ready to dish up ice cream," she said.

Slowly Rory straightened. "None for me tonight," he said and tossed the hoof pick into the bucket of grooming supplies. "It's a while to home on Walter, and I'll have a little bit of light yet, if I start now."

That was a surprise. Practically every night for weeks he had lingered and shared dessert with them, no matter that he happened to be riding Walter.

"You're sure? It's peach ice cream, with real peaches." Peaches were one of Rory's very favorite things. That was why she'd bought peach. She watched his face. There had been a certain coolness about him the past few days. Oh, she knew why, but she didn't want to think about it.

He shook his head, and his eyes skittered away from her. He lifted his hat and raked his fingers through his sweat-dampened hair. "You're gettin' low on hay. I'll have one of the hands bring you a load. How much longer do you plan to be feeding Dusty's horse?"

His questioning blue eyes settled upon her. Zoe shook her head and averted her gaze. "I don't know. Dusty will be here however long it takes until he can use his arm and his ribs are healed."

"That can be quite a few weeks yet."

"It won't be terribly long. Dusty's followed the rodeo since he was sixteen. As soon as he's able, he'll get some sort of work on the circuit. He's never stayed in one place longer than a few months."

She looked up to see Rory's gaze hard upon her. He said with intense quietness, "And that's all right with you? For Dusty to use you as a way station?"

Her pride flew at him. "He's spending time with his daughters, and as a friend, I'm giving him a place to stay," she ground out hotly. "He has nowhere else to go, and just because we happened to have been married once doesn't mean I shouldn't give him a helping hand when he needs it."

"No, it doesn't," Rory said. He looked downward a moment, then back at her. "But he has nowhere else to go because you make it easy for him to stay here with you." His tone dropped low. "You take care of him more like he's your child than as if he was ever your husband, Zoe. You not only feed him, you pay for the feed for his horse, even do most of the feedin'. You wash his clothes, pick up after him, see to most all his needs. And there's no other reason for you to do all that other than you *want* Dusty here."

Those words sat there a minute, drilling into her. Her cheeks and throat burned. She crossed her arms, then said, "I guess what I do is my business. No one else has to understand, or approve."

Fire flashed in Rory's eyes before they turned cold. He inclined his head. "No, no one has to do that." He turned away to mount Walter. "I'll have Sandy bring over a load of hay, enough for both horses for two weeks."

"I'll have a check waiting."

"Whatever suits you." He lifted the reins, then paused and gazed down at her. "I've been coming over here just about every day most of this summer. I've eaten quite a few meals fixed by your hands and done a few chores around here in return. And we've shared a few kisses and have wanted to share more than that. That's why I felt I had a right to say what I did."

He gazed at her, expressionless, while the words that he spoke told of how he felt in his heart.

A lump rose in Zoe's throat. She said, "You did have a right. And Dusty will only be here for a few more weeks. I'm just giving him a helping hand and the opportunity to get to know his daughters. That's all there is to it, and I don't have any feelings for him, other than . . . a sense of responsibility. I just can't turn him away. But it has nothing to do with you and me."

He gazed at her; then he shook his head. "As long as Dusty's here, I don't see a place for me." He gave her a cool nod. "Good night." And it was as if he'd said goodbye.

With the life slipping out her feet, Zoe stood there and watched him ride Walter through the wide door and out into the soft glow of twilight. Outside the barn, he tapped his spurs and lit out at a gallop. Riding away.

Whirling, Zoe stomped into the house. The screen door slammed behind her; she *never* let the screen door slam.

Mercy and Glory and Dusty were at the table, already eating ice cream. Their heads swiveled, and all three pairs of eyes stared at her.

"We went ahead and got started," Dusty said. "The ice cream was meltin' there on the counter."

"Fine." She turned toward the sink and saw the ice-cream container still sitting on the counter, growing soggy. Dusty had left it for her to take care of. She grabbed it up and stuck it in the freezer, slammed the door and returned to the sink to wash the stack of dishes. "You could have started on the dishes, Dusty."

The silence in the room was heavy as soot. Chair legs scooted, and out of the corner of her eye she saw Mercy go to the back door. Her small bare feet making a soft pattering, she went out onto the porch, then poked her head back around. "Where's Ror-ry?"

And Dusty said, "Rory's not comin' in?"

"He's gone home. Mercy, eat your ice cream. You girls need to get a bath."

She spoke sharply, and it came to her with as much surprise as it did Mercy. Zoe never spoke sharply to her daughters. Mercy's lower lip quivered, and Zoe went over and lifted her up, apologizing, saying she was just tired. She held Mercy tight, seeking comfort. She wondered how everything had gotten so mixed-up.

Chapter Thirteen

"You and Rory have a fight?" Dusty asked her.

"We had a little disagreement." She wasn't certain the exchange she and Rory had had could qualify as either a fight or a disagreement. But whatever it had been, it qualified as hurtful.

"Here are your jeans," she said and thrust at him the clothes she'd washed and folded. What Rory had said about her caring for Dusty as she would a child flashed in her mind like a garish neon sign. To make matters worse, before she thought, she said, "I'd appreciate it if you didn't just toss them on the floor."

"What'd you and Rory fight about?"

"That's our business. Good night."

She lay on the mattress with the girls. The bright moonlight made patterns on the walls, and the fan made a hum-clicking sound as it brought in the cool night air. Still, it was warm in the bed, with the girls' little bodies on either side of her. And Mercy had the habit of flopping her arm. She'd caught Zoe twice in the lip.

No, Zoe thought the second time Mercy smacked her lip, she didn't truly *want* Dusty in her house. She didn't have room for him; she wanted her own bed back.

Then why in the world did she allow him to stay?

Because she felt so responsible for him. She had once pledged her life to him, after all. And he just seemed to need someone to look out for him. Until the day they'd married, he hadn't ever had a checking account, because he didn't know how to keep a checkbook. He spent money until it was gone, never thinking about budgeting for tomorrow's needs. He could make coffee, and that was about it. He'd never kept a job beyond a few weeks, and he simply wasn't much good at anything except charming people. He simply liked having a good time and wished everyone else that same thing. It was pretty hard not to like a person like that.

None of those reasons had anything at all to do with her letting him stay because he'd gotten himself all banged up. All Rory's accusations came back to her. He'd been right, and well she knew it. She did take care of Dusty like a child, and she couldn't seem to help herself. She'd allowed Dusty to stay because she'd wanted him to. There had been unfinished business between them.

Zoe started crying at the memory of the things Rory had said. He had been cruel, had made Zoe sound like she was some sort of a weak-willed doormat of a woman. She cried quietly, because there was simply no privacy for boo-hooing in this small house. Turning onto her stomach, she buried her face in the pillow, knowing muffled crying wouldn't wake the girls. It did wake Fancy, though, who came over and nuzzled her head.

Rory didn't come the following day.

All that stuff he'd said was probably just his excuse for cutting and running, Zoe thought, glad for the anger that came, drowning the heartache. And it had been his idea to go down to the Classic in the first place! What in the world did he plan to do about that? Half of that fee had been her money, and she wasn't going to have paid it for nothing, which meant she would have to take Blue herself. Wasn't that going to be just fine and dandy! How would she manage with Glory and Mercy?

Then, suddenly, she felt lost without Rory. As if a part of her had been cut away. And she didn't understand that. What part in her life had he had, other than his interest in Blue? Maybe he'd helped her do a few things around the place, like put up that fence, fix the stalls, unclog her washer once, but she hadn't relied on him. She hadn't relied on him to help her make decisions, not for money, either. She hadn't *relied* on him for anything, other than coming around.

Memories of talking with him, laughing with him, even disagreeing with him, fluttered across her mind. And she realized she'd come to rely on his attentions. Rory Breen had become a part of her life simply by being attentive to her and the girls. With his interest and his caring, he'd eased her loneliness and brought a renewed confidence in herself as a woman. He'd brought a sense of hope back into her days.

She and Rory had developed a relationship as far different, yet equal, people. They had become, without her ever realizing it, companions.

She missed him. A lot. Like an arm cut off. And she found herself watching the road and the grassland for him to come. She realized that for a long time she'd been wondering if she and Rory could have a life together. She'd been thinking about that until Dusty had come, when she'd begun just taking one day at a time, because she'd been too confused to do anything else.

Dusty helped her take care of the animals. He took his arm out of the sling and easily managed the watering and feeding. He even brushed both horses. When she questioned him about his collarbone he said, "Boy, it's feelin' a lot better. But I'll make sure I don't put a lot of pressure on it." He was in chipper spirits.

Later he said, "You need cheerin' up. Let's go over to Raton. Tammy and Jody Carter are over there visitin' Tammy's sister. Let's go have dinner and see them."

Zoe shook her head. "I have a livin' to earn. Remember?" She didn't want to go anywhere. Deep inside she hoped that Rory would come.

He didn't. Not that day, nor the next.

Zoe didn't ride Blue those days. She thought he could use a rest. But mostly she didn't do it because she had no interest in doing it. She even quit thinking much about the Classic in Fort Worth, now only two weeks away. She went around fixing customers' hair, looking after the girls and Dusty and the animals, having to push herself to do anything at all. It seemed as if her gumption had up and vanished with Rory, which was stupid, and she scolded herself severely for thinking this. She reminded herself that she'd had this reaction to other upheavals in her life and that she had survived.

The first evening, when Zoe tried to round up the girls to take them inside for their baths, Glory hung back. She went over and sat on the front porch steps.

"What are you doin', Glory?" Zoe asked.

"Wai-tin' for Ror-ry." Glory pushed her little hands down between her knees.

Zoe swallowed. "Rory's not coming tonight, honey," she said, gently, remembering to sound her *g*.

Mercy looked up at her. "Why not?"

"Rory has some business to attend to for a few days. Come on in, you two. I'll put Palmolive in the bathwater, and you can make bubbles." If she didn't make a big deal of Rory's absence, like as not the girls wouldn't, either.

But Zoe was mad as a hatter. Rory thought he could just quit coming and be done with it. He didn't consider what that did to the girls. Mercy and Glory were certainly learning young that men simply took off whenever it pleased them.

The next day Mercy pulled a can of cream soda from the refrigerator and brought it to Zoe to be split with Glory. While Zoe was pouring the soft drink into two cups, Dusty came and got himself a can of cream soda. Suddenly Mercy stopped him, flinging herself to grab on to his arm, hanging there like a monkey.

"No...no!" she cried. "It's for Rorr-rry."

Dusty tried to reason with her. "We can buy more at the store, Glory."

"No! This 'un! And I'm Mer-cy."

"Put it back, Dusty," Zoe said. "I'll make you a glass of tea."

Late the following afternoon, when Zoe was straightening up the shop, Glory and Mercy came running in, crying that Rory was coming. Amazed, Zoe jumped to the window to see; sure enough, Rory was pulling into the drive. The back of his pickup truck was loaded with hay.

He'd brought it, not sent it with one of his ranch hands.

Zoe paused at the mirror, checking her hair and wiping dust smudges from her face, before she headed for the barn. About halfway across the yard, she slowed her steps. She couldn't let him know how eager she was to see him.

He'd backed the truck into the barn and was already unloading the rectangular bales. The girls sat happily atop the cab, dangling their legs against the rear window.

Rory looked down at her, and she looked up at him. There was a question in his eyes before he continued his unloading.

"I thought you were going to send this over with one of the hands," she said.

"Just as easy to bring it when I came to help you work Blue." He heaved a bale of hay off the truck. Sweat ran in rivulets down his temples.

"Do you want to work him tonight?" she asked, surprised.

"Sure." He paused, staring at her. "If you're ready to. If you've got things to do, I can exercise him some myself."

"No...I mean, I can work him with you. I just thought..." His eyes came round to hers again. "You haven't been here in days, and you didn't say when you were coming back."

He studied her. "I'm partnering with you on Blue for the Classic. I'll see it through."

She nodded, turning away as heat swept her cheeks. "I'll go change my clothes."

Rory watched her hurry away to the house, his gaze settling on her braid swinging down her back. He knew what she'd thought: that he wasn't coming back after their discussion the other evening. Well, he had thought about not coming back. It was a hard thing to face that the woman he'd begun considering as his, who a lot of people around had begun considering as his, had her ex-husband living in the same house with her. His gaze swung over to Dusty's horse, still in his stall, eating hay grown on Rory's ranch. And Rory knew grimly that he was right in his estimation of the situation. Zoe hadn't fully let go of Dusty, and maybe she never would.

Still, Rory had entered into taking Blue to the Classic with her, and he couldn't back out. And he guessed it wasn't time to give up on him and Zoe yet. And there were the girls, he thought, as his gaze came round to them, sitting there on the top of the truck, their golden eyes rapt upon him. He'd formed a friendship with them that he couldn't turn his back on, either.

"Come here." He reached first for Glory, plunked her on the hay bales, then lifted Mercy down. "I have three rolls of Life Savers in the truck. You find them, and I'll share them with you."

They grinned at him, then climbed the rest of the way to the ground and scampered to get inside the truck. A minute later they cried out with glee. Rory threw down a couple more bales of hay, then stopped to sit with the two little ones on the tailgate. With their characteristic solemnity, they gave him the candy rolls to open. Then they announced the color of the pieces they put into their mouths. Rory did likewise; it seemed the polite thing.

When Zoe returned to the barn, she found Rory sitting on the tailgate, flanked on either side by Mercy and Glory. All three of them were swinging their legs. She took the opportunity to gaze at them for a moment without them knowing, one big wide, masculine back and two small, feminine ones.

They worked Blue easy, because Rory said they didn't want to push him into making a bunch of mistakes with the competition growing so close. "There's no need to risk pulled muscles," he said.

Dusty came out to watch for about ten minutes, before retreating back into the house and the television—and taking the girls with him. Only Fancy was left, lying in the sand

and watching forlornly. Zoe had banned her from the house because of fleas.

Even alone, however, the mood was still strained between Zoe and Rory. They walked on eggs with each other, extremely polite, aloof. Zoe politely asked Rory to stay for a late supper, but he declined.

Just as he was ready to drive off, Mercy and Glory came running from the house, bringing his cream soda.

"I save-ed it for you," Mercy said.

"Are ya thirsty, Ror-ry?" Glory asked.

He crouched down and took the drink. "Why, yes, ma'am, I am. Thank you." He popped the top, very carefully, as it foamed over from being shaken. "I believe I'll take this with me."

"Will you be back to-mor-row?" Glory asked.

He glanced at Zoe, then shook his head. "Your mom is doin' fine with Blue. She can handle him. But I'll check back again in a few days, okay?"

When he drove away, Zoe knew that she was the one who had to make the next move. Only she wasn't certain exactly what that move was to be.

She could tell Dusty to go, she thought, but when and if she did, it had to be for the right reasons. It couldn't be because she feared losing Rory—for she wasn't certain she had Rory. Or that she wanted him.

On Sunday Dusty got restless and decided to drive to Raton alone, since Zoe wouldn't give in and go with him. She did suggest that he could take Mercy and Glory. "You could take them to see *Snow White*," she said. "I read that's playing over there. And they like that pizza place with all the games." But he wasn't much interested in doing that. Zoe hadn't figured he would be. It was one thing to play games here with the girls for an hour or so, and another thing entirely to be responsible for them for the better part of a whole day.

For the first time in almost two weeks she had the house to herself again. She hadn't known how much she'd missed it.

She brushed Blue and promised him they would ride that evening; she pushed the girls in the swing, and she watched for Rory. She pondered calling him about one of the calves that was looking poorly. But she couldn't bring herself to do it. He would see it quickly as the thin excuse it was, and it would seem as if she was begging him to come around. She certainly wasn't going to do that. If he wanted to come around, he would.

Back in the house, she made the girls some butter-and-sugar bread, then wandered into her bedroom. Dusty's clothes were thrown in a heap atop his big duffel bag. She folded and stacked them neatly. Then she cleaned his jumble of things from the nightstand and atop her dresser. With help from Mercy and Glory, and with a lot of playing and laughing, she changed the bed sheets and swept the room. Afterward, she and the girls propped themselves against pillows on the bed and read the adventures of *Tommy Turtle*. Zoe thought how she liked her own company and that of the girls.

And it occurred to her that while she missed Rory, she was almost relieved that Dusty was gone for the day. That pointed up something important to her, but she didn't want to think about it. It was almost frightening.

Closing the third book she'd read to Glory and Mercy, she said, "Let's get cleaned up and go in and have lunch with Jada."

"Yeah!" both girls cried in unison.

If Zoe had to swear on the Bible, she supposed she would have had to admit to hoping to run into Rory. She slipped on a cotton dress because it was the coolest thing to wear in such hot weather. And also because she looked pretty and feminine in it, which wouldn't hurt if she did happen to run into him.

Jada greeted them enthusiastically. "Well, my, my, if it isn't those Yarberry women. Prettiest girls in the county. Where's my kisses?" Bending, she exchanged kisses and hugs with the girls, and in return each girl received a stick of licorice.

"*Before* lunch?" Zoe said.

To which Jada breezily answered, "Oh, I can do that because I'm not their mother."

Zoe exchanged greetings with those people she knew as she and the girls followed Jada to the big round table in the back. Every stool at the counter was taken, as well as two of the four tables. Miss Loretta stopped Zoe to ask about having her white hair dyed red. For a moment Zoe was speechless. Then she assured Miss Loretta that she could most certainly dye it red, though she thought that Miss Loretta's white hair was beautiful.

"I want it red for my birthday," Miss Loretta said, "which is this Wednesday."

"Then you come on out Tuesday, and we'll make it red."

Miss Loretta said, loud enough for others to hear, "I don't want that trashy barn red Jada gets."

"I'll let you pick the color," Zoe said, which was all she could think of. Her eyes met Jada's. Jada was laughing. It took more than most anyone had to insult Jada, who always said that a person was only insulted if they allowed themselves to be.

Zoe was immediately glad to have come to see Jada. She hadn't realized how tense and blue she'd felt until her heart was lifted by Jada's sunny smiles and chatter. Over cheeseburgers and fries, Jada spoke of Frank Vargas and her latest date with him, which had involved a trip up to Colorado Springs. She also related the latest gossip: Millie Shatto had made Joe sleep down at the garage until he went to have a vasectomy. It took five days. Eldoree Winslow's daughter had had her purse stolen down in an Amarillo shopping mall, and one of the many Hunsicker children had been bitten by a snake. Every so often during their conversation Jada would break off and call greetings to customers coming or going. A number of them got a hug, too. She hugged Miss Loretta when the older woman rose to leave.

"I do that because it irritates the hell out of her," Jada said, "and there's nothing Miss Loretta likes better than to have something to squawk about."

The crowd had cleared by the time Glory and Mercy had worried their hamburgers to pieces, so Zoe allowed them to share a chocolate milk shake at the end of the counter, where they could spin on the stools.

After the girls had moved out of earshot Jada said, "I saw Rory at Kelly's last night." Her gaze was sharp.

"You did?"

"I just said so, didn't I? It was the first evening he's spent there since he started goin' to your place. Did you two have words?"

"A few." Zoe played the straw around the ice chips in her glass. "Was he drinking much?"

Jada shook her head. "No...matter of fact, he was guzzlin' cream soda, and he let off steam by breaking up a fight, not startin' one. He stayed late, though. What's wrong—did he get fed up with Dusty being around?"

Zoe nodded. "He and Dusty aren't exactly bosom buddies."

"Well, my, my, isn't that a surprise?"

Zoe gave her a dry look, then sighed. "I don't know quite how we got into it," she said, and went on to relate the bare details of their painful clash. "I guess I'm stubborn...but I don't like being told what to do. And Dusty has a right to see the girls, and I figure I should give them every chance to see their father. He may not be a great father, but it's important for kids to know their father loves them, and Dusty does, in his way. And he'll be gone soon enough. He's never stayed off the road more than six weeks in his life."

"I can understand all that," Jada said, "but I can sure see Rory's side of it, too. He feels as if a rival is being paraded in front of his nose—just like Krystal did to him."

"Dusty isn't a rival, and I certainly haven't acted like he is."

"Isn't he? You've certainly bent over backward for Dusty Dean."

Zoe shook her head. "I just couldn't turn him away. He asked me for help, and I couldn't turn him down."

Jada said quietly, "What are you gonna do next time he decides he wants to run home to you, Zoe?"

Zoe looked at her. She hadn't thought of that.

"You have to cut the ties sometime, darlin'. Dusty can't lean on you forever. You don't do either of you any favors by lettin' this go on. And I do believe Dusty Dean is the type you're gonna have to be firm with.''

Zoe nodded. She knew that, but it was as if she were telling her third child to go on down the road alone.

Rory saw Zoe's pickup truck in the lot of Cobb's Drugstore when he pulled into Kelly's lot. He lowered the windows and sat there, the breeze tugging at his hair while he looked from Zoe's truck to the front door of the drugstore at least four times. He debated going across to Cobb's. Nothing unusual about him doing that; he went into Cobb's all the time to visit with Jada, or get a cold drink or some item for Annie.

But he wasn't going to do that. It would just make things tougher. It was pretty stupid to keep hankering after a woman who still had a thing for her ex-husband. And he didn't need to butt in between Mercy and Glory and their daddy. No, he was a fifth wheel in that situation.

He was heading for the green door of Kelly's when he heard his name called. Jerking around, he saw Mercy and Glory waving to him from the concrete steps in front of Cobb's. Zoe stood behind them. Her eyes met his. Or at least she looked at him for an instant. From such a distance, neither of them could really make eye contact.

"Ror-ry! Ror-ry!"

Mercy and Glory sprinted forward, but Zoe quickly caught them, to keep them from running out into the road. Rory changed direction and headed toward them.

When he was across the road, Zoe let go of the girls, and they ran to him. He crouched down and hugged them to him, both at once. Their eager faces caused his heart to swell.

"Hello there, squirts." Still crouched, he pushed his hat back and looked at them. "You sure are dressed pretty today."

Glory pointed out the matching ribbons in their hair, and Mercy pointed to their polished sneakers. Rory was conscious of Zoe standing a couple of feet away, but he kept his gaze on the children.

"You been biz-zy?" Glory asked in that little child-adult way she had of speaking.

"Yep...just a little bit," Rory answered and slowly straightened.

"Are you comin' tonight?" Mercy asked.

Rory shook his head. "Hadn't planned on tonight, but maybe tomorrow, if your mama has time to ride." He looked up at Zoe.

She asked how he was, very politely. She looked cool and pretty as a picture in a pink print dress, with some frilly lace on the front.

"Fine. And you?" He spoke with as much cool politeness as she did.

"We're doing fine." There was flicker of pique in her tone and eyes. "We've just had lunch with Jada."

Rory wondered where Dusty was, but he sure wasn't going to ask. "I was just on my way to have ribs with Kelly. He's serving them on Sundays now."

"I've heard that."

"You might want to go over for ice cream. He's got three new flavors."

"We just had milk shakes at Jada's."

"Oh." It was getting awkward. Rory wanted just to jerk her to him and kiss the hell out of her right then and there.

A horn blared, drawing their attention. It was Dusty in his red-and-white pickup truck, coming down the road at the speed of the Zephyr Flyer. Rory would bet the guy was wearing those tall red-and-white boots. There was a faded blue car coming right behind him, followed by a blindingly bright turquoise truck. Dusty waved them on past with his hat, clutched in the hand with the broken wrist, as he pulled into the parking lot, sending gravel flying. The occupants of the passing vehicles honked, called and waved, arms fluttering from every window.

Dusty poked his fresh, grinning face out the window. "Hi there! Look who I found in Raton, Zoe." He leaned back to reveal his passenger.

"Hi, Zoe," a handsome young man said with a wave.

"Hi, Peter. How have you been?"

"Broke my leg."

Zoe nodded. "Seems to be the luck these days."

Dusty winked at the girls. "Hi, darlin's. I brought you a present." He pointed to the back of the truck, which held a big box wrapped in brown paper. Mercy and Glory jumped up and down, asking what he'd brought, and Dusty told them they would have to wait and see at the house. The arm that had been in a sling was propped easily on the opened window. He lifted lazy eyes to Rory. "How ya been, Breen?"

"Doin'."

"Well, we're havin' a little party tonight. You're sure welcome to come join us." He looked at Zoe then. "Did you recognize Jody's car? Found a bunch of the gang over to Raton, and they're lookin' forward to seein' you. You're comin' on home, aren't you?"

"Yes . . . we're coming home."

"I got everythin', darlin'. You won't have to lift a finger." He grinned handsomely at Zoe, then shifted into reverse and honked as he drove off down the road. Zoe stared after him.

Then Mercy and Glory tugged at her hands, wanting to go home and see what their present was. Zoe's eyes came round to Rory's. There was something in them, a darkness, a quietness, that he didn't quite understand. He did understand the aloofness.

"It was nice seeing you," she said.

"Yeah . . . good seein' you. I'll be round in a day or two to check on Blue."

She nodded. The girls waved at him as they eagerly pulled Zoe along.

Rory strode across to Kelly's. He didn't look back.

The vehicles were parked helter-skelter in the yard, and music was blasting from the house. When Zoe and the girls entered the kitchen, Dusty was pulling beer and soft drinks from a cooler on the table.

"Hey—look who's here!" He came over, put an arm around Zoe's shoulders and kissed her cheek, then bent to the girls. "And these are my daughters. Haven't they grown?'' He introduced Glory and Mercy, who gazed at everyone with wide eyes.

Zoe knew four of the seven people crowding into her small kitchen. While she exchanged polite greetings with everyone, Dusty bragged about Glory and Mercy and teased the girls about their present. He still couldn't tell them apart. Enlisting the aid of another man, he took the girls out to the truck to unload the promising box.

He'd bought them a big spring horse—Black Beauty. It made clopping and whinnying sounds. The men put it together on the lawn. Watching, Mercy and Glory hopped from one foot to the other.

The party moved outside, to the shady side of the house, where there was more room. The men came in for the kitchen chairs and then returned for the table. Spread across the counter were tubs of chicken, boxes of biscuits, containers of slaw, bags of chips, jars of pickles, three whole pies. Zoe set to work getting out plates and glasses, and Tammy joined in to help.

Dusty came behind Zoe and kissed her ear. He whispered, ''I only got beer. None of the hard stuff. I swear.''

She looked at him. ''Where'd you get the money?'' She waved her hand, indicating the food. ''And for the spring horse?''

''The horse was on sale—closeout—and I had a few bucks. Everybody chipped in for the food.'' He took her hand. ''Come on out and watch the girls. They're havin' a ball.''

She pulled her hand away. ''I'll be there in a minute. I'll get this stuff ready to serve first.''

Standing at the back door, Zoe watched the activity in the yard through the screen. Dusty was king of his realm, passing out charm and drinks, enjoying the moment. One of the women—Dusty had introduced her as Amy—came up beside him and put her arm around his waist. He put his around her shoulders. Amy had a model's tall, curvy figure and pale hair that hung to her shoulders and glimmered in the sunlight. Zoe had seen immediately that Amy was taken with Dusty. He treated her like he treated all pretty women, flirting with all his charm. As far as Zoe knew, when they'd been married Dusty had never actually cheated on her, but he had always loved exchanging attentions with women, most especially young women. Amy couldn't be over nineteen, the age Zoe had been when she and Dusty married. But, Zoe thought as she watched the two smiling and touching each other, none of the women Dusty gravitated to had given him what she had, which was security, stability. That was why Dusty had stayed with her and wanted to return to her now.

Zoe served beer and soft drinks, made iced tea, pried a chicken bone from between Fancy's teeth, cracked ice, washed dishes, put out a small fire in the grass, doctored Glory's scraped knee and a cut one of the men got in playful wrestling. To Tammy's friendly comment about Zoe and Dusty getting back together, Zoe said, "We're not back together."

"Oh," Tammy said with curious eyes but tactfully not asking questions.

The guests departed just before midnight. They left behind the kitchen table and chairs still on the lawn, trash and dishes from here to Colombia, and two very exhausted, dirty-faced, crying little girls. Zoe wiped their faces and hands with a wet cloth and stripped them out of their clothes. They were asleep upon hitting the mattress. Dusty helped her get the chairs and table inside, using his one good hand—and his arm that Zoe had suspicions about. Then Zoe bid him good-night and fell into bed with the girls.

Chapter Fourteen

It was near midnight when Rory returned home from Kelly's. He and Kelly had passed the Sunday-night hours playing chess and sharing a couple of beers. They'd kept each other company. And now that he was home, the loneliness settled upon Rory like a heavy, smothering quilt.

He went to the barn to find a bottle of Jack D. stashed in with the horse liniments. He hadn't gotten drunk in over two months. The only drinking he'd done had been a few beers with Kelly, and he'd begun to feel free. Until now. He thought of Zoe, looked at the bottle, turned out the light and carried the bottle with him. He climbed up on the bales of hay and sat watching the three yearlings out beyond in the moonlit corral. He ran his hand over the cool bottle. He wanted to get drunk; he wanted to drown the emotions eating at him. He wanted to block out the image of Zoe with Dusty.

"Rory? Are you in here?"

Matt's voice caused him to jump. He fleetingly considered not answering, then called softly, "Here. In the back." After a few moments Matt's figure came out of the deep shadows.

Matt looked up, saw him, and climbed up beside him . "I couldn't sleep, either," he said.

Rory held the bottle of whiskey out to him, as a sarcastic joke, because he knew Matt would decline. To his surprise, Matt took the bottle and drank deeply.

"What's wrong?" Rory asked.

Matt sighed deeply. "It's beginnin' to look like I can't get Annie pregnant."

That hung there for a long minute. Then Rory offered, "These things have to be left to Mother Nature's timing."

Matt shook his head. "I was tested today. My sperm count's low."

Rory really didn't know what to say to that. "I'm sorry, big brother." It seemed not at all enough to say. He started to point out they had Little Jesse, but thought better of it. Matt needed him to listen.

Matt shrugged and took another drink from the bottle, then handed it back to Rory. Rory looked at it a long moment. His hand shook. Then he recapped the bottle and set it aside.

"That stuff is too good to waste drinkin' it all at once," he said. "Besides, we each have enough problems, without havin' to deal with hangovers and Annie's worried eyes."

At that, Matt laughed dryly and draped an arm around Rory's shoulders. They sat like that for long minutes. And Rory felt closer to Matt than he had in a long time.

The sun was well up by the time Zoe awoke. She went to the kitchen, quietly closing the door behind her to encourage the girls to sleep as long as possible. She made coffee, fed the stock, gave the kitchen a lick and a promise, then showered quickly.

She was giving Darleen Hunsicker a cut and style by the time Dusty awoke. He poked sleepy eyes through the door, exchanged a charming hello with Darleen and asked Zoe if coffee was made.

"Waitin' in the kitchen," Zoe said. "Don't wake the girls."

"They're already playin' in the tub."

"Watch them, Dusty," she called after him.

Later, after she closed the door behind Darleen, she stood for a moment with her hand on the knob, thinking about what she would say to Dusty. Just as she was heading for the kitchen, the telephone rang. It was Amy, with the California hair, calling for Dusty.

He appeared, dressed only in jeans.

"It's Amy," Zoe told him with an amused smile when she handed him the receiver.

He looked sheepish. "Thanks. 'Lo, Amy... what's up?"

Zoe went to the bathroom to check on the girls, who were enjoying a bubble bath. She splashed water and exchanged kisses, then went on to the kitchen, where she poured herself a cup of coffee and sat to wait for Dusty.

He joined her ten minutes later. "Amy was wonderin' if we found her bracelet," he said and tucked his hand into his jeans pocket and shifted on bare feet.

"I haven't seen any bracelet, but I'll keep an eye out." Inwardly, she thought it significant that Amy had to speak to Dusty about the bracelet—and that it took a full ten minutes to do it.

He brought his coffee to the table and sat across from her. "The girls sure like their spring horse, don't they?" He grinned. There were shadows in his eyes, though, and Zoe knew he sensed she had something on her mind.

"Yes. They love it," she said.

He rose and poured them each fresh coffee. "I guess I should see about that pressure tank today. Water pressure seemed awfully poor this morning."

Zoe gazed at him. "Dusty, you can't stay here anymore."

He looked at her. The bleakness in his eyes stabbed her weak spot. "I've been tryin' to make it up to you, Zo."

She nodded and smiled tenderly. "I know... and that means a lot. I'm glad you came. There were... things we had to settle. And it's been good for the girls to get to know you. But we're not married anymore, Dusty, and you can't go on staying here indefinitely. I want to get on with my life, and you need to get on with yours." And I want my bed back, she thought irreverently.

He looked down at the coffee cup he cradled in his hands. After a moment he nodded. Then he grinned at her—it almost reached his pale eyes. "No one can say it hasn't been a hoot."

She grinned back. "No, no one can say that."

"I'll head out today, I guess, while I can join up with Pete. He's wantin' to head down to Belen and needs someone to drive, with his broken leg and all."

She watched his face and knew he'd already spoken about this to Pete. He'd been longing to go back to the life he loved. She asked, "Do you need any money? I have a few dollars saved."

He shifted his bare feet. "I could use what you can spare." He cast a crooked smile. "I'm down to a single sawbuck. I spent everything else I'd had for the girls' horse and eats yesterday."

Zoe reached into her purse.

"I'll send it back, Zo," he said as she handed him eighty dollars, all that was in her wallet. "I'll get a job with Benavides—he's supplying stock for the rodeo in Belen right now. He almost always needs extra help. And I'll be sendin' you money for the girls and all."

She thought how he did indeed mean it; no doubt he would often *think* of sending money. She watched him pocket the money and wondered what she herself was going to do without it—she would be short on the rent again. She sighed inwardly and thought that she could do it this one last time.

After another few seconds of standing there, he stepped to the doorway. He paused. "You'll explain to the girls, won't you? I mean, I really don't know much about little girls...." He looked helpless.

"I'll explain," she said.

"Thanks," he said lamely and headed away to the bedroom.

Zoe heard him murmur to the girls, more splashing and the girls giggling. "Oh, Daddy—I'm Mer-cy."

And so it had been settled. Zoe sighed, rose and began clearing the dishes. Soon she realized she was looking out the window—for Rory.

* * *

Late that afternoon they stood in the yard. Dusty kissed Glory and Mercy, and they hugged his neck. Then he stopped in front of Zoe. They gazed at each other, and he kissed her cheek.

"Good luck, Dusty. Send the girls notes, okay?"

He nodded. "Okay. I promise. Good luck to you and Rory down at the Classic. If you win, you'll be a rich lady next time I see you."

Zoe caught the speculative gleam in his eyes and thought, Don't you be trying to get your hands on my winnings, either. She had to smile; she knew him well.

"Bye... goodbye, Daddy...."

Zoe stood with the girls, waving as his truck and trailer pulled out of the drive. They watched the rig head down the road and the dust spiral into the air and blow away with the wind. Then the girls, with Fancy at their heels, raced to Black Beauty sitting in the small square of shade cast by the back porch. Zoe followed more slowly.

She felt as if a weight had been lifted off her shoulders, or as if she'd been going through a tunnel and suddenly was coming out on the other side. Life was ahead of her, and she was ready.

Her heart pattered with the thought of Rory—and what might be. Maybe. If she hadn't lost him. And though she wasn't certain she wanted to get into another relationship with a man. And thinking this, she smiled to herself. The heart played havoc, no matter how practical she tried to be.

Rory put off going to Zoe's until late Friday afternoon. He didn't want to face his feelings for her, his frustration at the situation with Dusty. But his honor compelled him to go to see her, to see how Blue was doing. He'd entered into showing Blue with her, and they were to leave for Fort Worth on Saturday. He had to see this thing through, despite his feelings on the situation. And he was drawn to her, too, and he damned himself as a fool.

The first thing he noticed when he drove into her yard was the absence of Dusty's pickup truck—and trailer. Zoe's truck was parked near the barn, but all appeared quiet. No sign of her or the girls.

Perhaps she'd gone off with Dusty. His chest squeezed, and anger flashed through him.

Curious, he went first to the barn. Blue was tied to the post. Dusty's horse was gone.

If she'd told Dusty to hit the road, why hadn't she called to tell him?

He heard footsteps and turned to see Zoe come through the wide opening. She stopped, stood there, her small figure silhouetted by the bright setting sun. They stared at each other.

"Ror-ry!" Glory and Mercy came from behind Zoe and ran at him.

"Hi ya, pumpkins." He scooped them up, one in each arm.

They babbled at him: they had just finished dinner, spaghetti, and Fancy liked spaghetti, too. Their daddy had bought them a spring horse; her name was Black Beauty, and she made noise, just like a real horse. Didn't he want to see her?

He told them he'd be to see her in a few minutes and set them on the ground. They ran out, and he and Zoe stood gazing at each other. She wore a thin denim shirt and worn jeans that hugged her thighs like a second skin. That fact lodged first in Rory's mind, followed by the way her bare neck disappeared into her shirt. His eyes returned to hers. Like a sudden, unexpected storm out of the north, emotion rose and swirled around them. And then he saw the anger flicker in her eyes.

"He looks great. How's he been working?" he said, indicating Blue and watching Zoe closely. He was talking about the darn stud, when what he really wanted to know was if Dusty was gone—and if she had sent him away.

"Good," she said and he knew she was mad and it was at him. He figured he'd find out why in the next few minutes.

Zoe tucked her hands in her back jeans pockets. As Monday had passed and then Tuesday, then Wednesday and then the rest of the week, each day dragging, her wondering *when* he was going to come had turned to *if* he was going to come. By gum, she'd about decided she was on her own—and now he showed up! She was surprised, delighted—and mad as a hornet.

"Did you come to see him work tonight?" she asked and slowly walked forward.

"I thought I might." His eyes were cautious.

"Won't make much difference how he does. If he doesn't have the idea by now, he isn't going to get it between tonight and Monday." Her words were sharper than a knife blade.

He blinked. "Then you don't want to work him?" His tone was equally sharp.

"I was just getting ready to," she said and walked over to grab the saddle pad.

Rory stepped quickly to grab the saddle.

Zoe flopped the pad on Blue's back and turned to take the saddle from Rory. "I can do it," she said, in the face of having Rory see how she would have to wiggle the heavy saddle onto Blue's back.

But he jerked it from her grasp. "Let me do it." He flopped it on Blue with annoying ease and bent to cinch it up.

Zoe stood back, fuming. When he'd finished he turned to her.

"Okay—what are you so mad about?"

She stared at him. "We are due to go down to Fort Worth tomorrow, and you're just now showin' up here, interested in how Blue is?"

"This horse was ready for showin' the last time I was here. All you needed to do since then was easy practice to keep him reminded, and you're perfectly capable of doing that. As a matter of fact, you've been tellin' me all along that you're perfectly capable of training him yourself." He brought his hand up to rest on his belt and leaned forward. "And if you needed me, you could have called."

"You could have called to inquire."

"I'm here tonight."

She broke the gaze and nodded. "Okay." She was annoyed with herself for getting so ruffled. She didn't want him to know how hurt she felt that he hadn't come around these past few days. If he'd wanted to come, he would have. "Do you want to ride first, or shall I?"

"You go ahead. I need to see the girls' play horse." And he turned and strode out the front of the barn.

He was here because of their pact about Blue. That was why and that was all. The thought brought a stabbing pain to her chest.

They worked Blue for an hour and a half, but not hard. Zoe rode first, and then Rory tried his hand. The tenseness remained between them and was transferred to Blue. At first he was stiff, pushy. Zoe strove to put all her irritation at Rory aside and concentrate on riding. Sit in the middle of the saddle; don't lean; keep limber; lift the rein to get his shoulder up. Ride; cut the cow. That was, after all, why they were here, and there was a lot of money at stake.

"He can't be any better," Rory said when they put Blue away. "And neither can you."

"But will it be good enough?" Zoe commented. She looked at Rory in the dimming twilight, at his strong jaw-line and the hair curling behind his ears. The tense self-consciousness returned.

"We're gonna find out." His tone was low, his eyes intent. "I figured we leave out of here around seven in the morning. I'll drive. Is that all right with you?"

She nodded. "We'll be ready. But . . . I thought I'd drive my truck down, too. That way we have two vehicles. You can go to your hotel when you want, and we can do the same."

"There's no need to do that. I already have us a suite at the hotel I always stay at down there." He held up his palm at her protest. "Two separate bedrooms and baths connected by a kitchen and sitting area, with a pull-out bed for the girls. And there is no bill, because the owner of the hotel is a friend of our family. We trade off—he comes up to our place to hunt and camp, he lends us rooms when we go there." When she still looked uncertain, he added, "Look, it's foolish to pay gas for two vehicles, have to park two vehicles. And going in one truck, we can trade off drivin', so we won't be so tired when we get there."

At last Zoe said, "Okay."

They walked outside. At the edge of the house, Glory and Mercy were still riding their "horsey."

Rory stopped, lifted his hat and ran a hand over his hair. "Ah...do you suppose you could give me a quick trim? It's been awhile, and since we're goin' to Fort Worth..."

He watched her hopefully. After several seconds a hint of a smile played over her lips. "Sure." She did, after all, still owe him about half a dozen cuts. But he sensed she wasn't averse to the idea, and for the first time he began to relax.

She called for the girls to come along to play on the front porch, where she could keep an eye on them. Rory fell in step beside her. As she opened the front door, she asked if he wanted a cream soda. "Mercy saved you another one."

And so again he sat in the chair. She laid him back and washed his hair, then clipped it. Her touch sent shivers down his spine. They didn't talk. Afterward, she walked outside with Rory. It was dark, stars bright above.

He stopped at the door of his truck. "I'll be here about seven tomorrow morning." He wondered powerfully about Dusty but wasn't about to ask.

She nodded. Her face was illuminated by the light from the window. The girls' tiny voices floated from inside and reached the back of his mind as he gazed at her. A warmth wrapped around them.

"I sent Dusty away," she said. "On Monday."

Rory took that in. "Monday?" That had been days ago. "Why didn't you call me?"

And she tossed back at him, "Why didn't you call me?"

They gazed at each other a long moment. Inside the house one of the girls yelled at the other. Rory came forward, grabbed Zoe to him and kissed her, rough, deep and hard.

He broke away and gazed down at her, his heart pounding. "I'll see you in the morning."

When Zoe went into the house, she telephoned Jada.

"I've reconsidered your offer to have the girls stay with you while I go down to Fort Worth. I'd like to take you up on it."

"It's about time you came to your senses," Jada said crisply. "Those babies could get trampled down there...horses all over the place. You can't watch them and tend to Blue, too." Then her voice turned gleeful. "And you and Rory can have time to yourselves."

"Yes to it all, Miss Know-it-all. We'll be dropping the girls off around seven."

Jada moaned. "Ye Gods and little fishes. Okay, I'll have my eyes open. Think they'll go back to bed?"

"No, I don't."

Zoe hung up and sat there. Glory's and Mercy's voices came to her; they were playing princesses. She dreaded telling them that she was leaving them behind. She had never been separated from them for so much as one night, much less three to five, depending. She didn't want to leave them now, but Jada was right about it being unsafe. Zoe simply couldn't keep an eye on them every minute and do what she needed with Blue.

And she did want this time with Rory. They were at a crossroads and had to decide which way they were going to go.

Zoe oohed and aahed over the luxurious hotel suite and marveled that Rory's friend would lend it to them—probably wrote it off his taxes, Rory told her—and then she spied the phone and went straight for it to call Glory and Mercy.

Rory watched her sitting on the bone-colored couch, one of the things she'd oohed and aahed about, with her shoulders all tensed. He worried that she was going to start crying again. His first shock that morning had come when she'd told him that they were leaving the girls with Jada. He'd certainly never considered that she would leave the girls; he'd *wished* it, but he hadn't considered it, because Zoe rarely let the girls out of her sight. He was highly pleased at this turn of events, though he was wise enough not to show it.

His second shock had come when they'd driven away and Zoe had started crying like Niagara Falls. He'd never seen her cry, not even when Blue had been so ill. Before they got too far away from Wings, he'd asked her if she wanted to return for the girls. "Noooo," she'd said through sobs. He'd felt really weird sitting there, driving on, with her all shriveled up against the far door. Made him feel like he was all to blame, for some unfathomable reason.

But the phone call went okay. She hung up and was smiling. The girls had accepted the separation, but not so completely as to make Zoe feel useless.

"Which bedroom do you want?" he asked.

She rose and looked from one door to the other and then back at him. They gazed at each other for one moment in which he *knew* she was thinking the same thing he was: that they were all alone here and there were beds in those rooms. Warmth rushed over him and lodged in his groin.

"It makes no difference to me. You choose." Her cheeks flushed.

"I'll take this one." He took up his bag and went off to the room on the right. And he told himself to quit having adolescent thoughts.

But those thoughts had lodged deep and kept popping up to taunt him throughout the evening.

He took Zoe to a friendly restaurant he knew of—and where they weren't likely to run into too many other horse people they knew—and overrode her protests about picking up the check by telling her that she could buy next time. He thought how it was their first real date.

Afterward, they returned to the stables to check on Blue, who wasn't happy in his strange environment and started calling to Zoe the minute he caught her scent. Zoe and Rory shot the breeze with some of the other contestants. The show had started that morning, but people were still arriving and would be coming and going all week long.

They came upon Etta and Frank Quevedo, who were there to support Frank's brother, who'd brought a horse. Etta had come along at the last minute. They saw Robert Walker and his latest fiancée, and Bruce Vickery, who'd once been a partner with Zoe's father and had to be at least a hundred years old.

When Zoe saw Yancey and Annalise Cordell's horse and learned Annalise and the horse were entered in the same division as herself, she began fretting. "Might as well go home," she muttered. "Blue doesn't have a chance against their gelding."

"Is that any way to think?" Rory countered. "Cordell's gelding is good, but he doesn't walk on water."

"No, but he does train in a swimming pool. They have one for their horses—and Annalise Cordell may qualify as a non-pro, but her horse is a product of their million-dollar training facility."

To which Rory said, "Funny, but I've never seen a cutting contest go on in a swimming pool—or a cow or a horse that could estimate the value of any facility."

She looked at him and started laughing, seeing the ridiculousness of her worries. But ten minutes later she was off again about some other horse that was sure to beat Blue. Her unusual agitation came as quite a surprise...and something of a pleasure; it gave Rory a chance to be strong for her.

However, the sexual thoughts that had whispered within him all evening appeared to shout the instant he opened the door to their hotel suite, and suddenly it was Rory's turn to get agitated.

Zoe went ahead of him, and his gaze swept down her spine. Her hair was loose and shimmered down over her shoulders, and her skirt lay quite nicely over her hips. She turned, and her eyes met his, then skittered away.

"I'm really exhausted," she said. "I think I'll go on to bed."

"Yeah...it's been a long day."

He watched her retreat to her room, practically running as she called good-night. He went to bed, but he didn't sleep much.

Zoe lay in the bed, propped on two fluffy down pillows, and stared at the shaft of light from the bathroom reflecting on the ceiling. She'd left the bathroom light on because, with the heavy curtains, the room was pitch-black.

A noise reached her, and she listened. It was either Rory moving around in the suite or someone outside in the hallway.

She imagined Rory lying in his bed, in the room just beyond the sitting room. She imagined going to him, crawling into bed with him.

She wanted to do that. Badly. She wanted to kiss him and feel his arms around her and feel his muscles and . . .

But she wasn't certain where that was going to lead, or if it would lead anywhere, or even if she wanted it to lead anywhere. She was simply afraid of the consequences, period. Ending up pregnant was certainly a worry, but what worried her more was ending up with another broken heart.

And so she rolled over and pulled a third pillow over her head. But doing that couldn't block out the pictures her mind insisted on conjuring.

Though the non-pro division Blue was in wasn't scheduled until Monday, they had come early so as to allow Blue time to get accustomed to his surroundings and settle down, and also to have plenty of opportunity to display him. To accomplish both, Rory and Zoe each rode him morning, afternoon and evening in the practice arena, where others came to show their horses or to view other people's. It was a popular gathering place.

And it was there that Zoe and Rory saw Annalise Cordell and her horse spinning like a top. Zoe watched with bleak eyes.

"So he can spin," Rory told her. "Spinnin' don't cut a cow. Now just get out there and ride Blue easy." He grinned, and she responded. He watched her; few women could ride with such style as she had.

That first afternoon a man made an offer of six thousand dollars for Blue. Zoe declined it quickly but later began having misgivings. "I should have my head examined. I should have taken that man's offer and run. Six thousand dollars!" She was getting agitated again.

"You'll be gettin' bigger offers than that before this thing's finished," Rory predicted. "You just have to hold out."

"Easy for you to say," she said. "You have six thousand dollars."

That struck him. He stared at her.

"Well, don't you?"

"I guess I do," he said, thinking of his bank accounts and feeling absurdly ashamed of everything over a thousand dollars.

She cast him a see-there look.

"And since I do, let me buy you a box of popcorn and a soda." He took her hand and held it tight. She didn't try to remove it.

They sat for hours in the arena and watched the cutting, evaluating the horses, criticizing the riders, guessing scores and complaining of the judges' blindness when they guessed wrong. They greeted a number of acquaintances, but Rory had no desire to join them, and Zoe didn't appear to want to, either.

Again and again their eyes met, and Rory knew that Zoe wasn't thinking only of horses and cutting, just as he wasn't. He recognized the questioning in her velvet-brown eyes. And the growing desire.

Were they, or weren't they? Should they, or shouldn't they? He kept asking himself those questions and wondering why things were so complicated. He couldn't recall a time when he'd found himself in such a dilemma over going to bed with a woman. It had always been so easy before: either he wanted to or he didn't; either she wanted to or she didn't. He'd never had this searching of himself and the consequences.

But this wasn't any simple little romance. The knowledge rose in him like a foaming tide. *This was serious, and suddenly it scared him to death.*

After a late dinner Rory, feeling a sense of self-preservation, offered to make a final night check on Blue and dropped Zoe at the hotel so she could telephone the girls. It seemed a good time to put some distance between them, too. Time for him to think. He didn't come to any conclusions, however.

And when he returned he found Zoe there, in the tiny kitchenette, in her bathrobe. A perfectly proper pink bathrobe that wrapped between her breasts and fell like a caress over her hips and legs.

It was the funniest thing, but the bathrobe and knowing full well there was nothing underneath it wasn't what did him in. It wasn't her hair falling all soft like that of an angel, either. Or her velvety eyes all filled with wanting and trying to hide it.

It was her bare little feet, with her dainty, pink-enameled toenails poking out beneath the hem of her robe, that sent all the practical considerations just shooting right out of his mind and a fever flooding his veins.

Chapter Fifteen

"No...no!" Zoe cried in a harsh whisper and twisted, but she was fighting herself more than him.

Rory held on to her. His eyes were hot with longing.

"You're a dumb ol' cowboy," she said between sobbing gasps. "And I have two babies...and we need to pay attention to showin' Blue."

His answer to all that was to kiss her. And all her objections faded as darkness before moonlight.

He kissed her, and she responded, eagerly, deeply, giving all she had and taking all she could. It was a kiss that unleashed it all—all the pent-up needs and frustrations and passions they'd both tried so hard to control. And once unleashed, those emotions raced away with the fury of wild horses. Forgotten was the open door of the small refrigerator behind her, the cubes of ice melting in the glass on the counter.

They broke apart, gasped for breath and kissed again. And again. His hands came up to cradle her cheeks, and they kissed yet again.

It was hot and wet and breathless. Exciting and frightening. And tender. It was the tenderness that got to her.

She gripped his shirt at his waist; it was warm. His mustache prickled, wonderfully so. There was the scent of him, which was musky sweat and manly cologne and night air, and the feel of him, which was strong and hard and pulsing. There was the sound of their clothing rubbing, cotton against cotton, hands atop cotton. The sounds of their quick breaths and pounding hearts.

His hands pressed her against his length, pushing her pelvis against his; his breath caressed her temple, his lips her neck. She thought she would shatter at any moment.

They spoke rapidly, in whispers, with eager gasps and quick kisses.

"Zoe...I have protection, darlin'. It'll be all right." He smoothed back her hair.

"It's the safe time for me." She stroked his mustache.

"Safe time?"

"Of my cycle. The infertile days."

"Oh. Does...that...really work?"

"It...sure...helps."

He kissed her until she felt her muscles melting. Then he lifted her into his arms and headed for his bedroom.

He set her on the bed in the dark room. They couldn't see each other, only feel. His hands were the callused hands of a hardworking man. They were strong, eager and ardent, yet gentle, too, as only those of such a strong man can be. She liked the way he kissed and the way he touched her. He made her catch fire.

They didn't get to removing all their clothes. Her robe fell open; he removed his boots, jeans and underwear. She slipped her hands beneath his shirt. The only sounds were of their heavy breathing and the bed softly squeaking.

And then they flew together in heat as white hot as the midsummer sun on the high plains.

"Oh! Why did you do that?" Zoe said in a raspy whisper. She shielded her eyes from the sudden light—the bedside lamp Rory had switched on.

He turned, blocking most of the brightness with his shoulders. "Because I want to look at you," he said, also in a raspy whisper. He tugged her arm away from her face and gazed down at her.

Zoe saw in his pale eyes the wonder she herself felt.

"I don't think it's ever been like this," he said, his voice echoing with raw emotion. He stroked her hair. "Not ever."

"Me, either," she said past the lump in her throat. Blinking her burning eyes, she reached up and stroked his mustache.

He kissed her softly and then smiled down at her with pleasure so pure, she thought her heart would burst. She returned the smile. Then she rubbed her toes on his ankle.

"Think maybe you'd like to take off your socks and stay a while, Mr. Breen?"

He hugged her to him, laughing. She didn't think she'd ever heard him laugh with such completeness before.

He removed his shirt and socks, she pulled her arms from her robe and together they slipped beneath the covers. She wasn't the least embarrassed; it all seemed natural. He turned out the light, and she nestled in the crook of his arm. He hugged her, then stroked circles on her arm with his thumb.

No promises were exchanged, no words of love spoken. Right then, in that moment, those things weren't needed. Zoe felt satiated. She was happy, and in love. She wanted no questions to spoil it.

The first thing Rory noticed when he awoke was gray light showing at the edges of the window drapes. The second thing he noticed was the damp heat from Zoe's body. He was curled around her, her little buttocks pressed against his groin.

He moved against her and immediately began throbbing. She stirred and gave a small sigh. His eyes adjusting, he could make out the pale skin of her shoulder. He caressed it, and a shiver went down his spine. She had incredibly soft skin, so different from his own. He'd been shocked at her passion. Such a small body to contain so much fire.

He kissed her shoulder. Gently, feeling coarse and rough next to her femininity, he pulled her thick, silky hair from her face. She sighed and stretched like a sleeping cat. He nuzzled her breasts; she moved against his lips.

"Rory?" she said in a drowsy whisper. Her arms came around his neck, and she pulled his mouth to hers and wrapped a leg around his. It was as if she were unfolding for him.

Pushing aside the questions that wanted to intrude, he made love to her, this time slowly and deliberately. He watched her move with his caresses and savored the fire building inside himself. He savored everything, lived totally in the moment. He gave her all he could and felt himself being the one filled.

"We've got to get to the stables!" she said to him and sprang from the bed.

Rory watched her breasts bob. For such a small woman, she had full breasts.

She caught him looking and turned red. In a huff, she wrapped the robe around herself. "We show today, you know."

Propelling himself across the bed, he grabbed her as she flew around the end and jerked her down and across him. "You and Blue don't show until afternoon at the earliest." He chuckled. "And you weren't so worried about Blue and showin' a few minutes ago."

"I was asleep a few minutes ago. You took advantage of me." She was laughing.

"Asleep or awake, you enjoyed it."

"Yes," she said.

He lost himself in her velvety eyes. "If you turn out pregnant, I won't let you be alone," he said. His tongue got stuck on the word marriage; it wouldn't come out. But he thought it.

"I know," she said. She stroked his mustache and thought how Dusty hadn't let her be alone, either, not that such a promise provided much. She'd taken the chance, and she had only herself to blame. She said, "Now, you just get that look out of your eye. We have a horse to show. We can't be hangin' around this bed all day long."

Wrestling herself away from him, she ran for her own room.

She gazed into the mirror. Her eyes were bright; she was smiling. *Oh, what good loving did for a person!* There was no denying that.

She loved him, she thought with sudden clarity. She loved Rory.

Her spirits dipped as her mind filled with questions. What now? Where did they go from here? Were these days here, away from everyone, all there would be—one of those four-day affairs? Or would they continue on into a long affair? Or would they go on to marriage? She swallowed and clutched her robe in a moment of panic. She didn't want to get hurt again.

She thought how he'd been with her. He'd been passionate and tender and loving. He was that kind of man. He wouldn't treat any woman badly. But that didn't mean he was in love with her.

And even if he should be in love with her, that didn't mean he wanted to marry her. And just because she loved him, she wasn't certain she wanted to marry him, either. He had a fondness for liquor, and he was a cowboy, after all. She'd known that all along, and here she'd gone and gotten involved with him!

The thoughts swirled in her mind as she hurried to shower and dress. And they kept intruding during the day. When Rory opened the truck door for her, she recalled how he'd swept her up into his arms. When he smiled at her over his coffee cup, she recalled how his lips had kissed her. When he brushed Blue, she recalled how his hands had felt upon her body.

Zoe exercised Blue at a slow easy lope in a wide circle with the other horses waiting in the warm-up ring for their turn to compete. Some riders notched out areas to practice their turns. Others sat on their mounts and talked quietly. At the far end of the arena the cutting competition was going on, but Zoe couldn't really see it clearly because of the judges' elevated seats and people and horses. She didn't want to watch, and she tried not to listen to scores as they were called.

She heard the number of the next rider. She was two away from her turn. There were over a hundred riders and horses entered in this division. Only the top scoring twenty of those entrants would be in the final go-round tomorrow. "We've got some job cut out for us, boy, to make it into the top twenty," she whispered to Blue and stroked his neck. Her heart pounded at the thought, and she shivered. *She wanted to make it . . . please . . . at least into that twenty.*

Rory motioned to her from the arena rail, and she walked Blue over. "Thought you might be ready for a drink."

"Thanks." She took the cold red-and-white cup. Her hand trembled. She deliberately relaxed her back, then her legs.

"Frank Quevedo's gonna be a herd holder for you," Rory said.

"I thought he and Etta were heading on down to San Antonio."

"Oh, he decided he'd stay and help you out. He's over there now, mountin' up." He lifted a hand, and Zoe turned to see Frank mounting a gray.

She smiled, and waved, too. That Frank would be there was comforting.

She returned the soft drink to Rory; he finished it off and then came down into the arena.

He moved her leg to check her saddle cinch. "Just had another offer for your stud."

"Who? How much?"

He grinned up at her. "Seven thousand. From Herman Miller. I told him to look us up if he's still interested after the finals."

She gazed at him and thought, Seven thousand. "Was he serious?"

"Oh, yeah, Herman's a gamblin' man—and he's always serious about it."

"How nice of you to make up my mind for me." She was irritated and thought, How like a man.

He just grinned at her. "Now you know there are others who think this stud's got a great chance out there." He ran his hand in a firm caress down her thigh, and the sensual sparkle in his eyes took her back to the early hours of the morning.

"You're not helping me keep my mind on cutting," she said.

"I'm tryin' to keep your mind *off* it, so you don't get all tensed up."

"I'm not tense."

"Darlin', I could play a tune on you, you're so tight." He walked over to Walter, tied nearby, and mounted.

Zoe knew what he said was so. Her number came over the address system, the announcer calling for her to get ready on deck as the next rider. Her heartbeat thudded as she adjusted her reins, though they didn't need it.

She said, "What if Blue shows badly right away? There'll be no more offers for him then. No one will want him, and I'll be flat broke. Did you think about that? If I sold him now, before he screws up, I'd be assured of hard cash."

"Too late to worry about that now." Rory settled his rear in his saddle.

Zoe sighed and gave him a dry look. She shifted her saddle, eased her legs, checked her reins and adjusted her hat. Seemed silly to wear a hat indoors, but it was the rules, as were her chaps. She was trying not to hear scores, but she heard the one of the contestant before her—210. That was damn good.

The announcer called, "True Blue Heart, owned and ridden by Zoe Padilla."

Rory raised an eyebrow.

"For Daddy," she said.

He smiled his slow smile and headed Walter off to take his position of turnback at the left side of the herd.

Zoe took a deep breath and clucked to Blue, sending him forward at a slow walk toward the herd. Blue was as quiet as they came, even though Zoe knew she was trembling slightly. She forced herself to relax, focused on the herd and pushed everything else from her mind.

It was a large, old-West–style bar in cow town. Lights glimmered in the mirrors and glass behind the long bar, fans twirled from the ceiling, and the band was into a new rendition of an old Hank Williams tune. The crowd was dense, and at least half the people were from the horse show.

The bar was one of the rare places on earth that served Coca-Cola in the small glass bottles, and that was what Zoe had. Rory had a long-neck beer. He'd ordered a soft drink first, but Zoe had told him to go ahead and enjoy a beer.

Zoe felt as if she were being drawn along with the flow of fervent energy. She felt pretty and womanly in her favorite blue blouse; Rory's eyes were warm upon her; excitement was all around her; and she and Blue had made it into the top twenty finalists.

The talk was of the scores from that day, of course, with discussion as to the merits of the judges' decisions. Zoe and Blue's score had been 213. She experienced a quiet glow, and a heavy sense of just how much of a long shot she and Blue were at winning this thing. That fact was more real to her than ever after seeing the horses and their owners and trainers. Tomorrow, for the finals, she would be competing against the twenty best out of today's competition. And at least eight of those had already outscored Blue, and Annalise Cordell and her gelding were among them. Zoe's hope of winning was down to a bare flicker, and that flicker kept alive only because she didn't want to let everyone down by giving up.

"Don't you lose heart, Zoe darlin'." Frank Quevedo bobbed his beer bottle at her. "I've seen the highest-scorin' fellas blow it in the finals. Anything can happen and usually does."

Etta nodded. "Years ago, Frank barely made the finals and then came away with second place." She nudged Frank. "Remember that?"

"Sure do." He laughed and went into the story.

A hefty, iron-gray-haired man with a wide grin came up, and Rory introduced him as Herman Miller. "Your stud sure did well today," the man said to Zoe. "I'll up my offer for him to ten thousand—right now."

Rory rested his hand on her back, but he looked downward, refusing to give her any guidance.

Zoe didn't know what to say. Ten thousand would do all she needed. And it was a sure thing.

"I'll even let you ride the fella in the finals," Herman Miller said grandly, as if doing her a favor. "You have paid the fees, after all."

Zoe smiled. "And if I win, you'll take the money."

"That's the game, gal." And he, too, grinned. "It's the gamble I like. The gamble is why I buy horses *before* the competition, not after, when I know what I'm gettin'." And Zoe knew he wasn't making an idle comment.

She thought of it all, thought how she was gambling not only with her future, but that of her daughters. She peered at Herman Miller, at his twinkling eyes. He believed, she decided. Giving a shake of her head, she reached for her cold bottle of Coke. "I guess not, Mr. Miller, but thank you kindly." She couldn't let her girls or Rory down by giving up now.

Mr. Miller laughed and bade them goodbye.

Rory took her hand and led her out on the dance floor, where he swept her into his arms. The band was playing a slow tune. His gaze captured hers; it was filled with admiration.

Zoe said, "I had no idea you could dance like this."

"Oh, ma'am, I love to shuffle." He winked at her, and heat shimmered in his blue eyes.

She put her head on his shoulder and lost herself in the music and the feel of Rory's body moving against her. As soon as the song ended, they said goodbye to the others and headed back to the hotel. Rory held her hand the whole trip.

Zoe called Jada, told her the day's news and then chatted with the girls. Afterward she showered, drew on her robe and gazed at herself in the mirror, wondering, What now?

When she opened the bathroom door, the light fell into the darkened bedroom, slashing across her bed. Rory, wearing only his jeans, was stretched out there.

He gazed at her, saw the surprise on her face, followed by the hint of a smile. In that instant her dewy youth stabbed him in the heart. Then she turned out the light, and the room was plunged into darkness. He heard the whisper of her cotton robe as she came toward him. Her shadow ap-

peared beside the bed. Rory drew her down beside him. She
leaned over and lay across his chest, resting her head on his
shoulder. He stroked her back; her robe was cool but
quickly warmed. Her hair was soft upon his cheek. The
scent of her quickened his desire.

"How are the girls?" he asked.

"They're fine. Jada took them to Amarillo today. There
was a small circus there. All three of them had quite a time."

"That's good."

They remained thus. The ticking of the clock on the
nightstand was loud. The beating of Rory's heart was
equally so. He continued to rhythmically stroke Zoe's back
and to savor the building of the heat between them. He caressed upward beneath her hair to the moist skin of the back
of her neck. He slipped her robe from her shoulder and
stroked her satiny skin. The sensual scent of her enveloped
him. His pulse pounded, hard. Then she lifted her head and
brought her lips to his. Her kiss was well-deep and wind-
strong. The heat inside him burst into a roaring flame.
Rolling her beneath him, he lost himself in her, in her scent,
in her velvety skin, in her womanly passion.

Afterward he cradled her in his arms. "I love you," he
said in a bare whisper. He listened. Her breathing told him
she'd fallen asleep.

He was glad; he shouldn't have said what he had. He
couldn't yet make a commitment. The wall remained there,
a wall of fear. A wall of experience, he told himself.

Somehow he just couldn't get beyond what had happened in his marriage to Krystal. And reservations were
prudent, he thought. The majority of the people he knew
ended up getting a divorce. He didn't think he could stand
to fail again.

Then he thought of the gamble Zoe was taking with her
horse.

What would she do if she won tomorrow? She would have
plenty of money then. Plenty for a new start, somewhere
besides Wings. Unless he married her. And then it occurred
to him, *Maybe she wouldn't marry him.*

* * *

Despite Rory's pleading with her to come back to bed, Zoe was up at the crack of dawn.

"The finals aren't even until tonight," Rory said.

"I know, but maybe this early I can have some good practice time on Blue without a lot of gawkers and distraction. He needs to be fed, anyway."

"Blue had plenty of hay last night to last him awhile." Rory went on to argue that distractions at practice were good for Blue, and that Zoe would be exhausted by the time the finals did start. However, nothing would do but for them to get to the stables.

"I can take a nap this afternoon," she told him. "You don't have to go—I could take your truck and come back for you after a while."

Rory shook his head and got up. He stood naked in front of her, but if she noticed, she controlled herself admirably. The hard fact was that she was completely taken up with riding in the finals—not with what was going on between them. "You're hell on my ego," he grumbled.

She whirled, her eyes wide with dismay. "Oh, Rory, I..."

He grinned. "I was just joking. Go on and get ready. I'm right behind you."

She was energy in motion, too impatient to even take time to make them coffee in the room. "We'll get coffee and breakfast on the way. If you're comin', come on."

He followed her. He had to walk smart. She smacked the elevator button three times, moving from foot to foot. Rory grabbed her to him, held her still and kissed her. He was gratified when he felt her melt against him and saw her eyes glaze for an instant. At least she did remember him.

Then they were down in the elevator and hurrying across the lobby and down the wide entry stairs. The stairs were polished granite and wet from an early morning rain shower—a combination dangerous to cowboy boots. Rory saw Zoe dip, heard her small cry. The next instant, before he could catch her, she'd gone down.

The first thing she grabbed was her knee, the one she'd injured weeks before.

Chapter Sixteen

Zoe sat on the bed, in her blouse and little blue panties, and tried to cajole Rory into helping her get her knee back into joint. But he was having none of it. She was a human—a *female* human—and he wasn't practicing his brand of amateur vet medicine on her.

Though she had a fit over the expense, he had the manager of the hotel get a doctor sent up to their room. The doctor manipulated Zoe's knee. When she let out a scream, Rory ducked quickly into the sitting room, where he couldn't see her until the doctor was done.

The doctor couldn't get the knee correctly aligned, either. "Without an X ray, I can't be certain," he said, "but I think the cartilage has shifted in there. You need to see a specialist."

"What about riding with it?" Rory asked, because he knew damn well she was going to.

"She can do whatever she likes, but she'll be doing it in pain. I'll leave some medication. That's all I can do."

Rory saw the doctor out, and when he returned to her bedroom, Zoe was testing out her knee. He watched her from the doorway. She couldn't bear any weight on that leg, which meant she would be hard-pressed to push on her foot in the stirrup when she needed to.

She turned and looked at him. Her face was pasty. "Will you help me get my jeans and boots back on?"

He shook his head, and she started to argue. He held up his palm. "Just listen to me for a second, will you?" She clamped her jaw and a tear trickled down her cheek. "I'll go take care of Blue and exercise him. You lie down and let your knee rest—and keep ice on it. There's a chance that if you take care of it, you'll be able to ride a lot better to-night."

Giving a reluctant nod, she lowered herself to the bed.

Rory cared for and worked Blue and from time to time called Zoe, checking on her and reporting on the stud. "He's workin' better than he ever has," he told her. She said her knee was getting a lot better. He knew she was lying.

Sure enough, her knee was only slightly improved when he returned to the hotel that afternoon. She tried to convince him it was great, though. The woman had a wily streak, he thought. He took an hour's nap, then ordered up dinner and showered.

When he came into her bedroom to check on her, he found her, dressed in her rose blouse, shiny satin vest, socks and lavender lace panties, trying to get into her jeans.

"Will you help me?"

He gave a large sigh and did, though his stomach knotted at each wince that swept her features. He was clumsy at the job; he'd never dressed a woman in his life. It had always been the other way around for him. And even with her help, he found it much harder getting a woman *into* her jeans than getting her *out* of them. By the time he'd gotten her boots on, he was sweating, and her face was as white as the sheet on the bed.

She wrapped her knee on the outside of her jeans, because her pants leg was too tight over the swollen joint for her to wrap it underneath. "My chaps'll hide it," she said. "And don't tell anyone. I won't have it said that the judges took pity on me because I'm a woman and hurt and all."

"Hey—I'm innocent."

"I'm sorry. I didn't mean to sound so hateful." She stroked his mustache. God, he loved it when she did that.

When he wanted her to take one of the pain pills, she refused. "If I take one of those things, I won't be able to stay in the saddle, much less ride. Get me the aspirin from my bag. It'll help reduce swelling."

Zoe was fifteenth in the lineup of twenty finalists.

When the time came, she limped down into the arena. Rory could tell she was doing her best not to limp, but there simply wasn't any way around it. Her features were set, and what he saw in her eyes made him wince inwardly.

He held Blue while she mounted from the right. He tucked her left foot into the stirrup, and then rested his hand on her thigh. "All set?"

She nodded and gave him a reassuring, if tight, smile.

He squeezed her leg, walked away and mounted Walter, heading out to take up his position as herd guard.

Zoe took a minute to settle herself on Blue. She clucked him into a walk, stopped him, turned him swiftly to the left. Her knee felt as if a hot poker had gone through it. She breathed deeply and thought how her father used to holler at her for relying too much on her legs for balance. Over and over he used to preach at her to ride by the seat of her pants.

She looked upward at all the people. She wondered why in the world she was doing this. What if she made a fool of herself by falling off? What if she wrecked her knee so badly she had to be laid up for days or weeks? Who'd take care of her girls then? Who'd earn the money for bills? Her pride had gone and done it to her again. Winning this thing was about as likely as her winning that magazine sweepstakes from that smiling man on television. Still, she had to do it and had to give it her best. By golly, she hadn't come this far to quit, or to fall out of the saddle or to pull some other silly stunt.

Lifting the reins, she sent Blue ahead and forced her thoughts from her throbbing knee. Her gaze fell on Rory. He looked relaxed, as if this were just another Sunday cutting at home. He was always relaxed on a horse; it was the living he had to do off one he seemed to find a strain. He looked at her a moment. No smile, but with such a light of pure excitement and faith in his blue eyes that she felt it clear to her heart.

She shifted her eyes to the herd, and all apprehension faded, as did awareness of the staring crowd and the judges, the time limit and the winning or losing. Even the pain in her knee was forced to the back of her mind. In that moment it became just her and Blue and the cattle.

They cut away eight cows, among them the brindle Zoe had chosen from up in the stands. In the process a cow bumped Zoe's stirrup, forcing her foot backward and putting pressure on her knee for aching seconds. Then she and Blue and the cows were clear. "That one...the brindle one, boy," she murmured. Blue understood, because that was the one he'd focused on, too. They allowed the others to peel away and slip back to the herd behind them. Seconds later Zoe sat atop Blue, staring at the brindle cow.

She lowered the reins, and the game was on.

For a moment the brindle hovered uncertainly, as if perplexed about what was going on. Then it sprinted—and Blue followed.

Back and forth, Blue matched the cow move for move. Focused, intent, captivated, Zoe whispered, "Get her, boy! That's it!" The brindle cow, the brown dirt, Blue's flying red mane, flashed in a blur before her eyes. The speed of Blue's movements jerked her around. Rory's and her daddy's voices echoed in her mind. *Push your rear into the saddle! Relax your legs! Stay centered!*

The cow circled, came back again and tried to duck beneath Blue's neck. But Blue was quicker. He crouched and feinted back, moving with the grace and sureness of a dancer. Adrenaline surged through Zoe. Then Blue and the cow were again face-to-face, only scant feet from each other. They swept left. They swept right. Zoe fought for balance. And then Blue held the cow with the power of his eyes as much as anything else.

Zoe became faintly aware of loud applause, of whistles and hoots, too. The go was over. With a shaking hand, she lifted the reins, and immediately Blue straightened and broke the gaze with the steer. As she rode to the side of the arena, an aching spread up from her leg, so deep that her head swam. Rory came up beside her. There was a grin on his face a mile wide.

"You just got yourself a horse worth twenty thousand dollars, darlin'."

With the strain suddenly dropping away, she felt a little lost. People were still clapping. Beneath her, Blue's chest heaved; his heat came up around her. Zoe thanked God that they had made it through, that she hadn't fallen off. She tried to ease her knee but couldn't. And added to that was a pain in her arm. She'd used it hard to push herself into the saddle. Barely aware of it, she stopped Blue at the official, who made the regulation check of Blue's bit. Rory appeared, holding up his hands to help her down.

"What do you think?" she whispered as she clung to him for several seconds.

"We'll know in a minute."

The pain in her knee was swamping her, bringing tears.

Rory slipped a halter on Blue, then took Zoe's arm. When the announcement came of a score of 219, a grand roar went up around them. Zoe had not won, however. She had tied with Annalise Cordell, and there were five cutters still to go.

Speculation was rife, as were the jokes. Two women in a work-off—that wasn't a common occurrence. Frank said he couldn't ever recall another instance of that happening. Women cutters remained in the minority, even in this day and age.

Horses that hadn't placed in the top five left the arena. Fresh cattle were brought in and settled. Judges stretched their legs. Annalise and Yancey Cordell came over to offer genuine good wishes and to inquire about Zoe's leg. She made light of it. The women even gave each other hugs; women were like that. Rory and Cordell exchanged grins.

Rory brought Zoe two more aspirin and rewrapped her knee.

"Tighter," she said.

He readjusted the bandage, then looked into her eyes. They were diamond bright with pain as well as excitement. Her cheeks were flushed, too.

"How's that?" he asked.

"Better."

He took her hand and helped her to stand. Her leg buckled, and he caught her. He bit back the comment that he didn't want her to ride. This was her call.

"I don't have to walk," she murmured through gritted teeth. "I only have to ride."

That made Rory think of her father.

He helped her into the saddle, practically lifting her up there. The knuckles of her hand gripping the horn were white. Rory couldn't stand seeing her in such pain. It made his stomach turn just to think of what her joint must look like. He had the urge to rip her off that horse and haul her out of there.

Instead he said, "That leg won't bother this horse at all. He adapts to you, and he reads you like a teenage boy reads a dirty book—quick and easy." She smiled at that.

He thought of her losing. Winning had come to mean so much to her; she would be crushed if she lost.

And if she won...*she wouldn't need him anymore.* Funny how that hadn't occurred to him before. When this was done, so was their loose partnership.

He mounted Walter, and together he and Zoe and Frank rode over to watch Annalise Cordell cut, and to study the cattle. After a minute Zoe pivoted Blue and worked him in gentle, smooth turns. Rory knew she was deliberately not watching.

Annalise Cordell and her golden buckskin were practically breathtaking, no doubt about it. Rory wouldn't have expected less from Cordell stock. The crowd applauded and hooted and whistled. The judges scored her a 221.

Minutes later Rory was again sitting in his place as herd holder. The huge arena was eerily quiet. In the seats up behind him Rory could hear the squeaking of a chair. He was somewhat surprised to discover his heart was beating double time. Zoe adjusted her hat and shifted her shoulders, then walked Blue forward. Rory saw the tenseness in her. Her eyes met his. *You can do it,* he silently told her.

Blue entered the herd; he was rule-book quiet and steady, and Rory didn't think even the harshest judge could fault him. He watched the tenseness go out of Zoe's back as the task absorbed her.

Together, taking up nearly a minute, Zoe and Blue cut six cows from the herd. They chose a deep black, with Brahma blood. She lowered her hand to Blue's neck, and the stud took over.

What followed was as fast, hard and beautiful a minute and a half of cutting as Rory had ever seen. Fluid and swift as spring water running over rocks, the stud moved, blocking the cow at every turn. His muscles rippled with controlled power, and his red mane and tail shimmered in the lights. Atop him, Zoe was supple and balanced, her compact body fit for the job. She and the horse worked as one.

Rory leaned forward and silently urged horse and rider on. *Push your rear in the saddle! Relax your legs! Stay centered!*

The steer circled, came back again and tried to duck beneath Blue's neck. Blue blocked him, crouched and shifted backward, moving with the grace and sureness of a dancer. When he got down in front of that cow about like a playful puppy, cheers erupted from the stand. *"Ooowee!" "Yeah!"*

The applause just about drowned out the sound of the buzzer. Rory noticed that all the noise didn't faze Blue. He continued to hold that cow until Zoe lifted the reins to call him off. Rory felt mighty proud, because he knew he'd had a great deal to do with turning out that horse, even if it was Zoe the horse would go through fire for.

He rode up beside her. Her eyes swung around to him. Her face was white as milk, her smile wide and trembling.

She slowly rode Blue over to the side of the arena and stopped at the official for the required bit check.

Rory dismounted, left Walter to take care of himself and went around to put the halter on Blue and help Zoe off. She shook her head.

Leaning toward him, she whispered hoarsely, "I can't get off.... I can't walk." She smiled a funny, painful little smile and glanced over to the officials. She put her hand out, and Rory slipped his into it and held tight.

The minutes of waiting ticked away. Again the arena grew eerily quiet.

The announcer's voice rang out. *"The score is 222!"*
Zoe had won, by one point.
She looked down at Rory, as if she couldn't believe it.
"You got it, darlin'."
When she rode across the arena to receive her trophy, she couldn't trot Blue as the other recipients had. In fact, Blue seemed to walk with extra care. Rory, sitting on Walter just outside the arena, watched them both through blurred vision. "Well," he said aloud, as if to Walter, "we saw what we could do with that stud." And he knew pride in Zoe—and in himself—for a job well done. And completed.

In the glare of the bright fall sunlight, Rory headed the gleaming white truck and trailer rig north toward Wings, up across the center of Oklahoma and then across the flat panhandle of Texas. He and Zoe and the two horses were going home with a lot more than they had come with.
A *lot* more, Rory thought emphatically. His mind skimmed over the five-figure check in Zoe's purse, and the trophy, the new champion saddle, the belt buckle and ribbon, gift bottles of champagne in the rear seat, the Western boots and hats for the girls on the floorboard, the champion horse in the trailer, Zoe's busted knee. And lastly he thought about him and Zoe, together. His thoughts lingered on that, tried to move on and came back to it again. It was a sweet, hot memory, that was for sure. And he mused again, yes, they were coming home with a lot more than they had left with.
They didn't talk much. More than once Zoe said how she couldn't wait to see the girls. She asked Rory if he wanted to split the check today, and he told her no doubt the bank would have to let the check clear before they could do any splitting, and at any rate, there wasn't a great hurry, at least on his part. She didn't say if there was on hers. He worked up to asking her what she was going to do with her half of the money. She looked at him for several seconds, then said she was going to buy some fancy face cream. That hadn't been an expected answer.
Mostly Zoe dozed, either on his shoulder or with her head pillowed on his thigh, as it was now. She'd been zonked

since her first pain pill last night—an hour after they'd gotten Blue settled and received congratulations from about a thousand people. Rory had received a couple of job offers for training horses, too. He'd been pleased but had declined.

So, he thought with a sigh and resting a hand on her hip, where did they go from here? They'd taken Blue to Fort Worth; they'd taken first place; they'd taken each other. What was next for them?

The options were few: they could go on like they had been . . . or they could live together . . . or they could get married.

He glanced down and found Zoe's dark eyes wide, gazing up at him. He returned his gaze to the road, his palm warm on her hip.

Something told him it was too late to go on like they had been. They'd gone past the wondering about it and wanting it stage and into the doing it. It was hard to backtrack from that.

And living together probably wasn't an option, because of Zoe's daughters; things could get sticky there.

That left marriage, and that option scared the hell out of Rory.

The road stretched ahead of him and the truck wheels turned, eating up the miles, and he continued to turn everything over in his mind.

Zoe knew Rory was thinking deeply. For one thing, he kept stroking the edge of his mustache, as was his habit when thinking over something. And, she supposed, she'd come to know him well enough in the past months to pick up on his moods.

It didn't take a mind reader to know what he was thinking about, either. She was thinking the same thing: What now? The climax of months of work, of hopes and expectations, had come about—in more ways than one, she thought with a silent, dry laugh.

So, where did they go from here?

Would he ask her to marry him—and would she say yes?

Another cowboy. Didn't she ever learn?

She had money now. She could move to Albuquerque and buy into a shop, get on the road to at least middle-class, maybe meet a nice steady teacher or grocer or maybe a veterinarian. She'd always thought a husband who was a veterinarian would come in handy.

Rory was the next thing to a veterinarian.

Her thoughts returned to the times they'd shared in bed. Those times with Rory Breen wouldn't be forgotten. Not ever.

In Amarillo and again in Clayton, Rory wanted her to stop in at the hospital, but she absolutely refused. She wanted to see her girls, to be home. She needed that now to get herself together. She felt so changed.

They spent very little time at Jada's, no more than it took to grab up the girls and their bag, which Jada had ready. With a promise of a long conversation tomorrow and with happy waves, the four of them headed on down the road, into the sunset, toward the shabby little place that had become home.

Fancy greeted them with eager barks and a wagging tail. Oren had fed her when he'd taken care of the cows. Even the gray cat came out to see them. The girls ran to play with both, then on into the house to ride Black Beauty. Zoe's and the girls' bags were taken inside, along with the precious trophy and ribbon and bottles of champagne. Zoe wondered what in the world she was going to do with all of them. Perhaps take a sip out of each one. But surely not alone.

Rory got Blue from the trailer and led him into his stall. Hobbling, Zoe brought the hose for fresh water. Rory frowned at her but didn't say anything. She wondered what, if anything, he would say before he left. They had slept together—and it had been hotter than a blazing inferno between them. Wasn't he going to comment about that?

She could say something, her mind whispered. But her pride refused.

Rory took his time seeing to Blue, emptying the truck of all Zoe's things, making certain she had everything she needed. The sun had dipped below the horizon and dusk had come by the time there wasn't anything else to keep him there. Yet he knew he needed to get things straight between them before he left. He just didn't know what to say.

She hobbled beside him as he went to his truck.

"Guess I'd better get Walter home," he said. "He's been in the trailer long enough."

"Yes, he's been patient."

They stopped at the truck; Zoe leaned on the fender to ease her throbbing knee.

"Oren and I will come for the cattle tomorrow. We'll turn them out and give Blue a few months of rest."

"Okay."

They gazed at each other. Rory bent and kissed her, quickly, just brushing his lips to hers. She didn't press for more. Her eyes were large and dark and unreadable.

"It was great," he said huskily.

"Yes," she said. Her eyes were warm, inviting.

Fleeing, he turned and opened the truck door. "I'll see you tomorrow." He would deal with it all then, that was what.

"Rory...don't go."

That certainly stopped him in his tracks. He looked back at her. She stood there, with frustration and uncertainty washed all over her face. The next instant he strode forward, grabbed her to him and kissed her, hard.

When they broke the kiss, his breath was short and his heart pounding. "I can't promise blue skies every day, darlin', but I can promise you a true-blue heart that won't be strayin' or runnin' off. I love you, Zoe. If you think we can make it, I want to marry you."

She hit his arm with her small, balled fist. "What kind of thing is that to say—if I think we can make it? *I* don't know if we can make it. Who ever knows that? And I'm scared to death." She lifted her face to him; tears were trickling down her cheeks. "But I know I love you...and I have a true-blue heart, too."

He was scared. God, he was scared. "I'll do my best not to drink, Zoe, but..."

She stopped his words with her fingertips. And then she stroked his mustache. "And I'll try not to be so opinionated, but the only promise we need to make is to love each other. That covers it." And the love shining in her eyes covered it all, too.

He said evenly, certainly, "Will you marry me, Zoe?"

"Yes," she answered quietly and just as certainly.

Rory kissed her and held her and knew that he wouldn't be leaving that night. And he knew that not only had this woman brought him love, she'd brought him the courage to find himself.

Epilogue

Jesse Breen's second son was wed there on the Breen ranch, in the shade of the cottonwoods down near the pond. The day was sunny but cool, the gathering small, just fifteen of their closest friends.

Aunt Ina came down to cook for those in the big house and prepare the reception, while Annie spent most days over at Zoe's. Zoe had had surgery on her knee and needed help with the girls. Sitting in a wheelchair, her knee in a splint, she wore a dress of mauve cotton cashmere knit and crocheted lace, and Glory and Mercy wore smaller versions of the same dress. Together, Zoe and Annie had made all three. Matt helped Rory put himself together, while Marnie and Oren took pictures of everything—even to sneaking one of Rory in his underwear. Jada was Zoe's matron of honor, Glory and Mercy were flower girls, and Little Jesse was the ring bearer.

Jesse stood up as best man for Rory. It was speculated that the situation could be a first—a best man standing up for his grown son while holding his baby daughter in his arms. Jesse preened, enjoying the opportunity to show off beautiful Mary Regina. And then Jesse couldn't find the ring and had to have Rory hold Mary Regina while he searched his pockets. It didn't bother Rory; Mary Regina giggled sweetly at him, and Zoe, used to accommodating children, laughed. When Rory handed Mary Regina back to Jesse, his gaze fell on Glory and Mercy standing aside with Annie. He beckoned them to him and lifted one in each arm. When it came time for his vows, he said them to the girls as well as Zoe. Jesse was button-popping proud of his son.

Jesse's gift to his second son and his new bride was the same as it had been to Annie and Matt—a bottle of champagne, which he prudently changed to sparkling grape juice, sitting in a silver ice bucket, and a new bedroom suite, which in this case he picked out and had delivered to the Ferguson place. Though the Ferguson place was hereafter to be called the Breen place, because Jesse added one more gift. He'd bought the old place from Otis Ferguson at last. Otis had driven a hard bargain.

Marnie said that more than being generous, Jesse was simply trying to run his son's life and keep him close. Jesse didn't argue; he couldn't argue with fact. Didn't matter, all were happy about it.

And that evening, after the guests had departed and the family was gathered in the living room of the big house, Jesse held Mary Regina and called Little Jesse, Glory and Mercy over to sit in the big chair with him. He had no trouble telling the twins apart—they were his granddaughters now, after all.

Marnie brought him a glass of wine, bent and kissed him quickly. "You do appear the very proud and handsome patriarch," she whispered and stood with her hand on his shoulder.

"And I have every right to be. They're a fine bunch, aren't they?" He ran his gaze over his sons and daughters-in-law, settling lastly on Oren. "Two down and one last one to go," he said.

Marnie looked down at him and laughed. "*Two* more to go, Papa," she said pointing at Mary Regina, who cooed up at him. "You have a daughter now."

"Good grief, I clean forgot!" The unwelcome image of Mary Regina getting married flashed in his mind.

And Marnie added wickedly, "And then it will be the grandchildren's turn."

Chuckling, Jesse took Marnie's hand and smiled at the children.

"On it goes," he said and tugged his wife until she bent her lips to his. He kissed her soundly—and it wasn't any old-fogy, patriarch kiss, either.

Little Jesse cried, "Look at Papa!"

*   *   *   *   *

Silhouette Books
is proud to present
our best authors,
their best books...
and the best in
your reading pleasure!

Throughout 1993, look for exciting books
by these top names in contemporary
romance:

CATHERINE COULTER—
Aftershocks in February

FERN MICHAELS—
Nightstar in March

DIANA PALMER—
Heather's Song in March

ELIZABETH LOWELL
Love Song for a Raven in April

SANDRA BROWN
(previously published under
the pseudonym Erin St. Claire)—
Led Astray in April

LINDA HOWARD—
All That Glitters in May

When it comes to passion,
we wrote the book.

Silhouette®

Take 4 bestselling love stories FREE

Plus get a FREE surprise gift!

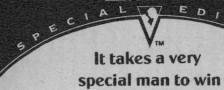

Silhouette SPECIAL EDITION™

It takes a very special man to win

That SPECIAL Woman!

She's friend, wife, mother—she's you! And beside each Special Woman stands a wonderfully *special* man. It's a celebration of our heroines— and the men who become part of their lives.

Look for these exciting titles from Silhouette Special Edition:

April   FALLING FOR RACHEL by Nora Roberts
Heroine: Rachel Stanislaski—a woman dedicated to her career discovers romance adds spice to life.

May   THE FOREVER NIGHT by Myrna Temte
Heroine: Ginny Bradford—a woman who thought she'd never love again finds the man of her dreams.

June   A WINTER'S ROSE by Erica Spindler
Heroine: Bently Cunningham—a woman with a blue-blooded background falls for one red-hot man.

July   KATE'S VOW by Sherryl Woods
Heroine: Kate Newton—a woman who viewed love as a mere fairy tale meets her own Prince Charming.

Don't miss THAT SPECIAL WOMAN! each month—from some of your special authors! Only from Silhouette Special Edition! And for the most special woman of all—you, our loyal reader—we have a wonderful gift: a beautiful journal to record all of your special moments. Look for details in this month's THAT SPECIAL WOMAN! title, available at your favorite retail outlet.

TSW2